THE

"A mix of cozy mystery and suspenseful general fiction . . . The suspense was high . . . I'd recommend this mystery."
—*Genre Reviews*

"Ada Madison is a talented writer who knows how to hook her audience from the very first page . . . A rich and satisfying read." —*MyShelf.com*

"This is [an] enjoyable academic amateur sleuth filled with puzzlers, brainteasers, and mathematician quotations. The cozy storyline is entertaining . . . Fans will appreciate Sophie's inquiry as she adds the clues and subtracts the red herrings to try to extrapolate the identity of the killer before she becomes a cold statistic." —*Genre Go Round Reviews*

THE SQUARE ROOT OF MURDER

"Math professor Sophie Knowles makes an auspicious debut in Ada Madison's delightful *The Square Root of Murder*. Petty academic politics and faculty secrets prove fertile topics in Madison's very capable hands."
—Miranda James, *New York Times* bestselling author of *File M for Murder*

"A clever puzzle, *The Square Root of Murder* is well plotted, and the reader will want to see more of Sophie. Madison has found the right equation for success in this entertaining series debut." —*Richmond Times-Dispatch*

"I strongly recommend *The Square Root of Murder*. It offers readers the familiarity of a cozy mystery with some interesting new twists. Five stars out of five." —*Examiner.com*

Praise for
THE PROBABILITY OF MURDER

Berkley Prime Crime titles by Ada Madison

THE SQUARE ROOT OF MURDER
THE PROBABILITY OF MURDER
A FUNCTION OF MURDER

A FUNCTION OF
MURDƐR

Ada Madison

BERKLEY PRIME CRIME, NEW YORK

THE BERKLEY PUBLISHING GROUP
Published by the Penguin Group
Penguin Group (USA) Inc.
375 Hudson Street, New York, New York 10014, USA

Penguin Group (Canada), 90 Eglinton Avenue East, Suite 700, Toronto, Ontario M4P 2Y3, Canada
(a division of Pearson Penguin Canada Inc.) • Penguin Books Ltd., 80 Strand, London WC2R 0RL,
England • Penguin Group Ireland, 25 St. Stephen's Green, Dublin 2, Ireland (a division of Penguin
Books Ltd.) • Penguin Group (Australia), 250 Camberwell Road, Camberwell, Victoria 3124, Australia
(a division of Pearson Australia Group Pty. Ltd.) • Penguin Books India Pvt. Ltd., 11 Community
Centre, Panchsheel Park, New Delhi—110 017, India • Penguin Group (NZ), 67 Apollo Drive,
Rosedale, Auckland 0632, New Zealand (a division of Pearson New Zealand Ltd.) • Penguin Books
(South Africa) (Pty.) Ltd., 24 Sturdee Avenue, Rosebank, Johannesburg 2196, South Africa

Penguin Books Ltd., Registered Offices: 80 Strand, London WC2R 0RL, England

This is a work of fiction. Names, characters, places, and incidents either are the product of the author's
imagination or are used fictitiously, and any resemblance to actual persons, living or dead, business
establishments, events, or locales is entirely coincidental. The publisher does not have any control over
and does not assume any responsibility for author or third-party websites or their content.

A FUNCTION OF MURDER

A Berkley Prime Crime Book / published by arrangement with the author

PUBLISHING HISTORY
Berkley Prime Crime mass-market edition / January 2013

Copyright © 2012 by Camille Minichino.
Math, puzzles, and games by Camille Minichino.
Interior map by Dick Rufer.
Cover illustration by Lisa French.
Cover design by Lesley Worrell.
Interior text design by Kristin del Rosario.

All rights reserved.
No part of this book may be reproduced, scanned, or distributed in any printed or
electronic form without permission. Please do not participate in or encourage piracy of
copyrighted materials in violation of the author's rights. Purchase only authorized editions.
For information, address: The Berkley Publishing Group,
a division of Penguin Group (USA) Inc.,
375 Hudson Street, New York, New York 10014.

ISBN: 978-0-425-25175-1

BERKLEY® PRIME CRIME
Berkley Prime Crime Books are published by The Berkley Publishing Group,
a division of Penguin Group (USA) Inc.,
375 Hudson Street, New York, New York 10014.
BERKLEY® PRIME CRIME and the PRIME CRIME logo are trademarks of
Penguin Group (USA) Inc.

PRINTED IN THE UNITED STATES OF AMERICA

10 9 8 7 6 5 4 3 2 1

If you purchased this book without a cover, you should be aware that this book is
stolen property. It was reported as "unsold and destroyed" to the publisher, and neither the
author nor the publisher has received any payment for this "stripped book."

ACKNOWLEDGMENTS

Thanks as always to my critique partners: Nannette Rundle Carroll, Jonnie Jacobs, Rita Lakin, Margaret Lucke, and Sue Stephenson. They are ideally knowledgeable, thorough, and supportive.

Thanks to Dr. Jeanne Trubek, mathematics chairwoman at Emmanuel College in Boston; and to Dr. Sally Dias, woman of many titles at Emmanuel, my friend and supporter. Both are outstanding resources for this series

A special word about experts who are ready to help at a moment's notice, with a word, a picture, or a seminar's worth of advice: educator Susan Durkin, chemist and ice climber William McConachie, medevac pilot Mark Ramos, and entrepreneur Mark Streich.

Thanks also to the extraordinary inspector Chris Lux for continued advice on police procedure. Chris is always available to answer my questions, often the same one for every book, or to share a laugh. My interpretation of his counsel should not be held against him.

Thanks to the many other writers and friends who offered critique, information, brainstorming, and inspiration; in particular: Gail and David Abbate, Judy Barnett, Sara Bly, Margaret Hamilton, Mary McConnell, Ann Parker, Jean Stokowski, Karen Streich, and Ellyn Wheeler.

My deepest gratitude goes to my husband, Dick Rufer. I can't imagine working without his support. He's my dedicated Webmaster (www.minichino.com), layout specialist, and on-call IT department.

Finally, how lucky can I be? I'm working with a special and dedicated editor, Michelle Vega, a bright light in my life, who is superb at seeing the whole without missing the tiniest detail. Thanks, Michelle!

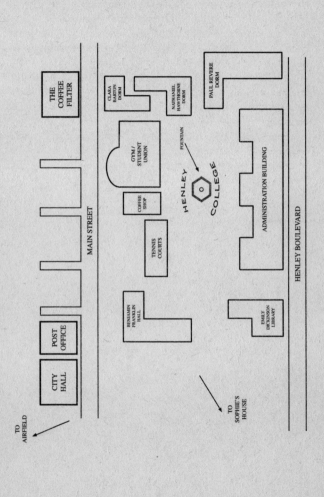

The laws of nature are but
the mathematical thoughts of God.

—EUCLID

CHAPTER $\sqrt{1}$

What's not to like about graduation ceremonies?

The speeches? Can't get enough of them. The flowers, balloons, parties, screaming coeds? Love them all. Every year I look forward to a long line of students filing by, one by one, switching the tassels on their mortarboards. I get a shiver of delight as I join the procession, my heavy silk and velvet robes weighing me down. What a pleasure it is to walk around the pathways of the campus and onto the great lawn, a trumpet voluntary ringing out through the stifling hot and humid air. I never want it to end.

Not.

Today, as the faculty sat outside on a makeshift stage, our uncomfortable folding chairs seemed to sway with every warm breeze.

Fran, my colleague in the Henley College Mathematics Department, nudged me.

"Professor Knowles, are you bored silly?" she whispered.

"Totally, Professor Emerson," I said. "Are you stuck to your chair?"

"Like white on the blackboards," answered Fran, who was old enough to remember chalk. "Can you believe this guy? Could he be less inspiring?" Fran gave a surreptitious nod in the direction of the podium where Mayor Edward P. Graves was holding forth as our keynote speaker. The *P.* was important to distinguish him from his father, Edward D., and his grandfather, Edward K., who had been our mayors before him.

At only thirty-nine, five years my junior, the current Edward Graves was in the middle of his first term as the youngest mayor in the history of Henley, Massachusetts. Sadly, however, it hadn't taken him long to pick up the walk and the talk of the average gray-haired politician. He seemed to have put on his smile at the same time as his highly polished shoes.

"Graduations are double milestones in our lives, because they celebrate the proud accomplishments of our past, while also looking forward to the future," the latest Mayor Graves said now, as if it were an original, quotable thought and nicely put. Hadn't Madeleine Albright said it better at my own baccalaureate, lo those many years ago?

Edward P.'s wife, Nora, perfectly coiffured, sat a row in front of Fran and me, across the aisle, knocking knees with the deans and other college and town officials. She'd already received a commendation from the college president, for her "generous, outstanding work with all the major charities of this city." Nora Graves kept a steady, pleasant look on her face, apparently neither bored nor sweaty, as Fran and I were. Even without the hat hair I was about to reveal as soon as I removed my velvet tam, my short dark hair would never look as good as our First Lady's.

I desperately wished I'd brought a puzzle with me, something with wires or magnets that I could put together by touch as I kept my hands under my robes. Too late now. I made a note to put a couple of pocket-size puzzles with my robes when I packed them away, so I'd be better prepared next year. And hadn't we already been on this stage for a year?

Mayor Graves had not been the unanimous choice for commencement speaker. We'd had a last-minute cancellation, and the dean had called an emergency meeting for a replacement. Many of us would have preferred a person of academic standing, like the originally scheduled speaker, who was a retired dean of a Boston medical school. Not that I'd been asked, but I'd have recommended one of any number of noted mathematicians in the greater Boston area. A sparkling equation would have made a nice addition to the commencement address.

I glanced across the aisle at art history instructor Chris Sizemore, to see how she was holding up. Chris had been one of the most adamant that we should have looked to educational institutions, not to city hall, for a speaker. Her chin rested low on her chest, her long brown hair falling like a veil over her face. She might have been asleep. Not a bad choice.

Next to her, Montgomery "Monty" Sizemore, Chris's younger brother and an adjunct professor in Henley's new business program, was awake, but agitated, and appeared to be commenting under his breath, perhaps doing business through his Bluetooth. Another decent choice.

The lunchroom rumor mill suggested that Monty had his own special beef with Mayor Graves over some consulting work his Boston-based company had done for the city of Henley. At issue this month was the waste management contract, with two contenders: one the mayor's choice, the other Monty's.

Groan. Why did I have to think of garbage now? Wasn't I hot and uncomfortable enough? Maybe that's why Monty was cringing, too, with his mind on which company would be granted the privilege of transporting our smelly refuse to the town dump.

All in all, surveying the faculty, noting the scattered smiles and frowns, it wasn't hard to figure out where each one stood on the dicey issue of commencement speaker.

The Henley College Faculty Senate debate had ended when the scales were tipped by an announcement: Cody Graves, the mayor's son, who'd be entering his senior year of high school in the fall, had already applied for admission to our college. The gossip from Admissions further hinted that a new gym might be in the offing—the Graves Athletic Center, to be exact—a critical addition now that men were admitted to the Henley campus. It seemed no one noticed the poor condition of our sports facilities until the first coed class arrived last September.

The prospects of a celebrity freshman next year and a new gym to follow outweighed any desire for academic integrity. Also overshadowed was any suggestion that the mayor's business dealings might be questioned—was there a waste management CEO among his campaign contributors, for example? It seemed the Faculty Senate was willing to risk a few boos from the crowd. None came. Instead, we entertained a strong but civilized undercurrent of disapproval.

From behind the podium, the town's top guy rambled on. "Today is not an end, but a beginning."

Another groan. I fanned myself with the fancy vellum program and considered texting Fran, sitting next to me. If our advanced calculus students could thumb their way through a lecture, texting across a classroom aisle, why couldn't we do a little business as we sat side by side? We'd already stayed quiet during the long ecumenical invocation, stood for the national anthem, and then sat again for speeches by esteemed college administrators and dignitaries from as far away as Boston (forty miles) and Providence, Rhode Island (twenty miles). Since the speeches began, I'd counted nineteen appearances by the word *future* and twelve by the word *beginning*, or forms thereof.

By far the best address today had come from one of the valedictorians, Kira Gilmore. Kira was also active in town politics, known to be one of the best workers at Mayor Graves's campaign headquarters. Too bad he hadn't sought her help with his speech. I imagined he was too busy pushing ahead with his career strategy of running for state senator before he completed his term as mayor.

I'll admit I may have paid more attention to Kira since she was a math major with a distinguished academic record and a professionally recognized senior thesis. Kira was what my mother would have called high-strung. I was sure there was a more trendy psychological term now for someone who was highly excitable and could make herself ill over the smallest bit of stress. She'd come to my office yesterday, the day before her graduation, and threatened to opt out of her place on the program.

"I can't do it, Dr. Knowles," she'd said. "There'll be so many people sitting out there, watching me fall all over myself."

I was ready with a canned routine that I used periodically on the privileged students of Henley College.

"Will your parents be among those sitting on the lawn tomorrow?" I asked Kira.

"Uh-huh, they got in from California last night."

"And, tell me, do you owe a lot in student loans?" I asked, knowing that Kira's hardworking parents had footed the entire bill for her degree.

Kira had looked perplexed. "Uh, no, I didn't take out any loans. I thought you knew that my mom and dad paid for—" She'd paused and ventured a tiny smile. "Okay, Dr. Knowles. I get it. My parents deserve to see me up there. It's not about me; it's about them."

"What a nice thought," I'd said.

In the end, as always, Kira had done beautifully. She'd

opened her speech with a quote she attributed to her grandmother—"If opportunity doesn't knock, build your own door"—and closed with one of her own—"Let's party tonight and change the world tomorrow."

I'd clapped loudly and whispered under my breath, *Nice going, Kira. MIT was so smart to accept you for grad school.*

With Mayor Graves still at the podium, I slid my hand through the slit on the seam of my robe and fumbled around for my skirt pocket where my phone lay among paper clips, coins, rubber bands, and a roll of antacids. Fran and I could at least work on some issues by text. I was chair this year and needed to remind Fran to give me her fall schedule for the bulletin. It would also be useful to have her recommendation for where my boyfriend, Bruce, and I might stay on the Cape next weekend, plus I wanted her recipe for lasagna. A whole array of important things needed attention. We shouldn't be wasting precious time.

My attempt at a covert action was disrupted by polite applause from the stage and from the lawn. The mayor had finished. I'd missed his closing lines, but I'd have bet they included the phrase *Go forth.*

"Notice who isn't clapping?" Fran asked me, as we both joined in the applause.

"Besides Chris and her brother? Lots. I'm just glad they're not booing."

As the mayor returned from the podium, he caught my eye and smiled. A big surprise. I recovered in time to smile back. He raised his eyebrows in a question and mouthed words that looked like "See you," a sentiment that did not at all fit our relationship, which amounted to crossing paths now and then at a charter school where I volunteered. Kira helped out at his campaign headquarters, but I'd never been there. I couldn't think of any other interaction we might have had that would have prompted a "See you" notice.

"What was that about?" Fran asked, removing any

doubt that the gesture was meant for me and not someone sitting behind or in front of me. Nor had it been a nervous twitch.

"I have no idea," I said. "Probably part of his twenty-four-seven campaign mode. A verbal handshake for a voter."

Mayor Graves stopped where his wife sat, took her by the elbow, and led her off the stage, walking toward the back. Who could blame them for escaping before the conferring of degrees? I envisioned him dumping his robes on the nearest empty chair and silently greeting everyone in the rows behind me with the same "See you" gesture he'd given me.

"Apparently, you rate more than the city's education bigwig these days," Fran said.

I knew what she meant. "I'm surprised he agreed to come," I said, glancing back at Superintendent of Schools Patrick Collins, who had his arms folded across his chest. I suspected he'd sat that way throughout the mayor's speech. It was a great way for academics at all levels to make a point without looking boorish themselves. Simply cross your arms and have people speculate as to what it is that you, in your great wisdom, disagree with.

"I wonder how that's all going to end," Fran said.

"Not well," I suggested, recalling a month's worth of newspaper headlines about the issues separating the superintendent of schools and the mayor. Poor Mayor Graves. I didn't understand why anyone would want the job of dealing with all the city's challenges, from its educational institutions to its waste disposal.

The current classroom dispute was over the performance and the funding of the charter schools in town. Bitter words were exchanged and documented in living detail. I felt sorry for the bald, aging superintendent who had to compete aesthetics-wise with our young, buff mayor and his full head of auburn hair.

My own experience as a volunteer at the Zeeman charter school, also known as Zeeman Academy, was mixed. I avoided the principal and the other administrators, who often seemed to be caught up in unnecessary paperwork and bureaucratic details, but I loved the students—full disclosure: I love all students—and kept at it as part of my lifelong mission for math literacy.

I'd chosen Zeeman because of its business orientation and well-known selection of internships for its older elementary school students. To me, mathematics was the ultimate field for everyone, offering both beautiful equations and the most practical, business-friendly methods, and I wanted to get that message across early.

We'd reached the exciting time in the Henley College commencement program when roughly five hundred students would be entered into the ranks of the college educated.

The practice of having every student's name called out ended a couple of years ago, when the exercises began to take longer than a two-credit class. Now students stood in blocks and degrees were awarded according to their major departments. Only the honors students paraded across the stage as their names were announced. Individual parchments for the gen pop of graduates were handed out later at separate, smaller department gatherings. My mouth watered as I thought of the catered appetizers that would be served to math and science graduates in my building shortly. Or longly.

During the transition at the podium, I heard a lot of shuffling behind me as some of those in the back rows felt they could follow the mayor's example and slip out unnoticed. Lucky me, sitting toward the front. Trapped. I mopped my brow in as ladylike a manner as possible and without knocking my tam off my head.

"I have an idea," Fran whispered through a barely open mouth.

"Anything. Show me what you've got," I said, as President Olivia Aldridge called for American Studies majors to stand. Only twenty-four departments to go, all the way past English and Political Science to Theatre Arts, and ending with Women's Studies.

I felt a poke from Fran and then something sliding across my lap. I pulled my robe over the new item, leaving only a small viewing space. I snuck a look and saw Fran's new smartphone with a wordplay game under way.

"I'm in," I whispered.

She'd started by forming the word *windy*. I checked the set of letters available to me and moved a word into place around her *i*: *tickle*.

Our phones were smart enough to know the value of each letter and kept score for us. It was twelve to twelve, and we were off.

Fran and I looked up now and then to clap for a student we'd taught, and finally to watch mortarboards soar through the air.

"Another class goes off into the world," she said.

I nodded. "I hope they're ready."

"The students or the world?" she asked.

"Both."

CHAPTER $\sqrt{2}$

In the air-conditioned comfort of Benjamin Franklin Hall, the math and science building, my feelings were different. Now I really didn't want the party to end.

This time the awarding of degrees was individual, some might have said drawn out, in Franklin's large lecture hall. Each math and science major, twenty-five in all, made an Oscar-like speech, thanking parents, roommates, the groundskeepers, and—big thrill here—us, the faculty.

To close the ceremony, the new graduates lined up to receive their official gift from the college: a letter opener with a replica of the college seal attached at the top. The blade was sterling silver, with a point sharp enough to open acceptance letters for grad school or jobs, we claimed.

"I'd love to have the contract for those," Fran said, as the last letter opener was removed from its box and oohed and aahed over. "Imagine the number of alumnae who have them."

"We should have done the calculation during the

speeches," I said. "Multiply one hundred years or so of graduates by—"

"Maybe next year," Fran said.

We repaired to the first-floor lounge to await food and drink from the caterers. With students, parents, faculty, and guests, the room was stretched to its limit and many took to the hallways.

At the close of every school year, I hated the idea of losing a class of senior math majors, plus all the science students I'd gotten close to over four years. I could, however, understand why they'd want to swear off grueling homework, pop quizzes, exams, and grades for the rest of their lives.

As always, there was a whole lot of clinging going on, and many promises were made while a mix of the graduates' musical favorites played in the background. Pitbull and Lady Gaga were prominent, as were the surprisingly long-lasting Black Eyed Peas, who dated back to before most of these students were born.

"I'll never, never lose touch with you," Jeanne Flowers, near tears, swore to Bethany Riggs.

"We totally have to hook up in California in August," Bethany said to Nicole Johnson.

"I'll tweet and text you every day," Nicole told Jeanne.

And so on, with Claudette, Heather, Jessica, and a dozen other flushed young women.

I could have written the script.

After fifteen years of college teaching, I usually came pretty close with my estimate—it would take two or three months for all but a few graduation-day promises to fall off to zero; only one month if European travel intervened.

Kira Gilmore, one of today's academic stars, rushed up to me and nearly knocked me over with her energetic hug. At close to six feet, a large-boned Californian, Kira towered over me, her five-foot-three math prof. Only a couple of weeks ago, Kira had impressed a professional mathematics society with a research paper based on her thesis—the application of mathematical models to political science. Knowing Kira's innate shyness, I was doubly proud of her performance.

"I'm coming back here so often, you won't even know I graduated," Kira said now. "You've been the best teacher and the best adviser, Dr. Knowles."

I thanked her and hugged her back. As much as I cared about her, I hoped Kira would not keep her promise. What I wanted most was to see her move on.

"Here comes the food," Nicole said, getting down to basics, and illustrating that the transition from starving student to sophisticated graduate wasn't immediate.

Group hugs broke up and cameras were put away for the moment as the caterers hired by the Franklin Hall faculty entered the lounge with large trays, a pleasing, aromatic trail in their wake. The food line formed as soon as the trays of delectables hit the table.

Our building, at the northwestern edge of the campus, was party central all year round, not just for graduation. Franklin Hall was famous for its Friday afternoon gatherings, celebrating the birthdays of famous mathematicians, scientists, and inventors. Besides commencement day, today, May fifteenth, was also Pierre Curie's birthday. You can imagine our double excitement, though Pierre had to take a backseat, his extraordinary scientific work commemorated with only a poster collage prepared by the physics and chemistry undergraduates.

Like the rest of the faculty, Fran and I had shed our hats and robes as soon as we could and left them in our offices. Most of my colleagues were a little more dressed up than on class days, but it was too hot for me to put anything heavy on my small frame. Fran looked especially elegant in one of her trademark flowing, multicolor pants outfits. She fit in well with the dressed-to-the-nines parents of the graduates, but I was probably more comfortable than any of them, in my simple halter-top dress.

None of the honorees had taken off their heavy black mantles. It made them easier to spot in the crowded room, which, I supposed, was the idea. I saw many proud, loving gestures as moms and dads adjusted the stiff white collars on their newly anointed daughters.

Our long conference table doubled as the buffet table at weekly parties, but those offerings were like table scraps compared to today's spread of gourmet appetizers. Instead of giant economy-size bags of cookies and chips, and dips of unidentifiable ingredients and questionable origin, the caterers had laid down a set of special hot and cold dishes. The faculty had sprung for clams casino, cherry peppers stuffed with shrimp, Swedish meatballs, and an assortment of olives, fruits, and cheeses.

For dessert, a large cake took up one corner of the lounge. Baked and decorated by Franklin Hall's under-classmen, the cake bore the message "LUV U GRADS" in blue and gold, to match the streamers and pennants around the room.

"Doesn't it bring tears to your eyes?" Fran asked me, faking a sniffle.

I uttered a phony sob for Fran's benefit, though in truth I really was more emotionally attached to my students than she was. Maybe because she had her own family to fawn over. For me, single, and an only child, Henley was my family. True, my boyfriend, Bruce Granville, and my best friend since childhood, Ariana Volens, were indispensable in my life, but I spent more time on campus than in Ari-ana's bead shop or with Bruce and his crazy schedule as a medevac pilot.

Once the food was served, the party groupings became reminiscent of middle school dances, where like stayed with like. Parents clustered together on one side of the room, eating at the small tables scattered around the lounge; the graduates gathered on the other side, balancing plates on their knees. Faculty roamed at first, greeting everyone, then we took seats wherever we found them.

On the parents' side there were exchanges of photos, both paper and digital, and plans for the future—the graduates' futures, strangely.

"Jeanne isn't interested in settling down until she finishes graduate school at least," Jeanne's mother said, while Dad nodded vigorously.

"Bethany won't stop until she's running the cardiology wing at some big Boston hospital," Bethany's father announced, spreading his arms to indicate the size of the medical facility his daughter would one day oversee.

A few of us knew better. We knew that Jeanne, a bio major, was expecting her boyfriend, graduating today from a college in Boston, to give her a ring and set a date this summer. Bethany's dream, well-known to her friends, was to move across the country to San Francisco as soon as she could pack up her jean shorts and flip-flops.

"I'll figure out what to do when I get there," she'd told us, but apparently not her parents.

If all went as usual, the parents of the grads would be the last to know.

It didn't do any good to try to remember my own dreams as a new college graduate. Life choices were never as simple as they seemed at twenty-one or twenty-two. If I hadn't moved back home to take care of my ailing mother . . . If I hadn't left the software company to teach . . . If I had followed my friend Ariana's path and gone into business for myself . . . If I hadn't met Bruce five years ago . . .

Crash! Clatter! Crash!

The sound of china and metal on tile brought all conversation and daydreaming to a halt. A mishap by one of the catering staff, was my first thought. How embarrassing for the person.

But it wasn't a young man or woman dressed in a black-

and-white outfit two sizes too large who'd caused the commotion.

It was Kira Gilmore. She'd dropped, or thrown, her plate and silverware to the floor, spilling olives, meatballs, and a clump of shellfish on the way, and was now in an agitated state not consistent with the party atmosphere.

"You shouldn't be mouthing off about Mayor Graves when you don't know what you're talking about," she yelled. The comment seemed to have been addressed to Nicole Johnson, who scooted her chair back from the circle of diners, still sitting and holding on to her plate of fruit and cheese.

"You have to admit he does have a nerve talking about service to the community when we know he's only using his mayorship as a stepping stone for his own advancement," Jeanne Flowers said, appearing to defend whatever Nicole had said.

"That is so unfair," Kira said, nearly in tears.

It seemed that Mayor Edward P. Graves had invaded the party, not in the flesh, but in conversation.

"Why doesn't he put his money where his mouth is and fund the charter schools the same as the others?" Nicole continued, apparently emboldened by Jeanne's defense of her initial remark. "Do you know that Zeeman Academy, my little brother's charter, might close next year because His Majesty, the mayor, thinks they're unnecessary?"

That was news to me, but then, my eyes and ears glazed over whenever I heard the Zeeman faculty discuss issues other than the latest teaching methods.

"Edward is not against Zeeman or any of the charter schools," Kira said, her face reddening. "His own son went to Zeeman up to eighth grade. He just wants the schools to be more accountable. No one gets it."

"Edward, is it?" Jeanne said, with a *neener-neener* sound that I associated with junior high kids. "He's such a hypocrite. You're just his groupie, Kira, and you see what you want to see."

"As if your boyfriend is perfect," Kira managed, though her heart wasn't in it.

I didn't really want to hear what college students thought was wrong with one another's passions of the month, but I was concerned that Kira was in distress. Her reaction went far beyond what might be expected of a loyal Henley resident, even one who was an award-winning campaign worker for the mayor's state senate run.

The girls' voices softened finally, and the rest of the guests made awkward attempts to return to their conversations. The efficient catering staff came in with spray bottles, cloths, and sponges and relieved Kira's befuddled parents, who had started to clean the mess she'd made.

"What do you think that was about?" I asked Fran, who'd taken a seat next to me. I was still holding on to the notion that a math major, even one who'd graduated, was my responsibility. And I couldn't help wondering why one of Henley College's top students was defending the mayor as if she were—

"She's seeing him." Fran broke into my thoughts, stabbing at a clam at the same time.

"What? Seeing him, as in . . . ?" I tried to erase the image that was forming. "Kira? Seeing the mayor? Are you sure?"

"It's obvious," Fran said.

"Not to me."

Fran rolled her eyes, a reminder that I seldom got the subtleties of who was hooking up with whom these days. Was it that long ago that I was twenty? Answer: *yes*. But Fran was older, and a grandmother, so I couldn't blame my age and state in life for how often I missed cues regarding personal relationships.

Though no one said so, Kira's outburst had put a damper on the party. The good cheer and harmless gossip that were present at the beginning had dissipated. Guests began saying their farewells and wandered off in family units, presumably seeking a less charged environment.

There's some good in every ill wind, my mother, Margaret Stone, used to remind me. She was right this afternoon. The fact that the party was cut short meant all the more leftovers for the students who were staying in the dorm until official closing time next week. The caterers and a few of us faculty and undergrads helped pack up the savories.

"You really don't want these meatballs and peppers, Dr. Knowles? Dr. Emerson?" a sophomore chem major asked, eyes wide.

We shook our heads. "It's all yours," Fran said.

"There's sooo much cake left. I could hack off a piece for you," a freshman bio major said, licking her lips and wielding a knife that looked more suited to a slab of beef.

"It's our gift to you," I said, and accepted another farewell hug.

Fran and I decided to retreat to our respective offices for some downtime before going out to dinner with a group of math majors and their parents at seven thirty.

We headed down the hall, still chatting about the Kira Gilmore–Edward Graves issue, whispering all the way. We stopped abruptly when our longtime janitor, working overtime today, came toward us, pushing his big barrel of cleaning equipment.

"Afternoon, Doctors," Woody said, sticking to his respectful guns, despite the many times we'd encouraged him to call us by our first names. "Congratulations to you all."

"Thanks, Mr. Conroy," I teased.

Woody reached into one of the many pockets in his overalls and pulled out a shiny key ring with a tiny soccer ball dangling from its chain. He held it up to show us both, then offered it to Fran.

"I saw this little thing as I was checking out of the hardware store. I thought of your young grandson, Dr. Emerson. Do you think he might like it?"

Fran took the key ring with a gracious smile. "How sweet of you, Woody," she said. "I'm sure he'll love it."

"Glad to hear it," Woody said, sounding relieved.

I didn't for a minute think that seven-year-old Derek needed a key ring, but all that mattered was that Woody thought so.

"If you hurry to the lounge, there might be some treats for you," Fran said.

We knew the girls loved the old guy, and why wouldn't they? He'd jump at a chance to change a light fixture for them in the dorm or rig up an extra connector for the lab or chase down an alleged mouse in the supply closet. They'd be happy to share the bounty with him today.

"Thank you kindly, ladies. You're always thinking of me," Woody said. He tipped an imaginary hat and pushed his barrel at a slightly faster pace toward the lounge.

"He's still trying to make it up to you," I said, when Woody was out of earshot.

"Two years later," Fran said, pocketing the key chain. "I forgave him a long time ago."

No one expected Woody ever to forgive himself, however, for inadvertently tossing important papers from Fran's office into the trash. She'd stacked a set of research notes on the floor on top of a broken three-ring binder. The arrangement looked so battered and messy that Woody had assumed it was all trash and hauled it away.

Poor Woody had been so distressed over the matter that he'd had our copy center make up two signs, "TRASH" and "NOT TRASH," and handed them out to every Franklin Hall faculty member. We laughed at the gesture at first, but the signs had come in handy more than once.

Fran and I had arrived at the intersection of the building's two corridors, resigned to the office work that awaited.

"Today should count for double overtime for us," I added.

"As if it matters to our paychecks," Fran said. She let out a sigh. "At least we got the degrees handed out without incident."

"And made a little dent in the food." My priorities were showing.

"And we won't have to deal with the mayor for another year," Fran said.

We parted ways. "That's the good news," I said.

CHAPTER $\sqrt{3}$

The town of Henley, incorporated in 1775, liked to think of itself as the Cambridge of southern Massachusetts, part of the rich tradition of academic hubs in the Commonwealth.

As such, about a two-block area around the campus in all directions was populated with coffee shops, pizza parlors, and small bookstores, plus an array of boutiques, some of which were affordable for the average college student, some not. I'd noticed that since the advent of male students to the Henley campus this year, several stores had added more athletic equipment and small electronics to their inventories. With parents in town, I expected business in all of the shops would be booming this weekend.

Unlike Harvard Square, however, or MIT, we had little choice in the way of grown-up restaurants. The Inn at Henley boasted the nicest table linens, the classiest music, and the most expensive entrées. The ones I'd tried had been worth the price. Tonight the place was packed with college faculty, graduates, and their families. I was glad Fran had

been smart enough to book two long tables weeks ago, a
job that technically was mine as department chair. Fran
was also smart enough to know I wouldn't think of it in
time. Again, I chalked it up to her highly developed skills
as a mother, grandmother, and household organizer.

"I love the charming nautical theme," Nicole's mother,
Nannette, said, as we settled in our places. From her oohs
and aahs at the fish nets hanging from the ceiling and the
large tanks of live fish at the entry, I gathered that her family was new to the Inn.

The Johnsons, who were natives of Henley, were one of
those matching-initials families, including Nicholas (Dad)
and twelve-year-old Nathan. I was sure they wore matching
colorful shirts when they vacationed in Hawaii. Or even on
Cape Cod. Even as I thought this, I realized the Johnsons'
situation didn't allow for many vacations. Nicole, the first
in her family to graduate from college, had been on a
financial-aid package that included work study in various
offices on campus.

"Cool sharks," Nathan said, as we looked over the
menu. Everyone seemed relieved when he pointed not to
the live fish tank, but to the oil paintings along one wall.
The three other N. Johnsons agreed.

I'd sometimes wondered what my parents would have
named a second child. Would my math teacher father have
prevailed again and added another famous mathematician
to the family? My patron was eighteenth-century mathematician Sophie Saint Germain. Thus my complex set of
initials: S. S. G. K. No monogrammed towels for me. I
envisioned a brother called Isaac Newton Knowles, with
the nickname Ink. Just as well he never materialized.

At tables next to our two at the Inn of Henley were
Judith Donohue, head of biology, with her majors, and on
the other side, Robert Michaels, chemistry chair, with his.
The table for physics, the fourth and smallest department
represented in Ben Franklin Hall, was far across the room,

making it inaccessible for the cross-table talk that was prevalent at gatherings like this.

We faculty encouraged and relied on talking among people at different tables, since it was always a little stressful to be around students' families. The crosstalk kept us from serious discussion of any one topic at a single table. Otherwise, there was too much potential for pushing parents' buttons. We had only the students' interpretation of the religious or political persuasion their parents adhered to and how tightly they adhered. Graduation and similar celebratory dinners, therefore, were never the relaxing events they were designed to be.

I was surprised that Kira and her parents joined us as planned, after the awkward incident at the Franklin Hall party. The animosity between Kira and her friends who'd bad-mouthed the mayor seemed to have been forgotten, and they were back to their usual chummy young selves.

The presence of the other majors and their parents helped the situation. The girls from four or five neighboring tables gossiped about who wore what, if anything, under her gown and what the guys might wear in a few years. Not exactly conversation worthy of young women with Bachelor of Arts degrees, but peaceful at least. And there was no talk of any "thing" between Kira and the mayor. I was ready to believe Fran was losing her touch on the reading-people front. Surely not every public official was guilty of preying on attractive young volunteers.

Having Nathan, a preteen, fish-and-chips boy at our table helped the conversation, since there were always the politically neutral Xboxes, soccer games, new apps, and 3-D movies to chat about. Nathan thought I'd be interested in his latest game, involving simple algebraic equations that had to be solved in order to gain access to a box where there was a key to another box, where there was another equation, another key, and so on. Not especially thrilling for me, but I was pleased that it was math- and not

war-related, and we all got through the main meal without
any plates of food being thrown to the floor.

I'd been sneaking text messages to Bruce once in a while
throughout the day, keeping my boyfriend up to speed on
the various dramatic moments. I refrained from phoning
him on days like today when he came off a twelve-hour
shift at Henley Airfield and slept on and off. He wasn't due
back at MAstar—Massachusetts Shock, Trauma, and Air
Rescue—the company he piloted for, until nine tomorrow
night, barring a national or even a citywide emergency.

"No food spilled," I'd thumbed, winding my way back
from a visit to the restroom with stops at the physics and
sociology tables.

"Fun time?" Bruce texted.

"U bet," I thumbed. "Ur up?"

"Up. Miss U."

"Me 2."

Chris Sizemore reached out to take my hand in greeting
as I approached the art history table. Several of the majors
had been creative with their mortarboards and wore them
now. I admired a Van Gogh–like sunflower on one and a
Monet-ish blue cathedral on another.

"Loved that scholarly speech, didn't you?" Chris asked,
rolling her baby blues. "Aren't you glad we hired the
mayor?" she added.

Too bad she couldn't simply enjoy her students' clever-
ness. I chose to smile and pretend temporary deafness.
"Can't hear you. Too noisy in here," I said, cupping my ear.

Chris's brother, Monty, was also in the group. Having
no business graduates yet in the new program, he'd apparently adopted his sister's majors today. As an adjunct,
Monty had no vote on faculty issues, but he'd had an opinion anyway, one that matched his sister's. He waved at me
and shouted, "Follow your dream," which I recognized as
a phrase the mayor had used two or three times in his
address. I felt another pang of sympathy for the mayor,

having to deal with controversy on all sides, from Superintendent Collins to businessman Monty Sizemore and his sister, and who knew what in between.

I let their comments float alone on the air and gave the Sizemores big waves as I went on my way. I breathed in the aroma of the many chunks of lobster rolled in buttery toast, an Inn specialty. I hoped the brother and sister combo behind me wasn't ruining the dinner for the graduates with their sore-loser grudges.

I got back to my table just as things were about to take a turn for the worse there. Apparently, someone had unthinkingly asked young Nathan how school was going, and his father had stepped in to respond.

"Don't get me started," the highly volatile Nicholas Johnson warned, but then started anyway. "Nathan goes to Zeeman Academy."

"Dad?" Nathan said in a soft, pleading voice, and everyone knew what he was asking.

I'd never had Nathan in class at Zeeman, but Mr. Johnson wasn't interested in what I was doing there, anyway. He went on, on his own track.

"The curriculum has been slowly deteriorating, although Mr. Richardson, our principal, is trying his best to keep things going. Our esteemed mayor will do nothing to help. He challenges everything Mr. Richardson tries to do. The budget is at about sixty percent what the regular schools are getting. Faculty are being let go, and the whole shebang will probably be out of business by the time Natalie's ready for first grade."

I hadn't known about Natalie, the fifth N. Johnson, and marveled at the span of ages in the family, until Nicole clarified. "Natalie's my cousin. We're kind of a clan on the western side of town. They talk about the Johnson and Johnson and Johnson company," she said, with an attempt at a light laugh. The new graduate was clearly trying to move from the topic of charter schools.

I never expected Zeeman Academy, my volunteer project this year, to be a main focus of graduation day. Twice a
week, I drove across town, in between my college classes
and office hours, and spent an hour or so with middle
schoolers. Besides helping their regular teacher, often over-
burdened with too many students, I led the students in
doing puzzles and games I'd developed to show how much
fun math can be.

The enterprise provided fun times for me as well. I'd
researched educational sites and found myself getting
hooked on math games. From simple arithmetic functions to
pre-algebra reasoning problems, the games were lively and
instructive for the most part. So what if the "rewards" for
correct answers involved sound effects, balloons, critters,
and spaceships. I harbored the vague notion that one day I'd
take on the task of creating more sophisticated games for
kids, with more fun math and fewer whistles. When Bruce
and Ariana heard me suggest that lately, they both declared
sophisticated games an oxymoron. To my dismay, Ariana
also challenged *fun math* as a legitimate phrase.

I'd been aware of tensions between the Zeeman Academy administration and the city officials, but I'd blocked
out the details as much as possible.

At dinner now, after Mr. Johnson's tirade, all eyes had
shifted to Kira and her dessert plate. We all seemed to be
thinking the same thing: A hot fudge brownie sundae
would make quite a mess on the sea blue carpet of the Inn
at Henley. I pulled my lemon sorbet closer to me and kept
two hands on the plate under the bowl.

"It's beyond me how that man got into office. Oh, wait,
he's part of the family, with a capital *F*," Mr. Johnson said,
continuing his rant. "His father, his grandfather, probably
eventually his son will—"

"Let's not get into that now, dear," Mrs. Johnson interrupted, while Nicole made a visor for her eyes with the
palm of her hand.

"You mean you don't want to talk about how Graves is determined to make his way up the ladder on the backs of our kids?" Mr. Johnson continued.

Mrs. Johnson put her hand on her husband's arm, a universal signal from one spouse to another, meaning *Cool it, Sweetie*. Hubby finally got the message and focused on his drink. He retained his sour look, however, making a point that he was not pleased at being cut off. I was glad I wouldn't be riding home with them this evening.

During the Johnsons' display, Kira's parents, the shyest of the group, took long swallows of wine. Kira, bless her, excused herself from the table and headed for the restroom. Nicole and two other new graduates followed her.

And the second party of the day came to an abrupt, awkward end.

After witnessing a few tearful good-byes among the students and participating in more keep-in-touch promises, Fran and I walked out of the restaurant and into a pleasantly chilly night. Fran would be driving me back to campus where Bruce would pick me up. My own car was in the shop downtown having its dashboard warning lights reset to "Don't stay on all the time."

"Do you like my new wheels?" Fran asked, as I buckled myself into her shiny minivan. "I bought this to accommodate my grandkids and their teams. There's a game console in the back."

"That's great. You can always use the experience to advise the first student who submits a thesis proposal for the application of mathematics to the mechanics of video games."

"Do you know someone who wants to take that on?" Fran asked.

"Not yet, but I can almost guarantee that some guy from the freshman class will want to do it in three years."

"I'll be deep into retirement and soccer-grandmother duties by then."

"Nuh-uh." I couldn't bear the thought of the department without Fran. "You'd miss days like today."

Fran blew a raspberry unbecoming a mathematician grandmother, and clearly indicating that she was too young to retire.

Bruce assumed his hunky stance as soon as Fran approached the parking lot near Franklin Hall. He leaned against the front fender of his new black muscle car, his arms folded across his chest, his dark hair rustling in the slight breeze. All he needed to complete the picture was pointy leather boots and a cowboy hat, but instead he wore his usual off-duty khakis and a black polo shirt. I couldn't see his grin, but I knew it was there, and I loved it.

Ten minutes later, with Fran on her way home, Bruce and I were next in line at Jimmie's "Not Just Ice Cream," across from the east side of campus. I almost chose a red velvet cupcake, to go along with the new dessert craze in Henley, but in the end walked out with my usual chocolate-chocolate milk shake.

"No dinner at the Inn?" Bruce asked. He who had dined on granola bars and orange-colored chips all day was satisfied with a waffle cone of butter toffee ice cream.

"The classier the restaurant, the smaller the portions," I explained.

We strolled the campus, now minus the ugly temporary stage, taking the long way to my office and Bruce's car, both on the west side. Most of the buildings were dark, with only a smattering of students in each of the three dorms.

I was surprised to see lights on anywhere in the Administration Building, but especially on the ground floor of the faculty offices wing. The humanities profs weren't lucky enough to have their own building as we in the math and science community did, so their offices were jammed together at the back of Admin. Some dedicated English or history teachers were working late tonight. I doubted they were poring over the fall syllabus. More likely, cramming to get grades done so they could take off and not show up again until Labor Day.

During my early days at Henley, I'd thought it strange that the imposing Administration Building, with its English Collegiate Gothic architecture, faced away from the rest of the campus. I was used to schools where the main building opened onto a quadrangle of sorts. But Henley's Admin fronted on the busy Henley Boulevard. Once I learned the history of the college, I realized that the only way for the school to grow from that single building a hundred years ago was to plant its newer structures in back. Later a fountain was built a few yards from the rear of Admin, and now it served as the center of campus.

Bruce and I drifted toward the fountain, enjoying Jimmie's ice cream, ready to take turns sharing "how was your day" stories that didn't fit into text messages.

"The Bat Phone was quiet until about four this morning," Bruce said. "Then this semi on I-495 by Hopedale runs into an SUV coming back from the Cape." He used his hands, tipping his waffle cone precariously, to mimic a collision that I knew couldn't have had a happy ending. "This little kid, maybe six years old, was asleep on the backseat. No seat belt." Bruce uttered a sad grunt. "We flew the boy and his mother to County General. An ambulance took the dad and the semi driver, but . . ." He shook his head and drew a long breath.

We sat down on one of the curved concrete benches surrounding the fountain. I put my head on his shoulder and rubbed his back for a few quiet minutes.

"Did anyone make it?" I asked.

"The little boy, Ricky, is badly injured, but he's going to

be okay. So's his mother. But the father, who was driving, is gone. And the semi driver doesn't have a scratch on him." He turned and brushed the concern from my face with his hand and a slight, resigned smile. "How about you?" he asked. "How was all the pomp and circumstance?"

"Really?" I asked Bruce, our shorthand for "Do you want me to tell you silly, distracting commencement day stories?"

Outbursts like Kira's, disputes over petty politics and whatever else was going on in the schools or at the mayor's campaign headquarters, paled in the light of Bruce's Bat Phone duties.

"Really," Bruce said. "Tell me some campus gossip."

My most upsetting moments today, besides our aborted parties, had come from Elysse Hutchins, a student who was unhappy with her final exam grade and wanted me to reconsider.

I launched into the reasons for my annoyance with Elysse—she'd disputed points I'd taken off her exam for not following instructions on a statistics problem. She'd blasted me in an email after I explained my reasoning for the grade and declined to change it.

"She's a transfer student and I've given her special attention all semester," I said. I remembered all the times I'd sat in front of the whiteboard with the thin, pixie-haired blond, reviewing math methods long after office hours were over. "I've gone out of my way to make up for any gaps caused by the transfer."

"I'm sure you have," Bruce said, trying hard to pay attention, but not fully engaged.

I switched topics and brought up the tension over the performance of charter schools and the way they're funded. "Some of the families were accusing Mayor Graves of neglecting the charters," I reported.

"The charter setup is made for disaster," Bruce said,

coming to life again. "You know what I mean from working at Zeeman, but the problem is system-wide. I remember
when my niece was in a charter school in Boston. My sister
was on the board and went nuts trying to keep it together,
with more reporting and paperwork than teaching going
on, and no one seemed to care about discipline or stan-
dards. It was always a question of 'Who's in charge?'
You've got a school that is and isn't under supervision of
the district and the superintendent of schools."

"I wouldn't want Pat Collins's job," I said, remembering
the superintendent's glowering visage on the stage today.

"He goes home to a cushy residence on the Cape,
remember. During my pilot-to-the-stars days, I picked him
up now and then to take him to a meeting here, but I guess
now he has a home in Henley, also."

"It's hard to say who's right in all this. It's probably not
all the superintendent's fault. Not the principals' either," I
said.

"Nothing works if there's no clear line of authority."

Thus spoke a retired air force man.

By ten fifteen, according to the old chimes from Franklin Hall, we decided it was time to leave. We stood and
brushed off particles of dust and leaves deposited by the
breeze, ready for the walk to Bruce's car, marveling at how
still and lovely the campus was. The graduation hubbub
and the squealing from one of the last all-female graduating classes were over. Who knew what kind of celebratory
sounds the male grads would make in a couple of years?
Perhaps they'd simply say, "Good job, bro," and knock
knuckles.

Seemingly out of nowhere, we heard clumping noises—
dragging sounds on the lawn and then shuffled footsteps on
the pathway, coming from the direction of the dorms and
the east end of the Administration Building.

"Help!" a low, pained voice cried. "Help me!"

We turned and saw a man in a light business suit

staggering toward us, as if he would topple over on the next step. He looked a lot like the mayor, with auburn highlights showing up under the campus security lamps.

On closer inspection—it was the mayor.

I could hardly believe it. He teetered and swayed till he got to the edge of the fountain, where we'd been sitting, then fell in, headfirst. His commencement speech wasn't that bad, I thought, that he had to get himself wasted. How embarrassing. What was he thinking? He should be grateful that it was Bruce and me who were here and not someone from his opponent's campaign or parents with a decidedly negative opinion of him to begin with.

Bruce didn't stop to judge or make a guess about what had happened or why. He snapped to it, on full alert, as if he were back in the air force in Saudi Arabia, or at the MAstar helipad rushing to get to an accident scene. He made it to the fountain in three long steps and lifted the mayor out by the shoulders. He laid him facedown on the grass.

I was confused—why didn't he put him on his back? That's what television emergency crews did when they gave CPR. Faceup.

Then I saw the blade sticking up in the air.

I drew in my breath. What had happened?

"Your sweater." Bruce addressed me more calmly than I would have thought possible. "And nine-one-one. Make sure you give the address."

Bruce was on autopilot, so to speak, issuing commands. I was grateful for his reminder that the emergency dispatcher might not be able to trace the exact location of my cell.

I dug in my purse for my phone, shrugging off my cotton sweater at the same time. I stuck the phone under my chin talking to dispatch, hopping around the fountain, trying to free my sweater from my arms, as if I'd been hired to do a frantic, comic dance.

I handed my sweater to Bruce, who promptly wrapped
it around the shiny silver blade, close to the wound in the
mayor's back, and applied pressure to the surrounding
area. At first the blade looked to me like a knife, then a
screwdriver or some other tool, and finally I recognized it
as a letter opener. One of the special Henley College letter
openers, in fact. The same letter opener that the Mathematics Department and every other department handed out to
its majors on graduation day. My eyes were locked on my
sweater, steadily soaking up the mayor's blood. Finally, I
turned away from the unlikely, gruesome sight at our beautiful fountain.

I thought I heard low cries of help and indecipherable
words from the mayor as he lay on the ground, but it might
have been the rustling of the nearby trees, or my mind in
trauma.

At one point, Bruce stood for a moment and twisted his
body in all directions, taking in the campus. Stretching, I
assumed. I had always thought I'd like to see Bruce in
action, at his job. And although Bruce simply piloted a
helicopter, he assured me, and left the medical ministra-
tions to the flight nurses, I saw now that he was ready to fill
in wherever he was needed. I had a new appreciation for
my boyfriend and his grace under pressure and knew I'd
never again need an up close demonstration of his skills.

By the time the emergency workers arrived, I felt I'd been
holding my breath all evening.

The noise and lights from the vehicles and crew turned
the campus inside out, from its serene late-night ambience
to a loud and busy scene. I hadn't noticed the small crowd
gathering, approaching as near as they could get to the
fountain without interfering with the workers or battling
with the police.

I stepped back and surveyed the groups. I saw students

in various sleepwear outfits huddled together, most of them texting or speaking on cell phones and snapping pictures. Some of the students waved at me, but I kept my head down and pretended not to see them. It didn't seem the right occasion for meeting and greeting, and they did have the good sense not to make their way over to me. I couldn't tell whether it was clear to any of the spectators that the body sprawled out on their campus lawn was that of the mayor, the man who'd addressed them from a stage only a few hours ago. But I wouldn't have been surprised if the scene had already gone viral, no matter who they thought the victim was.

My lovely white sweater was now in an evidence bag, as was other detritus of the mayor's plunge. After conferring with the police and dispatched crew, Bruce had jogged across the campus to my office, unsolicited, to pick up a jacket for me. There was no reason for my chill other than the rupture of my quiet campus, but I was grateful as he wrapped me in my own hooded sweatshirt. It wasn't the freshest item of clothing I owned, the garment of choice after my occasional bout of exercise, but at least it wasn't bloody.

"Did the mayor say anything while you were . . . down there with him?" I asked Bruce.

Bruce shrugged. "He said, 'Sophie, something something.'"

I took a quick step back, recoiling from Bruce's response, nearly tripping on an uneven patch of grass, and almost ending up sprawled on the ground. "What? What something something?"

Bruce shrugged. "I couldn't get anything else."

"Was he asking for me? Do you think he wanted to talk to me? Or was he just pointing me out? What did he mean?"

Bruce took my hand to steady me. "I don't think he meant anything by it, Soph. Just, maybe, you were in his field of vision."

"But you were the one rushing to help him."

"He doesn't know my name; he knows yours." Bruce took a breath and, I was sure, called up the protocols for distraught witnesses in his MAstar handbook. "You know, he was mumbling. He might not even have said your name, Soph. I don't know why I sounded so sure. Now that I think about it, he might have said, 'Off me,' like 'Get this knife off me.'" Bruce made *off me* sound uncannily like *Sophie*, but I wasn't buying it.

"You said—"

Bruce patted my hand before he let it go. "I'd better run back and see if I can be of any help to those guys. You'll be okay for a little while?"

I nodded, as much as I hated for him to leave. I glanced up at the back of Admin and saw that whatever offices had been lit up a few minutes ago had gone dark. Probably whoever was working over there realized there was more excitement down here. No kidding.

I took a deep breath and turned from Admin, which now looked like an enormous haunted house.

I didn't believe Bruce's *off me* theory for a minute. Did the mayor think I was the one who'd stabbed him? I felt a new chill. I zipped my jacket all the way to my neck and threw the hood over my head. Had the mayor been on his way to see me when someone put a pseudo-knife in his back? Why would he want to see me? Why would someone stop him by stabbing him?

I wanted answers, but I'd have to wait until he was recovered enough to ask him.

It seemed the mayor was still in my life for a while longer.

CHAPTER $\sqrt{4}$

The weeks after graduation, before the start of summer school, were supposed to be the most relaxing for the faculty. Sure, there was research to get back to, and prep for the interim classes and the fall term, but there was also time to bid the campus good-bye for a while and hit the beaches or the mountains, both of which were plentiful along the eastern seaboard.

The presence of homicide detective Virgil Mitchell, Bruce's best friend since college, pushed that dream away. Virgil had arrived about the same time as the ambulance, patrol cars, and fire truck. Though I'd seen a letter opener sticking out of the mayor's back, I hadn't fully processed the idea that someone had deliberately stabbed him or that he might not survive the attack. Even now I held on to the possibility that he'd fallen on the letter opener, never mind the shaky physics involved, or that a party game had gone bad. Virgil would figure it all out and declare it an

accident; the mayor would end up good as new after a brief
recovery period; and we could all go back to normal.

Someone in uniform thought it was a good idea for
Bruce to ride in the ambulance, so off they went, leaving
me with my imagination. I was free to run rampant over
the idea that a city official who might be dead might have
said my name as one of his last words, and might have been
trying to ask me something. Or tell me something. Or . . .

I needed to calm down, to do a statistical analysis of
the theories. I chose one of Bruce's several interpretations,
the least worrisome, as the most likely: I happened to
be the person the mayor saw as he stumbled toward the
fountain looking for help. It made sense—Bruce was wearing a black polo shirt; I was wearing a white sweater. I
knew enough physics to do a little riff on the pattern of
reflection from the lamp near the fountain.

When Virgil approached, I collapsed for a moment on
his hulking chest. Virgil was large in size and in heart, and
this wasn't the first time his presence had provided comfort. Just seeing someone who was like family, who'd shared
many a meal in my home, brought a measure of relief. He
gave me a brief hug and walked me away from the scene
(why hadn't I thought of that?), toward the back of the looming redbrick Administration Building.

We sat on a bench looking away from the fountain. My
mind wandered to irrelevant details like whether I should
call Ariana, who was combining bead shop business with
a vacation in San Diego, and how convenient that a hazmat
team had arrived to rid the water of the mayor's blood.

"Tough night, huh?" Virgil said.

"Is he going to be all right?" I asked.

He handed me Bruce's car keys. "Bruce said your car
isn't here, so you'll need these. He'll get a ride to your
house a little later."

"I thought he was just drunk—the mayor, I mean—but
the wound . . ." I closed my eyes as if the image of blood

spurting everywhere was in front of me and not in my head. "Did someone do that to him?"

Nice going, Sophie. It's a good thing it was Virgil and he was used to hearing dumb things escape my lips.

"You were here at graduation, when the mayor gave his speech?" Virgil asked. He bent over, leaning his forearms on his wide thighs, bringing himself down to my level.

It would have been hard to find two more physically different men than Bruce and Virgil, except that they both had widow's peaks of dark hair. There was my fitness freak, ice-climbing boyfriend on the one hand, and his somewhat lumbering, oversize buddy on the other. But in temperament the men were so much alike, both able to respond to crises with professionalism and compassion.

Thanks to his bent-over posture on the bench, I was able to meet Virgil's eyes. "It was a beautiful night. All the graduation craziness was over. Bruce and I got ice cream and thought we'd stroll around for a while." I felt my throat choke up. "I'm sorry to be such a flake right now."

"Take your time, Sophie." Virgil gave me a minute. "You heard the mayor's speech?"

I finally became aware that I hadn't answered Virgil's question. "Yes, pretty much all of the faculty were here. The mayor gave the keynote address."

I didn't mention how I now regretted all the criticism I'd levied against the poor man, how Fran and I had gossiped like schoolgirls during his talk. I found myself hoping Mayor Graves would be well enough to address us again next year. I swore that I'd pay attention and clap the loudest, and whatever it took, I'd strong-arm the whole rest of the faculty into doing the same.

"Do you have any idea what time the mayor left the campus?" Virgil asked.

"His speech was over at three fifteen. I don't know if he left the campus right away, but he left the stage with his wife at that time."

Virgil grinned. "Looked at your watch a lot, huh?"

At last, I felt a smile creep onto my face. "Nothing personal."

"I've been to a few ceremonies like that. I get it. Bruce indicated that the mayor mentioned your name before he fell? Any idea why?"

"Bruce said that?" What happened to "get this knife *off me*" instead of "*Sophie*"? "No. I can't imagine why he would have said my name. I don't think I ever heard the mayor call me by my first name."

"But you had conversations with him in the past?"

Ring, rring. Rring, rring.

The old-fashioned sound from my smartphone, the unlikely ringtone suggested by my new age friend Ariana, the one with multiple body piercings and rainbow-colored hair. To look at our fashion choices, you'd never know we'd been best friends since our days at the same schools, from K to twelve. I wished she herself were here now and not just her selection of ringtone.

I snuck a look at my phone's screen, in case there was an even more important person than a homicide detective wanting to talk to me. I was surprised to see Monty Size-more's name. If the mayor's fall had already made the Internet news, Monty would want details right away. I hoped he and his sister weren't gloating at the fate of his nemesis.

I wasn't sure why, but Monty had always struck me as somewhat shallow, a wheeler-dealer who liked to be on the inside of things, always checking to see if he had the attention of the highest-ranking person in the room. Fran said it was just my perception, because I had misgivings about anyone who wasn't an academic, and Monty was definitely a businessman first, an instructor second.

"It's one of the faculty. I'll call him back later," I told Virgil. Before I could switch my phone to off, I noticed another incoming call, this one from Fran. Their calls were more blows of reality. There was no way Monty or Fran would be trying to reach me at this hour unless they'd heard the news. Or seen it on YouTube. I clicked off. I'd call Fran later. And maybe Monty.

"We were talking about how you've had interactions with the mayor on a personal level in the past," Virgil said.

A big leap. This was Virgil in action as an interrogator, never minding the fact that his interviewee this time was a woman who provided a comfortable den for him to hang out with his buddy, and all the pizza they could eat.

"I wouldn't call our interactions personal. You know I volunteer at the Zeeman Academy, a charter school that seems to be a focus of his lately. His son, Cody, was a student there through the eighth grade. He'll be a high school senior in the fall."

"But the mayor is still involved in the Zeeman school?"

I nodded. "Whether as the mayor, or as an alumni parent, I don't know. He's dropped by my class a few times. But it's always 'Professor Knowles' or 'Dr. Knowles' and 'Mayor Graves.' We're not on a first-name basis."

"When was the last time you saw him at that school?"

An easy one. "Friday. I guess that was just yesterday." I blew out a breath, as if it were my first in a while. "It was the last day for the eighth graders. The school is K through eight. We had a little send-off with cake and punch and kind of crafty diplomas, even though there's still one more week of school for the other grades. I personally don't like it when kids have five graduations on the way to college, but"—I stopped—"why am I telling you that?"

"No problem," Virgil said, taking a stretch break himself, giving me time. "The mayor was at the party?"

"He'd been at the school and he was on his way out, I think, and stepped into the lounge for a minute."

"He have any cake? Say anything to you?"

I thought a few seconds. "He had cake, said hello to me. He shook my hand, the way politicians do, and said

something like 'good job,' nothing specific. He never called
me 'Sophie.' He left within seven minutes."

Virgil smiled, though I wasn't sure why.

An emergency worker called Virgil away and I was left
with my thoughts. I became aware of many more uniformed officers now, spread over the campus, speaking to
the students and some parents. As ugly as the temporary
stage had been, I'd have given anything to have it in my
view now, rather than the unmistakable lights, vehicle
rumbles, and chatter that signaled calamity.

Unlike me, most faculty and administrators had called
it a day hours ago. Except for whoever had been working
on the ground floor of Admin while Bruce and I ate our ice
cream. I wondered now if whoever it was had seen anything useful. That person would have had a good vantage
point. I made a note to mention it to Virgil, though I figured that one of the swarm of officers would make the dis-
covery as they continued to interview everyone.

A news crew had also arrived, with enough lights to
give the area around the fountain a garish look. I wondered
if they knew more than I did about the incident, and how
they would spin it.

"Zeeman Academy is way over on the west side of
town, right?"

I started, unaware that Virgil was back.

"On Brier Road, yes. It's a new facility, whereas the
other two charters in the county took over older buildings.
They were traditional schools that either closed from a
decline in population or were converted by a bona fide
charter."

"Again, do you know what his interest was in that particular school?"

I shrugged. "Maybe because his son had been a student
there, but, as I said, Cody left Zeeman three years ago."

"How often would you say the mayor comes around now?"

I strained to remember the occasions when the mayor

had shown up at Zeeman on days that I was present. "Almost every week lately. He spent most of the time looking over papers, I'm not sure what kind, in the principal's office."

"Who's the principal there?"

"His name is Douglas Richardson."

"You like him?"

I paused. "I guess so, yes. He's kind of mid-career, ambitious. I know he's grateful for a college presence at the school. Joan Bradley from Henley's English Department has set up a program there, also. She got the kids interested in putting out a newsletter."

An enormous wave of tiredness came over me. I pinched my eyelids and took a deep breath to help me wake up.

"We're almost done," Virgil said. "It's important for me to get all this down as soon as possible."

"I understand."

"The papers you mentioned the mayor was looking at, were they like ledgers? Bank statements? Was the mayor tracking some financial problem?"

"I don't think so. From what I overheard in the lunch-room, he was checking the records for applications to the school, acceptances, test scores, that kind of thing."

"Any idea why?"

"I'm sorry. I didn't pay that much attention. I'm not sure exactly, but with special schools like Zeeman Academy, there are always issues around numbers. They need a certain number of applications and acceptances to stay in business. And their test scores are always scrutinized. Some schools inflate grades to look better on paper. I'm not saying that happens at Zeeman, just that it's a general problem throughout the system and in any city."

"But it could be happening at Zeeman?"

"Sure. It's possible but I really can't say."

I felt a chill and stuck my hands in the pockets of my sweatshirt. I doubted the temperature had changed.

Another wave of exhaustion came over me. It seemed I'd been sitting on the bench, struggling to remember things, to answer Virgil's questions, for hours. Never mind that probably less than fifteen minutes had passed.

"And Mayor Graves would be on which side of that?"

"Of what?"

"Would it be to his advantage to inflate the grades or not inflate the grades?"

I shrugged and shook my head. "Hard to say. It would depend on the rest of his agenda for education." I gave Virgil a pleading look. "Do you think we could continue this tomorrow?"

"I know you're tired and this is tough." He patted my hand. "Just a little bit more, Sophie, I promise. Can you give me your impression of where the mayor stood on this issue of inflating the grades?"

I took a deep breath, trying for a second wind. "Not really. I try to stay out of school politics when I'm not actually on the faculty."

"I suppose there's enough of that here." Virgil swept his arm in a large arc, taking in the Administration Building in front of us. "A lot of politics?"

"You said it," I replied, thinking of the debate over whether we should have invited the mayor to speak at commencement in the first place.

A flash of panic shot through me. "No, it couldn't be."

"You think of something?"

I regretted my outburst, but there was no going back. I had to tell Virgil about the mayor's being at the center of conflicting opinions among the faculty. I gave as casual a description as I could, but Virgil wanted names.

"You seriously think someone on the Henley faculty would stab the mayor because he or she didn't get to choose who would be the graduation speaker?" I asked.

"You'd be surprised at the motives I've come across."

"But he's already given the speech, so what would be the point?" I asked, fully awake now.

"As I said, you'd be surprised. I have to cover all bases, rule people out, Sophie. You know that."

"If we attacked someone every time we lost a vote at faculty senate meetings, you'd be setting up camp here full-time." Now I was heating up, defending my colleagues.

"You were on the losing side of that vote?"

I thought Virgil might be joking. Then I saw his serious expression in the light from the floods on the Administration Building in front of us.

After a few stuttering sounds, I admitted, "I lost, yes, but it was no big deal."

"Why didn't you want the mayor to speak?"

"It wasn't so much that I didn't want the mayor to speak. I wanted someone else to speak. Some of us thought that an academic or a researcher would have been a more appropriate keynoter at a baccalaureate ceremony."

"Who was the other candidate?"

"It wasn't that kind of vote, with one guy against another. Our speaker cancelled. They're scheduled way in advance. In fact, we'll already be looking at candidates for next year at our summer faculty meeting."

If I'd been in a joking mood, I'd have asked Virgil if he wanted his name on the short list of potential candidates.

"Who was the scheduled speaker?" he asked.

"Dr. Muriel James from Harvard Med was supposed to give the address, but she had to have surgery last week, so we needed a replacement."

"Besides you, who else was against the mayor?" Virgil flipped his notebook to a new page and held his pen over the clean sheet. I imagined many a guilty person being intimidated by the gesture. So was I. I cleared my throat.

"No one was *against* the mayor." I thought I'd made that

clear, but apparently not. Was my friend Virgil taking advantage of my weakened state?

Virgil tapped his pen. "Who voted 'no' then?"

"Is this legal? Don't you need a warrant for this?" I asked, about 75 percent kidding and the rest serious.

Virgil was 100 percent serious. "Names, Sophie."

As uncomfortable as I was exposing colleagues, I saw no other choice. I did my best to remember the faculty members, besides me, who'd argued for a different speaker.

Henley was less than an hour away from more than a hundred colleges, universities, art schools, law schools, med schools, and divinity schools in the greater Boston area. There was no question that among the Henley faculty, we had enough contacts to talk a professor at one of them into collecting a fee for a fifteen-minute commencement address.

In a way, we were all against the mayor. The aye votes were really votes to cooperate with our president and deans who saw money coming to the school in the form of a new building.

I gave Virgil ten names from the losing side, as he wanted to put it. Four representing science and mathematics—Fran's and mine included—and six from assorted humanities departments.

"Anyone stand out as more determined than the others?"

"More determined to do what? All these questions, Virgil. Has the mayor died? Was he . . . murdered?"

Virgil slapped his notebook lightly against the palm of his hand. "Anyone react more strongly than others at the meeting? Make threats. Anything like that?"

I took a deep breath. The kind just before you might lie to the police.

I thought of Chris Sizemore, who'd stormed out of the meeting after the vote to invite the mayor. She'd thrown the paper with the single-item agenda into the trash and said something like, "This is a big mistake." I never figured out why Chris's reaction was over-the-top, but she was quick-tempered at the best of times. She was also young and ide-alistic, which accounted for a lot in my book.

I analyzed Virgil's questions. *Did anyone react strongly?* he'd asked. Now that I thought about it, Chris may have sim-ply *rushed* out of the room, which was different from *storm-ing* out. Maybe she was late for another meeting. Or maybe she had a bathroom emergency.

Virgil had also asked if anyone had made threats. I wouldn't have called *This is a big mistake* a threat, just an opinion. It wasn't as if Chris had wielded a gun while she said it. Or a letter opener.

In any case, Chris's name was on the list I'd already rattled off to Virgil. If there was anything more to her out-burst, he'd rout it out.

Hadn't I heard that the wife was always a prime sus-pect? Nora Graves had probably had to put up with a lot as Henley's First Lady, while her husband had his eyes on a senate seat, and perhaps an eye where it shouldn't be. I tried to imagine the beautifully put-together Nora Graves coming down on her husband's back with enough force to kill him. I couldn't see it, especially when I inserted their teenager, Cody, into the picture. I wondered if the Henley PD ruled out wives with children.

While I was thinking of names I should give to Virgil, Kira Gilmore came to mind, but Virgil was asking about volatile behavior against the mayor, not in defense of him. No need to bring her into this right now. I was sure Virgil and his team would interview all the students present, if they hadn't already. Kira was the last person I could think of who'd be able to hurt someone.

"Sophie?" Virgil asked. "Anyone stand out?"

"No," I told him. "No one in particular." I took a breath. "Do you think I could go home now?"

This time he nodded, but he gave me a look that said he'd be back with that question and more.

I felt I'd done my duty, or close enough, by Virgil. Maybe he would return the favor.

"What do the doctors say? Can you tell me anything about the mayor's condition?"

"Not at the moment."

"You can't tell me at the moment or you don't know?"

Virgil smiled. "Anything else I can do for you?"

I shook my head. I knew when to call it quits. For now.

I looked toward the crowd, still milling around the fountain, just outside the crime scene tape. The news crew hadn't packed it in yet. A stiff young man was being recorded for his fifteen minutes of fame. How much more could there be to say about the incident? Enough to fill a whole news hour, I supposed.

I didn't want to walk close to the gathering by myself, especially since I'd spotted a few students I knew. I was in no mood to chat, and even less inclined to be interviewed by a woman with so much hair spray the breezes were redirected when they hit her "do."

"Would you walk me to Bruce's car?" I asked Virgil.

Virgil rose and extended his arm. I guessed I looked like I needed help.

CHAPTER $\sqrt{5}$

I pulled up to my house and parked Bruce's car in front. My little blue cottage was dark except for the small flood-light that clicked on when I walked toward the door. I'd hoped to find candles burning in the window and Bruce waiting with a cold drink. Or a hot drink. Anything to welcome me. You'd think I'd been the needy one lying in a hospital bed, or called to duty on my evening off.

I could almost smell a little bruschetta snack. It had been a long time since my stuffed scrod dinner, and the clerks at Jimmie's didn't make milk shakes as generously as they used to.

Inside, I was tempted to walk past the blinking number eleven on my answering machine and head straight for the shower. I was sure my cell phone, now turned back on, also was bursting with voice mails and texts. I didn't think I could handle them, especially after the grueling interview with Virgil. I'd get to them later. Right now I had to clean up. Though I knew it was physically impossible, I felt I had poor Mayor Graves's blood splatter all over my clothes.

Rring, rring. Rring, rring.

But even at a few minutes before midnight, I couldn't ignore a summons in the present, especially when I saw that it was Bruce calling from his landline. Uh-oh, he'd gone home. There'd be no shared drinks tonight.

"Hey, Sophie. I've been leaving messages everywhere. You okay?"

"I just got in. I had my phone off while I was being grilled by Detective Mitchell." I hoped I sounded lighter and breezier than I felt.

Bruce chuckled. "I left the hospital just as Virge was coming in."

I couldn't believe I'd been whining about going home when Virgil still had a long night ahead of him.

"Is the mayor . . . ?" I held my breath.

"Gone." One word, in a voice that was soft and low.

I carried my phone to the den, flicking lights on all the way, and fell onto the couch. My body seemed to sag another six inches, from the inside out. "How awful, Bruce."

"Yeah, everyone did their best, though it didn't look good from the start. He suffered an intrathoracic hemorrhage when his right lung was penetrated."

"By the letter opener?" I couldn't imagine a benign instrument like the Henley College letter opener being the cause of a mortal wound. It never seemed that sharp when I used it for its intended purpose. "How could a simple letter opener do all that damage?"

"Anything can do a lot of damage in the right hands. Or the wrong hands. Guys in prison use whittled down soap, remember. It's a matter of the amount of force, in the right spot, with the right . . ." Bruce paused. "You don't need to know this right now, do you?"

No, I didn't. "It's okay. I'm so sorry. What a terrible thing for his family." I felt I should also offer condolences to Bruce, who'd lost two people in one day, first a little boy's father in a car accident and now the mayor. I couldn't imagine the letdown if your job description was to keep people alive and you failed. "You must be beat."

"Uh-huh. I came straight home. One of the EMTs was coming my way and drove me. Hope that's okay?"

"Of course it's okay. I wish I could do something for you. I can swing by with your car anytime tomorrow," I offered.

"Nuh-uh. That won't work. Larry's going to pick me up in a few hours. We all have to be boots-to-the-ground first thing. There's no telling how people will react when they wake up to this news. It's all over the Internet already, but most Henley citizens are sleeping."

"They're not expecting riots in the streets, are they?"

"You never know what backlash there might be. The murder of a city official is not your everyday crime."

There it was. *Murder.* The official word from a more or less official person, though I'd already lost all hope of a freak accident as Virgil was questioning me.

"The more tension, the more potential for accidents," Bruce continued. "Plus, until they know why this happened, security will be beefed up for everyone on the mayor's staff and family and the whole city council. Every kind of emergency vehicle is going to be on standby."

"Medevac helicopters included," I said.

"This is me, saluting."

I could hear Bruce's voice fading. And though I had many more questions—How is the city's First Lady holding up? Who is the mayor's successor? Do the police have any leads on who killed him or why? Were there fingerprints on the letter opener?—Bruce didn't need my particular version of grilling, even if he might know more than I did.

I told myself it was good that Bruce wasn't worried about me. Why should he be? It wasn't as if a good friend of mine had died. As I'd told Virgil, the mayor and I weren't even on a first-name basis. And as long as wishing he would disappear from the stage during his speech didn't count as inflicting bodily harm, I should be able to get on with the weekend without a debilitating reaction.

The self-to-self pep talk didn't take. An unexpected wave of guilt washed over me. True, I'd had nothing to do with the mayor's stabbing, but had I done everything I could to help him? At least Bruce and the team of medical workers could say that they had.

I had to ask. "Did he regain consciousness?"

"No, he never . . ." Bruce paused and I knew he'd figured out my predicament. "Sophie, I know what you're thinking. There was nothing you could have done to save the man. Less than nothing."

Instead of a small lecture on what *less than nothing* meant, mathematically speaking, it was my distress that came rushing out. "I should have gone to the hospital with you, or at least when I was finished with Virgil. Maybe I'd have been able to talk to him, find out why he said my name."

"Sophie, about your name—"

"You can't deny it, Bruce. If you told Virgil about it, you must have been pretty sure that's what he said. What if he wanted something from me? Something that could simply have made his last moments peaceful, or even helped ID his killer?" I paused, entertaining a flash of a thought. "In fact, why didn't he say his killer's name instead of mine?"

"I'm coming over," Bruce said.

That's all I needed to hear. "No, no. I'm sorry I brought it up. I'm exhausted myself and I'd be asleep before you got here," I lied. "And anyway, you don't have a car."

"I could take the helicopter."

No wonder I loved him. Who else could have had me laughing at the end of this conversation?

"Good night, Bruce," I said. "Call me if you need anything."

I hardly heard his "Thanks. I love you" before the dial tone.

I, on the other hand, was fully wired, even after a shower and a cup of warm, purportedly sleep-inducing tea. I made a note to tell Ariana her special no-fail green brew had failed me.

There was no dearth of items on my to-do list. I had a stack of resumes to review for the new associate professor position we'd budgeted for in the Mathematics Department, and deadlines to meet for the magazines I submitted puzzles to on a regular basis. I needed to sketch out a couple of exercises for my last week at Zeeman Academy and recover my momentum on my differential equations research, which always suffered at the end of a school year.

None of these projects called out to me.

Maybe a little TV would do it. I plopped on the couch in the den and scrolled through the programs I'd recorded. I hadn't realized how many crime dramas were on the list. Usually they were my favorite genre, but not now, when there was a real crime drama in my life. I had a feeling the murder of Mayor Graves would take considerably longer than one hour to be solved.

Feeling the need for more personal contact, I decided first to call Ariana, who was winding up her business at a bead show in California. The night was young for Ariana, where it was only a few minutes before ten o'clock. She was my best friend and owner of A Hill of Beads, my venue for exploring my creative side, as she called it. As if making a bracelet from wire and pieces of glass was more creative than composing a wordplay puzzle or solving a fourth-order differential equation.

I was surprised to hear her voice. Could my socially

intense friend be alone in her hotel room on a Saturday night?

"Another bomb of a date," Ariana explained. "Besides that, I've seen enough new products to last a year. One more tray of hammer-faceted beads or pewter findings and I'll be dizzy. I did pick up lots of great beading books for the bookrack in the store, though. You might like to look through them first."

"I can't wait."

"I hear your attitude. Anyway, I have great hopes for tomorrow. I signed up for volleyball on the beach."

"Of course you did." I pictured Ariana in an outfit that showed more of her piercing and ink than usual. For the trip, she'd highlighted her long blond hair with green stripes in honor of Aestas, the Roman goddess of the summer.

"Get it, Sophie?" she'd asked, showing me her latest look as I drove her to the airport. "Aestas is often pictured standing by an emerald throne."

She knew I'd never get it, and also that it didn't spoil our friendship one bit.

"I got your text messages," Ariana told me now. "Boring graduation speeches, huh? What do you expect from a—"

"You need to hear what happened, Ariana." I stopped her before she'd regret a putdown of a man, or category of a man, who was now dead.

I hated to spoil my friend's good mood, but I knew she'd want to hear what was going on in her hometown. I briefed Ariana on the murder of our mayor, stopping for a long breath now and then. I left out the parts about his thorax, but included the part about his calling me by name.

Ariana was silent, most likely invoking Aestas. I gave her time.

"I'm just so, so glad you and Bruce are safe," she said, her voice soft and full of relief.

What? Why wouldn't we be? Had Ariana misunderstood

my story? It was Mayor Graves who'd been attacked, not Bruce or me.

With a start I saw that Ariana's mind had gone in a direction that had never occurred to me—the stabber could have been wandering around the hallowed halls looking for victims, with a stash of letter openers, scissors, knives, or other weapons at the ready. Maybe the mayor wasn't targeted at all, but was simply a handy, random victim, the first of many. I wondered if Virgil had thought of that. Now I realized that Bruce had thought of it—when he stood and surveyed the campus, he wasn't just stretching, he was scanning for the attacker.

I swallowed hard and got up from my sofa. It wouldn't hurt to take a look around my own house. "We're fine," I told Ariana, carrying only my cell phone as a weapon against an intruder.

"I wish I were there, Sophie. Do you need me to come home?"

I expected nothing less from my sweet friend who was willing to give up volleyball on a sunny beach to take care of me. "No, no," I said, still making my sweep of the small three-bedroom house I grew up in. "It's not like the mayor and I were close friends. I don't know why this is hitting me so hard."

"Why wouldn't it? It happened on your campus, right in front of you. And, most important, he called out specifically for you, Sophie, as he was dying. You can't take that lightly."

"I guess not." I finished a circle of the kitchen and the hallway of bedrooms, one of which I'd outfitted as my office, ending up mildly at ease, back on the den sofa. "You know what, Ariana? I wish I could have kept all this from you until you got back. I shouldn't be putting a damper on your vacation."

"Shhh. It's a business trip. In case the IRS is listening."

Ariana was always good for a smile. "Business trip it is.

We can talk about what's going on here on Wednesday. We'll have the whole ride back from Logan, and then some."

We agreed to let the matter go, though Ariana closed with, "Relax, Sophie." Ariana stretched out the word "relax" till it became a massage on its own. "I'll pour cleansing energy into the phenomenon."

I knew better than to ask what she meant.

I skipped through most of the emails that had been downloaded throughout the evening. Usually I checked frequently on my smartphone, but tonight had been different. I scanned several emails regarding final grades from students who couldn't wait the two weeks until grades were officially posted. Paula Mattson, a bio major who'd taken my statistics class, simply admitted, "I can't stand not knowing how I did," and her best friend, Wendy Pruit, advised me that while I was figuring out Paula's final grade, I might find it convenient to calculate hers, also. *Thanks, Wendy. So thoughtful of you.*

Simple, polite requests didn't annoy me as did the email that popped up from Elysse Hutchins, threatening to issue a formal complaint about me to the dean if I didn't adjust her exam grade to account for full credit on the statistics problem she'd blown. The last thing I needed was to go through a grievance process with the administration. I entertained the notion that I should just cave and give Elysse whatever grade she wanted. There'd be no decisions tonight, however.

Several emails with one-word subjects like "OMG," "Unbelievable!" and "howdathapen?" were on the list. I didn't need to open them to figure out the content.

I took a break to prepare a small plate of crostini and bruschetta, left over from Bruce's midweek visit, to eat in the den.

I devised a formula for the task. Read three emails, listen to one voice mail, take one bite of crispy toast and tasty sauce. Repeat the sequence until the task has been completed.

A cross-section of faculty and students had left messages through one medium or another, some on more than one. Though I would have loved to answer Fran, one of the many who'd tried to reach me while I was with Virgil and following, I refrained from a middle-of-the-night call. I'd expected to see or hear something from Kira Gilmore, the mayor's staunchest defender, either through email or by phone, but so far I hadn't come across anything from her. I wondered if she'd heard the news. If she was staying in the hotel with her parents before they flew back to California, she might not be up-to-date.

The email from Henley College president Olivia Aldridge read as expected, with an expression of sorrow at the loss of "a young leader with such promise, who'd already given so much," and a mention that an official condolences note and flower arrangement would be sent to the mayor's family. The president wanted to assure us that campus security was already being scrutinized and improvements were in the works. Whatever that meant. Most prominent in the email was a warning to the faculty and staff not to talk to anyone "outside the HC family," and to avoid speaking to the press, especially. All questions should be referred to the college's Office of Government and Community Relations.

I got the message.

I was sure Ariana and Bruce were considered to be part of the Henley College family, and I had no desire to call around to anyone else with the news.

I'd run out of emails, but there were still a few more voice mails on both my landline and my cell.

More OMGs caused me to press delete before the poor student got her entire message out. At some point I'd have to step up and offer whatever I could by way of comfort and a willing ear to my charges.

I scanned my phone screen and saw that I had one message left, from a private caller, around noon, long before any of the action on campus, both good and bad. I almost didn't bother hitting the arrow, but decided I might as well complete the job. I touched the screen and heard a male voice. A first, other than calls from Bruce. None of the guys in my classes had tried to contact me. Apparently males took things like grades and campus crime more in stride than females. Good to know, in case something like this incident happened in the future.

I heard a vaguely familiar voice. "Dr. Knowles. Sophie, if I may. This is Ed Graves. Looking forward to seeing you at graduation today." *Throat clearing.* "I need to talk to you."

I stopped the message. Ed Graves? Mayor Graves? Not only a first name this time, but a nickname? The world seemed to go into a Fourier transform where casual acquaintances became bosom buddies. Or maybe the bruschetta had soured and clouded my hearing.

I played the message again, and listened further.

"I need to talk to you. Someplace outside my office. Something's troubling me about Zeeman and I'd like to enlist your help." A pause here led me to believe the call had ended, but eventually he continued. "Please call my direct line, 508-555-0137, so we can set up a time. In the meantime—"

The mayor was cut off by my message limit. I clenched my jaw and cursed the technology that didn't allow him to finish, as if it were the fault of the electrons, or whatever rattled around in my phone. I wrote down his direct number out of habit, even as I realized I'd never use it.

I played the mayor's—Ed's—message once again, and noted again the time it had come in—12:20 PM. I couldn't seem to stop myself. I played it twice more all the way through. Maybe I'd hear a word or phrase that would explain why he'd chosen to involve me on the last day he was alive. I hated that I didn't know what would have followed *in the meantime* if my message limit hadn't intervened. Each replay was creepier than the last as I tried to match the voice on my phone with that of our keynote speaker of a lifetime ago.

A dying mayor had asked for my help. Twice in one day. Two times too many. I had to know why.

Virgil was my best bet. I'd play this message for him and he'd be able to put some things together and satisfy my curiosity. Too bad it was one thirty in the morning and he wouldn't be sitting in his office. Also, too bad it was one thirty in the morning and I still wasn't sleepy.

I left a cryptic message on Virgil's office voice mail, to the effect that I needed to play a cell phone message for him, whenever he'd be available tomorrow. "If you have plans to go hiking in the hills, please call me first," I ended. As long as I'd known him, Virgil hadn't even taken a long walk on a flat road. I hoped I'd given him a smile that would get us off to a good start when I played the mayor's message for him and then quizzed him about the investigation.

I wrote down what I knew about Mayor Graves's weekend, in case it would help Virgil. I'd seen the mayor in the hallway at the Zeeman Academy around two in the afternoon on Friday, then he'd stopped in at the eighth graders' farewell party at three thirty.

On Saturday, there had been a small reception before commencement exercises, starting at one o'clock, for invited guests and department chairs, in the college president's conference room. The mayor and his wife attended, along with members of the town council and school superintendent Patrick Collins. What I knew now was that before the reception, the mayor had called me. What I didn't know was *why*. Why me, and what was wrong at Zeeman Academy?

I couldn't remember anything unusual about the president's gathering. No outbursts, no smashed china that I was aware of. The volatile Chris Sizemore and her brother had skipped the reception, and the rest of the faculty were well behaved, as were all of the council members.

One thing I recalled was a brief, but typical, show of animosity between the mayor and Superintendent Collins, who seemed to have imbibed a little too much of President Aldridge's punch. The two men were off in a corner, and no one except someone like me, who was bored by cocktail talk, would have noticed their confrontational tones and body language. After a minute or so, the two men reentered the main reception area, smiling like old friends. I'd always marveled at how politicians could do that—play golf together and pal around, or seem to, even in a cutthroat campaign or after a heated debate.

I questioned whether, in the light of events today, I should tell Virgil about the incident. I wished I had a guidebook. Was it worse to withhold something with only a small chance of being important to the investigation, or to implicate a perfectly innocent public servant like the superintendent of our schools? What if the argument was over a baseball play or the merits of a local restaurant?

At the end of the reception, the mayor had donned the rented robes we'd provided and joined the procession onto the stage with the faculty and staff. He gave his speech, then took his wife and left at three fifteen.

The next thing I was sure of was that he'd stumbled toward Bruce and me, with the silver blade of a letter opener in his back, just after the enormous tower clock struck ten fifteen on Saturday night.

Whatever he'd done in the seven hours in between had cost him his life. Or so it seemed.

As gory as the end of the timeline was, putting things in order worked its magic and I was finally able to sleep, this year's commencement day almost put to rest.

CHAPTER $\sqrt{6}$

I woke up disoriented, as if I were lying in the middle of a puzzle that had me stumped. Not an anagram, or a cross-word, or a brainteaser, any of which I'd have a chance of solving. This was more of a rebus that I couldn't figure out, with cartoon drawings of sharp objects and grass and rolled-up diplomas interspersed with mathematical symbols.

I pulled myself together with French press coffee and a banana.

I'd expected to work while waiting for Virgil to call, but discovered I didn't have my briefcase at home. The pre-man-in-the-fountain plan had been for Bruce and me to go to my office after our late-night ice cream stroll and collect my briefcase and robes. Instead, Bruce had gone off in an ambulance with the town's highest-ranking official and I'd driven straight home alone in his car.

I dreaded going back to the crime scene so soon, even on a sunny day like today. It would be a while before the lovely spray of water at the heart of the campus would have its charm restored in my mind. But there was a limit to the number of hours I could survive without my briefcase. I'd reconsider later in the day.

I pulled out my clipboard, which always had an unfinished puzzle on it, one that I was either creating or solving. This one was due to an editor at a children's games magazine in a week. I'd chosen a bakery theme, then constructed a puzzle around cupcakes, pies, birthday cakes, tarts, and many kinds of cookies. I proofread what I had so far, wishing I had a real treat to go with my coffee.

A call from Bruce, already at work, brightened my mood. The morning briefing at MAstar was over and he was waiting for his assignment.

"We're probably going to sit around the trailer all day watching videos until the Bat Phone rings."

Fortunately, Bruce was a big movie fan and considered himself very lucky that he got paid to watch endless loops of his favorites.

"I'm sure you guys will dig out all the old war movies," I teased.

"I drew the right straw, so we're starting with *Tigerland*."

"I knew it. And it's not Vietnam you're interested in. You just like staring at Colin Farrell's widow's peak and pretending you're looking in the mirror," I said.

"Guilty," he said.

Buzz. Buzz.

My doorbell. I was glad I'd opted for a pair of capris and a decent Henley Math Department T-shirt this morning instead of staying in my pj's, which had been my first inclination.

I looked through the peephole. Virgil Mitchell, from the HPD, in his light summer suit, stared back. He looked more rested than I did. Best of all, he was carrying a box from the donut shop.

"Your best bud is here," I said to Bruce. "I hope you don't have to bail me out later."

We signed off as I pulled open the door to let Virgil in. I tapped the box. "Really?"

"I love being a cliché," Virgil said, handing it to me.

The delicious, unhealthy smell took over my nose and I could hardly wait to dive in. The box had barely hit my island counter when I lifted the cover.

"Two jellies. How did you know?" I asked, squeezing cherry-colored foodstuff (I hoped) into my mouth while the other hand poured coffee for Virgil.

"You made it clear years ago." He smiled. "I figured we'd listen to your phone message over breakfast. As long as you don't tell Bruce the menu."

I brushed powdered sugar from my T-shirt. "I'll vacuum every trace. He'll never know we veered from the health-food regimen."

"Feeling any better this morning?" he asked.

The question caused my good humor to collapse. My light mood was over. "Not a lot."

"It's tough when anyone loses his life too soon, especially when you witness it."

"You deal with this all the time," I said.

He pointed to the box of donuts. "There are rewards."

I laughed and thanked him for the break.

We'd settled across from each other at my breakfast nook, overlooking the patio where my glorious lilies of the valley, late-blooming tulips, and impatiens held sway. How could it be so cheery outside when I wasn't ready for it? Warm as it was, I wanted to hide under the lavender comforter on my bed.

"I'll get my phone for you," I said to Virgil.

"Do you mind if I turn on your TV? I didn't see a paper yet. Don't know if this would make the *Globe*, anyway."

"He was our mayor," I said, feeling I'd made my point.

Virgil, who'd spent a few years of his career in Boston, shrugged. "It's Henley," he said.

I handed Virgil the remote and went to retrieve my phone from its charger.

Since our local newspaper had cut circulation to a weekly appearance, the metropolitan *Boston Globe* was our only option for timely news other than the Internet and television. There were those who didn't think we needed labor-intensive, slow-moving print media anymore, but I wasn't ready to give myself over completely to i-living. I could only guess how far cell phone photos of last night's drama had traveled through the ether.

When I returned to the kitchen, Virgil was watching the footage shot by the local news crew. I wondered how the anchors managed to look so perfectly groomed before ten in the morning.

"Do they know more than you do?" I asked Virgil.

"The only reason I'm listening is to find out. See if they have another source, see if they have misinformation, whatever."

In the upper left corner of the screen was a cameo of a very young-looking Edward P. Graves. It might have been from his high school yearbook, the guy most likely to succeed. I'd have bet money that he was also prom king, president of student government, and quarterback. In the center of the display was the Henley College fountain, sans bleeding body, and our beautiful campus, with its old brick buildings, stately trees, and inviting pathways.

On location, an unsurprisingly attractive woman wore a somber expression over her navy blue jacket. She spoke slowly, honoring the gravitas of the feature. "Last night, this idyllic campus setting was the scene of tragedy. Only a few hours after receiving an ovation for his forward-looking commencement address to graduates of Henley College, Mayor Edward P. Graves, third generation of the . . ."

An ovation? Forward-looking? I waved my hand to get the reporter's attention, as if I she could hear my critique of her script. "Why do they have to spin it like that?" I asked Virgil. "Isn't Mayor Graves's death just as tragic if his speech was boring and hackneyed?"

Virgil bit into a long cruller, sending granules of cinnamon and sugar across his wide chest. "It's what they do."

"Why is every murder victim suddenly the best person who ever walked the earth? Graves was not our most inspired mayor, his speech was boring, and he probably got as many votes because of his name as anything else." I took a breath. "But still it's beyond terrible that he was killed."

I could feel my face heat up as I talked over the television news show. That was it, I realized. It was a news *show*, part of the day's entertainment, not a source of trusted information. The best question of the moment was—why was I angry at a woman who was just doing her job?

"Sorry," I said to Virgil. I placed my phone on the table between us. "Hit the pound sign whenever you're ready."

Virgil gave me a calming look and put his hand on mine. "You know, no matter what's on this phone, Sophie, there was absolutely nothing you could have done about the mayor's death. You're not the one responsible."

I'd heard that before. When would I believe it? How badly off was I that I needed a cop and a shrink? But Virgil had it right. I did feel as though I'd let the mayor down in some way. I could only try to compensate by helping find his killer, starting with sharing the phone message with Virgil.

"You're right," I said, and hit the pound sign myself.

I'd muted the television set, which now showed a video of Mayor Graves on the Henley campus yesterday, marching from the Administration Building to the rickety temporary stage. He cut a somewhat dull figure with his rented black robes, compared to our faculty and administrators, who wore the colors from educational institutions all over the world. Competing with Harvard's unique crimson outfit were robes in different shades of red with black stripes on the sleeves; hood trims of pale blue, yellow, and maroon; and various shapes of mortarboards and velvet tams with gold tassels. The biggest hit every year was the enormous yellow lampshade-like hat from the Sorbonne, worn by the chair of our Modern Languages Department, Bob O'Connell.

"This is Ed Graves. Looking forward to seeing you at graduation today."

I was startled by the mayor's voice, having gotten caught up in the televised commencement pomp. I turned my attention to my phone, where Virgil's head was about two inches away from its speaker. I lowered my head also, though I didn't have as far to go.

"Something's troubling me about Zeeman and I'd like to enlist your help." By now it seemed I was as familiar with the mayor's voice as I was with Bruce's or Virgil's.

As I'd done last night, Virgil touched the screen to replay the message a couple of times. I sat still, arms crossed, wishing I felt like finishing the rest of my jelly donut.

Impossible as it seemed, on the last replay I heard something new. Not the part that was truncated after *in the meantime*, but a sound I hadn't heard before.

"Did you hear that?" I asked Virgil. "Is that a train in the background?" There was no train that ran through Henley or even close. "Where do you think he is?"

"The lab guys will figure it out."

That was handy, but I wanted to know now.

I'd forgotten about the timeline. I grabbed paper and pen from one of my kitchen drawers with miscellany and sketched the day out from memory for Virgil.

"This is the mayor's schedule yesterday. Twelve twenty, he calls me. One o'clock, he attends the president's reception. Two o'clock, he joins the procession to the stage. Two fifteen, ceremonies start. Three o'clock, the mayor gives his speech. Three fifteen, he leaves the stage with his wife. Ten fifteen—"

"Good," Virgil said. "This is helpful."

"I'm wondering where he was when he made this call. He was at the reception right at one. I remember that because there were only a few of us there that early. He couldn't have been too far from campus. Is there a train within a half hour or so of Henley?"

Virgil shrugged and repeated, "The lab guys will figure it out." He put my phone in his jacket pocket. "I'll have to take this." My look must have revealed the separation anxiety I was feeling, nomophobe that I was. "Just kidding," he said. "I know you're glued to this thing." He put the phone back on the table with a "gotcha" smirk.

"If you need it . . ." I said, taking it back and holding it on my lap with both hands.

"I just need your phone number and your password." He scratched his head. "Oh, yeah, and your permission."

"Done."

I wondered if Virgil knew how much I appreciated his humor.

"You and I talked about Zeeman Academy last night," Virgil said. "You think any more about it at all? Any idea what the trouble is that the mayor's talking about in that message?"

I shook my head. "I told you, I try to keep out of the politics. I'm there as a guest instructor." I remembered the schedule and snapped my head up. "But they're still in session. I have two classes there this week, tomorrow and Wednesday. I can ask around, look around—"

"You can look at nothing but your own blackboard, or whatever they use these days."

"Whiteboards and dry-erase markers," I said, ever helpful.

"Yeah, thanks. Do I make myself clear?"

Shades of my mother, Margaret Stone, when she was

laying down the law to her unruly only child. The only thing missing was Mom's slightly crooked index finger wagging at me.

"Of course. What did you think I was going to do?"

Virgil blew out a loud breath and rolled his eyes. "Just don't play cop, got it?"

I saluted.

I refilled Virgil's cup, mostly to keep him in my kitchen for a while longer. I started with an innocuous question.

"Did someone get sworn in already to replace the mayor?"

"Sort of. The procedure is that the senior person on the council, that would be Deidre Eddington, is automatically acting mayor until there's a slate of candidates and a vote in the fall."

Eddington? I doubted she was any relation to Sir Arthur. My mind took a welcome trip to a time in the future when an astrophysicist like Sir Arthur Eddington or, better yet, a mathematician might be mayor. It wouldn't hurt to bring a little scientific method and logic to the seat of government.

"So there's no swearing-in ceremony or anything?"

Virgil shook his head. "There might already have been a private one. It can happen immediately, since it's understood when you're elected to the council that you'll step in if needed according to the town charter."

My next question was harder. "I'm still puzzled by the mayor's calling out for me, Virgil. If he knew he had only two or three words left in him, why wouldn't he have named his killer? Do you think he didn't see the person who stabbed him?"

"Maybe."

"Or he could have used his cell and called nine-one-one."

"We picked up his phone a few yards from where he fell. Most likely fell as he tried to use it."

Information at last. I pushed on. "Or he saw Bruce and me and knew he'd have help soon."

"Maybe."

"It doesn't sound like a stabbing, though. I mean, you might shoot from behind, but if you're stabbing someone in the back, you have to get close, right? How do you know the guy isn't going to turn at the last minute? And how do you know you have the exact right spot to kill someone? Do you think the attacker didn't mean to kill the mayor, just hurt him?"

"Maybe."

"You're not going to tell me much, are you?"

Virgil smiled and checked his watch. "I gotta go."

Big surprise. I closed up the box of donuts, resigned to Virgil's silence. "Your buddies will enjoy these. You should take the donuts to the station."

He held up his hand in a gesture of refusal. "That's where donuts are born."

I laughed. It had been worth the information-free interview just to have a few smiles this morning.

"Have you talked to Mrs. Graves?" I asked, one last shot as I opened the door for him. "Maybe I'll make a condolence call."

"Don't do it, Sophie."

"I just said maybe."

"She's not home, anyway."

"Not home?" I asked.

"Stay out of it, Sophie. Please?" Then, as if I'd agreed, he said, "Thanks."

"You're welcome," I said, knowing Virgil could tell I didn't mean it.

I felt I'd done a day's work navigating around Virgil's questions and responses. If it weren't for check-in calls from

Bruce and Ariana, I might have gone back to bed. I was considering it again, when Fran called.

"Finally," she said, when I answered.

I gave Fran a complete report on my life, from the time she dropped me off at Bruce's feet, right up to Virgil's visit, the remnants of which were on my counter in the form of donuts. Going over the details wasn't fun, and, with Ariana already up to speed, I was glad I couldn't think of anyone else I'd need to share them with.

"The mayor left you a voice mail?" Fran asked. I couldn't tell whether she was favorably impressed that the Honorable Edward P. Graves had called me personally, or whether she was wigged-out over it. She clarified right away. "Too creepy."

"That was my first reaction, too, but now I'm used to it and I'm trying to figure out what it means."

"Maybe that's what his nod to you was all about?"

"Nod?"

"At the graduation ceremony. When he turned from the podium at the end of his speech, he caught your eye and said something, remember?"

I squeezed my eyes shut, hoping to ward off a headache. "Yes. How could I have forgotten something like that?"

"Because a lot of *somethings* related to Ed Graves have happened since then," Fran said.

"I think all he said was 'See you,' but maybe it's all connected. I should tell Virgil. Or maybe it's a big nothing."

"Do the police know anything?" she asked.

"If they do, they're not telling." I reminded Fran of the frustrating session with Virgil, whose light cologne still hung in the air along with the heavy aroma of donut.

"The problem with someone in the public eye like that is there's no shortage of people with motive," she said.

How well I knew.

Beep. Beep.

My call-waiting signal. I looked at the screen on my

landline handset. Kira Gilmore. If it had been any other student I probably would have let the call go to voice mail, but after her performance at two parties yesterday, followed by the events of the evening, I was concerned about Kira's emotional state. I'd thought about calling her several times, but hadn't felt I could do it with any degree of calmness.

I bailed on Fran, promising to call her back, then clicked on with Kira, whose voice was weighed down with grief.

"Dr. Knowles, what am I going to do?" No preamble. It was as though I'd cut into a conversation she'd been having with herself for as long as she'd known about the mayor's death. Edward's death, to her.

"You must be so sad, Kira," I said. "So am I. I've been thinking about you. Are you still on campus?" My real question was, are you on a ledge somewhere?

"I'm in the dorm. My parents went back home at, like, dawn, this morning. They don't even know yet. I won't be able to reach them for another couple of hours. I might stay on to work at the campaign headquarters for a couple more weeks to close—" Her words came to abrupt halt. A gasp followed quickly, then, a wail. "To close the doors. There's no more campaign!"

Kira's sobs took over the line. I tried to fill in with soothing words.

"I know it's hard, Kira. This will take time for you to process." *Nice going*, I thought. As if grieving was like collecting data for an experiment. "Are you still in your room? I thought the dorms were closing today." A white lie.

"Who would do this, Dr. Knowles? He was the nicest, most amazing man. There's nothing left for me now."

If Kira was at an eight out of ten on the freaked-out scale at the party yesterday and the dinner last night, she was now at sixteen.

"Would you like to get a coffee, Kira? I can meet you downtown."

"I don't know. I'm just . . . There are still cops on

campus. I didn't go down there, but I could see them from
the window in the lounge."

The dorm lounge, where various potential weapons
were stocked. Knives, electrical appliances, and a handyman's box of common tools. Maybe even a letter opener.

"Kira?" I thought I lost the connection, until I heard a
soft weeping. "Kira, I know you were . . ." I struggled for
the right word. *Close* didn't sound appropriate. Neither did
friends. I wished Fran's term *seeing him* wouldn't keep
blocking out my internal thesaurus. "I know he meant a lot
to you." *Citizen-wise*, I almost said.

"We had something very special." A pause for raspy,
erratic breathing. "No one gets it."

Uh-oh. "I get it, Kira. I do. Look, it's so hot here, I was
just going to leave for an iced mocha. How does that sound?
Why don't we meet at the Coffee Filter?" I heard sniffles
from the depths. "How about fifteen minutes from now?
It's air-conditioned there and I'm stifling in my house."
Gray lies.

"I don't know. I—"

"Oh good. Thanks," I cut in. "My friends are all working or out of town and it would be great to have someone
to talk things over with."

"There's no one here either," Kira said. "They all went
out for breakfast like everything was normal. Jeanne,
Paula, Bethany, even Nicole."

"Then it's up to us, Kira. We can talk about it or just be
quiet together if you want."

"Ummm . . ."

"Hey, I haven't talked to you much since you're officially a Henley College alumna." I managed a weak "Ta
da," and added "You promised to visit often, remember?
This can be our first non-teacher-student visit."

I was encouraged by what might have been a small
chuckle, which might have meant simply that she saw
through my falsetto cheeriness.

"Okay."

Whew. "I do need a favor, though. If you can do it. I know you have that new graphing app installed on your phone. I have to pull things together for a class on graphs at Zeeman this week." Lies, lies.

"I have the app."

"I'd be really grateful if you can go over it with me." I paused for effect, then an afterthought. "Or, if you just want to talk, that's okay, too."

I hoped I got it right, following suggestions from all the counseling workshops I'd been to over the years. The first thing I'd learn not to say is any form of "This, too, shall pass" or "You're young yet and still have your whole life before you." I'd learned early on that teaching math to people barely out of their teens wasn't just about the math, but about life. I felt confident that I'd done better than the clichés, especially since the circumstances were more traumatic than the usual crises that threatened to put students over the edge—breaking up with a boyfriend, the lack of a prom date, or a B-plus instead of an expected A.

I went through my mental checklist. I'd coaxed Kira out of her physical location; given her something to do for me, so she feels committed to the meeting; left an opening if she's just looking for a sympathetic ear. I waited for the response.

After a long pause, Kira answered my request. "Ummm. I don't know."

"It will take me about fifteen minutes to get to the Coffee Filter. See you soon," I said, not too cheery, not too down, as if I'd misunderstood her hesitation.

Kira's "Okay," wasn't as enthusiastic as I'd hoped, but at least she hadn't hung up on me.

The Coffee Filter was barely a five-minute walk from Kira's dorm, the Clara Barton, on the northeastern edge of campus. I didn't want her to be alone any longer than necessary. I tried to think of someone who'd be on campus on a Sunday, especially this Sunday, with a "no more teachers, no more books" air about it. No administrators would be there, and no smart-thinking faculty would step foot on the pathways that wound around the buildings on the day after graduation.

I worked my way down my mental list to the staff and perked up. Woody, our all-purpose maintenance man. His main beat was Franklin Hall, but I knew he'd do anything for his employer family.

I called his cell phone, supplied to him by the college for janitorial emergencies. I felt my need at the moment more than qualified.

"Awful thing, Dr. Knowles," he said to me. I knew what he meant and I knew his old gray head was shaking in disbelief at the murder of Henley's mayor.

I hated to rush past Woody's feelings of sympathy, but I needed him to move fast.

"You know Kira Gilmore, Woody?"

"Course."

"She's been hit pretty hard by the mayor's death, maybe even more than the rest of us. Do you think you can stop at Clara Barton dorm and . . ." I was at a loss for what Woody could do. What excuse could he have for dropping in?

"I'm in front of Nathaniel Hawthorne, right next door. I'll look in on Clara Barton and see if anybody needs any boxes for movin' or somethin'," Woody said. "That do, Dr. Knowles?"

I wondered if Woody were a closet therapist.

"Perfect. I'm scheduled to meet her at the Coffee Filter on Main in about fifteen minutes."

"I understand. She'll be there, Dr. Knowles."

"Thank you so much, Woody."

"No, Doctor, thank you."

Some people just made everything seem easy. I needed that right now.

CHAPTER $\sqrt{7}$

I tapped my steering wheel with more than my usual impatience in heavy traffic. If I'd gone online before leaving, I'd have known enough not to take my regular route to campus. Checking road conditions on my phone now would be too little, too late. I'd have to wait it out and hope for the best.

Our creatively named Main Street ran parallel to Henley Boulevard. Both were long east-west streets, both bordered the campus, to the north and the south, respectively. I'd driven east toward town, taking Main. I skirted the highway, expecting to pass the city hall and post office buildings, and end up directly across the street from the back of the campus, where the Coffee Filter was located.

That would have been the quickest route, except it was blocked. The beautiful city hall, with its gold dome, rivaling that of the State House in Boston, was the site of one of the largest gatherings I'd ever seen in our town. Moments before I was forced into a detour, I saw that the steps of the building were lined with mourners carrying items toward the top landing, where a kind of shrine was taking shape. I identified flowers, wreaths, posters, candles, and large photographs, probably from the mayor's campaign. I'd thought vigils were held only at night, but apparently when a city official was involved, they were all day, also.

Had I missed a memo? How did such events come about? I supposed if I'd checked my email this morning, I'd have found an invitation or notice in some form. News spread a lot faster these days. Barely twelve hours ago, the mayor was alive and calling my name in front of the fountain; now his murder had been broadcast far and wide.

As pleased as I was about the tribute to the mayor and the great turnout to comfort his family, if they were even here, I was upset at being caught in it. I was afraid Kira would use any excuse to bolt and I feared for her safety. It was always a touchy time when a vulnerable young woman's dreams were dashed, for whatever reason.

The detour forced me to drive away from the Coffee Filter, and I found myself becoming increasingly anxious. I didn't want to be late. I worried that Kira was sitting there alone, with all this hubbub only four short blocks away. Maybe in her current state, she hadn't even looked to her left as she'd crossed Main, and so she hadn't seen the crowds. In a way, I hoped she was oblivious to them. Who knew how she might react? I could picture her running down and joining them happily. I could also picture her running toward them, hysterical, calling them disrespectful or irreverent or making an even more pointed accusation. Henley's finest were out in full force and seemed ready to haul away anyone who disrupted the proceedings. I didn't want to visit Kira in jail any more than I wanted to find her in the hospital.

I called Kira's cell and left a message saying I was getting close and would see her shortly. I hoped that was true, on many levels.

It took three turns around the block to find a spot for Bruce's car, partly because of the crowd, but mostly because I didn't drive it that often and I needed the equivalent of a space and a half to park comfortably.

I slammed on my brakes when I saw a car backing out of a place two doors down from the rear entrance to the Coffee Filter. I was determined to wait, mindful of the times I'd seethed when a guy in front of me pulled the same selfish trick. Exigent circumstances, I told myself, as I listened to the honking behind me.

I parked the car, silently thanking the city council for voting for free parking on Sunday, and dashed toward the coffee shop.

It took a minute for my eyes to adjust to the dark room. The cavernous space was fairly empty, from a combination of a depleted student population and a major attraction four blocks away.

My jaw finally relaxed when I saw Kira, alive, at a corner table. I put on my most casual demeanor and walked toward her. I became even more relieved when I noticed that she was texting. From my perspective across the room, it might have been any other day, time to make a date with a friend or tweet about the great chocolate croissants at the Coffee Filter.

Kira looked up from her thumbs and greeted me. "Hey, Dr. Knowles," she said, then looked down again. "I just have to finish this."

What? At forty-four, was I already too old to deal with the mood swings of college students? Should I be happy that Kira was back to normal, whatever that was for her, or annoyed that I'd spent a lot of nervous energy on unnecessary worry about her well-being? As long as she wasn't texting her last will and testament, I should be satisfied.

Since there seemed to be no more urgency, I gestured that I'd step to the counter and order a coffee.

The Coffee Filter was a student's delight—a huge, dark

room with old wooden tables that you could feel free to put
your feet up on, or even carve your initials in, yet the latest
in Wi-Fi service and trendy drinks were available. Most of
the baristas, male and female, were students themselves,
equipped with piercings, streaked hair, many layers of tank
tops, and tattoos, fitting the clientele. It occurred to me that
Ariana would also fit right in and be hired on the spot. Not
so much Bruce. Definitely not Virgil.

I dug out my coffee card and walked to the counter,
mentally scratching my head over what to do and say next.
If Kira was out of the woods emotionally, where was she
exactly? At the river, with a load of rocks in her pockets?
Or focusing on a promising future as a mathematician,
which should be enough to cheer up anyone?

I took my iced mocha to the table and sat down across
from my star pupil. I thought of quoting phrases from her
own speech yesterday, phrases about courage and facing
challenges and gumption, though I didn't remember that
she'd used that last word specifically.

"I'll put this on vibrate," Kira said, working her smartphone, then setting it beside her iced drink. She looked
directly at me. Close up, I noticed her eyes looking a little
glassy. I wished I knew more physiology, a subject so much
more complicated than linear algebra or topological
invariants.

"Same here," I said, fiddling with my own smartphone.

"Thanks for siccing Woody on me," Kira said, with a
grin.

Woody? Was he the reason Kira was sitting here? If our
old janitor had done that good a job at therapy, he should
get a raise, and maybe a more lofty title. If we could give
an honorary degree to a baseball player, as we did last year,
we could give one to our own dedicated maintenance man.
I knew Woody's birthday was coming up in a few days, on
May twentieth, the same day as Cher's—I kept track of
such things even for people who didn't get a Franklin Hall

Friday party—and resolved to at least get him a better present than last year's pound of chocolates.

"I'm glad you're feeling better."

Kira's face collapsed. "As long as I don't think about it, I'm okay. Woody said to fill my mind with other things."

"That was good advice."

Kira smiled. "He even said I should buy myself a graduation present, maybe new shoes."

"A wise man," I said, thinking about Woody's physical presence—partly bald and gray, tall and gangly. Though closer in age to a man who might be Kira's grandfather, the general resemblance to her father was clear. Mr. Gilmore, like Woody, was also a shy, retiring man who, you knew, would be able to fix your bicycle as well as have good sound advice for you. I thought of calling Woody and telling him to drop his broom and get over here now in case Kira relapsed.

We took sips of our drinks and I let Kira take the lead as we commented on the selection of coffees and teas and the whiny, unidentifiable music coming over the too-loud PA system.

"They're getting ready to put away the student music and bring on the tourist music," Kira said. I agreed. Henley was just close enough to the Cape for easy access for summer visitors, and just far enough away to have less expensive motels.

I remembered that I'd brought something for Kira. As I'd run out the door of my house, I'd grabbed a puzzle, Kira's favorite kind, a wooden sliding block puzzle that, when solved correctly, would reveal an M. C. Escher drawing. I pulled it out of my purse and gave it to her now.

"Oh cool. Thanks, Dr. Knowles."

"That will keep you busy for three minutes."

She laughed, looking at the misoriented black-and-white segments. "I don't know. This looks challenging."

"Maybe six minutes, then."

Still on small talk, I expressed the hope that the crowd down the street didn't all suddenly need a shot of caffeine. I immediately regretted the comment. I rushed to move off the topic of the crowd, lest we get to its raison d'être.

"How about that graphing app?" I asked.

"First I need to tell you something," Kira said, causing a little blip of energy to run through me. "I don't know if I should go to the police with this or not."

Uh-oh. "What is it?"

"I think I know who killed Edward."

I drew in my breath, realizing how unlikely it was that her next words would be reliable. But I gave her a look that said "I'm all ears."

"Nicole," she said, sounding sure of herself.

"Nicole Johnson? What makes you say that? I know her parents are angry over Nicholas's school situation, but—"

"What was happening at Zeeman, the money running out and all, wasn't Edward's fault. He was trying to work with the principal to make it a better school. He cared about all the schools. But they blamed him for everything that went wrong."

"That doesn't mean Nicole, or any of her family, killed him." I refrained from calling the idea absurd, in deference to Kira's precarious state.

"I found something," Kira said.

Another questioning look from me brought more nonsense from Kira. "Nicole and I have lockers next to each other in the gym. And I saw a knife in there last week."

"What kind of knife?"

Kira frowned and swallowed a couple of times. "A large one."

If I'd been texting this story, I'd have written LOL next. "Kira, do you know what weapon the killer used?"

"They said he was"—her voice faltered; I needed Woody—"Edward was stabbed. So I figured it was Nicole who did it. With her knife."

Was this a board game? Poor Kira. Virgil and his homicide division pals should have it this easy, catching lies. When she heard about a stabbing, she'd naturally assumed the weapon was a knife. My heart went out to a young woman desperate enough to accuse one of her best friends.

"And you didn't tell the police last night that you saw a knife in Nicole's locker?" I knew the police had canvassed all the dorms already but I couldn't count on Virgil's letting me in on a detail like this.

I let out a long breath when she shook her head *no*. I could just imagine the dip in her credibility if she'd told the officer this wild story. It would have called into question any real information she might have and possibly caused nasty repercussions for Nicole and her family.

"The cops just took all our phone numbers and where we'd be in the next few days and asked some questions, like where we were and did we see anything unusual. We're supposed to call them if we think of anything else." Kira hung her head, already remorseful, I guessed. She seemed to be breaking down again, the way I'd heard her on the phone. "I wouldn't have let Nicole go to jail, honest, Dr. Knowles."

"I know."

"I don't know why I said that now about the knife. There wasn't a knife in the locker except for the plastics ones from the lounge." She looked at me, her eyes pleading. "I'm not a liar."

"I know," I repeated, with a feeling of helplessness.

"I'm just so mad at Nicole and her dad for saying those things about him yesterday." More sniffles. "I loved him."

Another decision to make—whether to quiz Kira on what she meant; what, if anything, she and the mayor had together. Did she have a crush, a full-blown fantasy, or had there been a real, mutual relationship between them? Or some fourth variation that was part of the youth culture? A simple *Loved him in what way?* would have sufficed, but I couldn't bring myself to ask.

I had the crazy thought that going coed might have one more advantage than we'd considered at the grueling faculty meetings to decide the issue for Henley College. Maybe having dating material sitting right next to the girls in the classroom would prevent this kind of older-man infatuation in the future. Probably not.

I'd been pleased when Kira had become involved in city politics, but it hadn't seemed to help much with her emotional growth and, in fact, may have twisted it. I feared now for her survival without the built-in camaraderie and safety net of college classes and dorm life. I knew she'd be able to cope with the toughest graduate school curriculum intellectually, but I worried that the environment of a large institution would force her further and further into herself.

I put my hand on hers. "Give yourself some time, Kira." I knew I was perilously close to platitudes, but I was running out of creative advice.

"I feel like I have to do something for Edward."

I forced myself to adjust to calling Mayor Graves "Edward," at least while talking to Kira. "If you really want to help find Edward's killer, you'll tell the truth. When the police come around again, just tell them all you know about the problems at Zeeman Academy. Did he talk about it with you in any detail?"

"You think that's the reason he was killed?"

"Why don't you tell me what you know."

Kira rambled on about the conflicts among the mayor, Superintendent of Schools Patrick Collins, and Principal Douglas Richardson of the Zeeman charter school.

"Edward was convinced that Principal Richardson was inflating the grades and the test scores, making it look like the kids were doing better on the state tests than they actually were. The school has to put out a report every year—they call it their Report Card—and it covers teacher qualifications, student achievement, and accountability to the district. Edward thought Principal Richardson was fudging the marks."

I got it. Charter schools depended on funding from outside the school system, so unless they could show good performance, they'd lose money.

Kira went on. "No one wants to give donations to a school with poor grades, not even the parents of the kids who go there, right?"

I nodded my agreement, as if I'd given this issue a lot of thought and had a well-informed opinion. "But the state funds the school no matter what." I'd gotten that much from my brush with education sites online.

"Yeah, but only partly. And that's what everyone wanted Edward to do, to get more funding from the state no matter how the kids did on the state tests."

Whether this was pillow talk or not, I felt I could trust Kira's information this time, unlike her fiction of a few minutes ago. I knew that many aspects of charter schools were not as transparent as the typical public school. There was a less rigid chain of command, as air force vet Bruce had pointed out, and possibly, therefore, more opportunity for off-the-books dealings.

I thought of the mayor's message to me, that I might be able to help with whatever was troubling him about Zeeman. But if Kira was right and there was a grade inflation problem, how would I have been able to help? I didn't even assign grades to the students in my little corner of the school curriculum, let alone involve myself in overall grade reporting. I simply dropped in for a couple of hours twice a week and showed fidgety youngsters how much fun math could be. Since the regular teacher always stayed in the classroom with me, there was never a serious discipline problem, and since I wasn't being paid, I had few interactions with anyone in administration.

That was how I liked it. Dealing with one administration at a time was enough for any teacher, including me. I was sure administrators felt the same way about working with faculty bodies.

I decided it was safe to quiz Kira a bit more. She seemed to have settled into her own version of stable. I knew she'd have a better grasp of the politics than I did. It would be nice to go into Zeeman tomorrow with a little more of a handle on the situation than I'd had up to now.

"Do you know what made the mayor suspicious of the grades? Did someone tell him?" I asked.

"The grades from all the district schools eventually go through Superintendent Collins. He was the one who suspected something first, because Zeeman has more than its share of problem kids and he couldn't believe how high the grades were, so he told Edward. But then Principal Richardson told Edward something about Superintendent Collins that Superintendent Collins didn't want found out, and poor Edward was caught in the middle."

It was a dizzying triangle. Everyone had something on everyone else, which seemed not uncommon in political situations. And which was why I tried to steer clear of them.

Maybe in fact it was more than a triangle—a quadrilateral. "Why are the Johnsons, Mr. Johnson especially, so upset with . . . Edward?" I asked.

"Edward wanted to step in and yank Principal Richardson out of there. He could have put him in jail, actually. Since there's money involved, that makes it fraud. If Edward could have proven it, the city could have taken over the charter. But Mr. Johnson wanted the mayor to just leave the principal alone and throw more money at the school. He thought that would fix the problem of poor grades. Edward wanted to save the charter by having a clean slate. He wanted to report the test scores as they were and work to raise the kids' grades legitimately." Kira had already shredded two brown Coffee Filter napkins as she

talked. She picked up a third. "Isn't that the best thing for
the kids?"

It seemed so, but as with all political issues, I fell easily
for the latest spin that made some sense. I couldn't help
wonder, though—was all this connected to the mayor's
message to me? Had he intended to tell me something that
would make his case for having Principal Richardson
charged with fraud? If so, what was it?

I wanted to take notes on the three-, maybe four-party
war, each one having something on the other. I quickly
eliminated Nicole's dad as I remembered his driving off
with his family after the dinner at the Inn. There wouldn't
have been time for him to drive all the way across town to
where the Johnsons lived, drop off his wife and son, and
drive back to stab the mayor. Nasty as he'd been during
dinner, I couldn't envision him leaving the car running,
with Nannette and Nathan inside, while he dashed on campus to commit murder.

The superintendent and the principal, however, were
another story. I wouldn't have been surprised if either of
them knew a little tidbit about the mayor that wasn't fit for
a layperson's ears. My slightly jaded view of the political
system at all levels said that's how the machine worked.

I thought I'd test my theory on Kira, my current political consultant.

"Is there anything that either of the men knew about
Edward that he might not want revealed?"

Kira's eyes went wide, her face reddening. "Of course
not," she said.

Uh-oh. Could Fran have been right, about that "seeing
him" thing? Or was Kira embarrassed that someone might
actually believe her fantasy?

How to deal with Kira's mixed signals? She'd obviously
wanted everyone to think she and the mayor were close.
Now that I was calling her bluff in a way, she was pulling

back. I saw all the signs of a dreamer, afraid of losing the dream to reality.

Before I could decide how to proceed, Kira took over again. "There was also that other issue, the waste management contract. The one Mr. Sizemore was trying to force down Edward's throat."

A transparent tactic on Kira's part, but I was as happy to move off the hot politician-intern button as she was. Kira was smart enough to know that I was looking for motive in the mayor's stabbing, and that, right now, she was my best bet for information.

"I remember reading that there were competing bids," I said, wishing I'd cared more at the time about who'd be hauling away my trash on Friday mornings.

Kira nodded. "There's the W. Thomas Company that Edward prefers, and the Stewart Brothers that Mr. Sizemore wants to give the contract to," Kira said. "It was strange, because they'd always been simpatico on contracts. Mr. Sizemore would do his management consultant thing, making assessments and all, and then make a recommendation, and Edward would agree. But not on this waste management deal. Then, the next thing I know, Edward decides to award the contract to W. Thomas, never mind Mr. Sizemore's recommendation of the Stewart Brothers, and then terminate Mr. Sizemore himself."

"Wouldn't a city contract just go to the low bidder?" I asked.

"It's not that simple. Let me tell you, it's impossible to keep bids secret anymore. So they have to offer up other value-added things. Like, Thomas would add an extra pickup at the holidays, and the Stewart Brothers would provide a special green waste container free of charge. That kind of thing."

Kira went on a bit about waste management, impressing me with her understanding of city businesses. I'd never considered how lucrative the waste business was until I heard her expound in what were probably words she'd heard from the mayor.

"Think about it," she said. "You pay them to take away your trash, and then they turn around and sell it."

It was obvious as Kira explained it. There were all sorts of ways to sell waste, whether as recyclables or as fodder for research into chemical treatments.

I found myself imagining Kira doing doctoral work as an extension of her undergraduate thesis, applying mathematics to politics. I saw her extending the work she did, moving on to analyzing strategies and voting systems using sophisticated statistical methods.

I tried to imagine what the real relationship was between Kira and the mayor. He seemed to have confided in her a great deal, perhaps simply because she was smart and would provide an excellent sounding board.

In my mental meanderings, I'd missed the fact that Kira was now quietly sobbing. I took her hand and uttered a soothing platitude.

"I'm okay," she said. "I miss talking with him."

It was clear that the mayor of Henley had loved my student for her mind. I wished I could ask him what his other intentions had been.

CHAPTER $\sqrt{8}$

The arrival of a wave of people in small clusters, most likely from the event at the city hall, made it impossible for Kira and me to continue our chat. It was just as well. Our session had run its course.

A gaggle of young people surrounded our table, and Kira introduced me to her friends from Mayor Graves's campaign headquarters, mostly young women. I recognized one or two from campus, but none were my students. As we greeted one another with expressions of sympathy and disbelief at the loss of their hero, I couldn't help assess their potential as killers. Could the mayor's murderer have been the guy in the black cargo pants who had a suspicious, glassy-eyed expression? Or the one so well built that he could easily apply great force to the handle of a letter opener? Or the tall blond girl with yellow and white plastic daisies on her flip-flops who avoided making eye contact with me?

It was a wonder cops and homicide detectives like Virgil ever trusted anyone. Maybe they didn't.

Eventually I was able to slip away from the Coffee Filter, amid much hugging and many tears. I felt comfortable leaving Kira with her friends, notwithstanding the fact that one of them might be a murderer. Until now, my political naiveté had made me immune to the idea of strife in a political campaign. I'd imagined a campaign headquarters as a hotbed of goodwill with enthusiastic, dedicated citizens, young and old, all pulling together for the same candidate, in a spirit of camaraderie. I remembered Kira talking about a cake her coworkers brought in to recognize that she'd taken in more pledges of contributions than any other volunteer.

I supposed many people thought of college campuses similarly—a peaceful community of teachers and students, all after enlightenment and knowledge for its own sake—which was far from the truth. While I never regretted my decision to leave the world of software start-ups, I had to admit that campus politics were every bit as complicated and often as nasty as at any institution outside the ivory tower. Every faculty senate meeting had its share of petty grievances and intense turf wars. Should the History Department take the Modern Languages Department's schedule into account when planning its curriculum? Since the Chemistry Department offers "Science for Poets" to fulfill the science requirement, why doesn't the English Department offer "Shakespeare for Scientists" for the language requirement?

The recent faculty debate over commencement speakers came to mind, and brought me back to our deceased mayor.

I imagined that, more than for most citizens, the list of suspects for the case of a murdered mayor must be as long as the city phone book. Poor Virgil and his colleagues at the HPD.

Before I could talk myself out of it, I left Bruce's car behind the Coffee Filter and headed for my campus office on foot. My plan was to walk down Main Street to the northwest pedestrian gate, directly outside Franklin Hall. I could thus avoid laying my eyes on the bloody fountain. It would forevermore be bloody to me, I realized, no matter what kind of filtering system or treatments the hazmat team brought to bear on it. I'd enter Franklin, retrieve my things, and return to Bruce's car by the same route. Lugging my robes and briefcase back to the car, even as the day grew warmer, seemed light duty compared to being drawn to the tainted center of campus.

People were still streaming from the city hall toward the Coffee Filter, among them some faces I recognized. The most unexpected were those of Monty Sizemore and his sister, Chris. They were dressed as if for tennis and, come to find out, that's exactly where they'd been—playing on the college tennis courts across the street. They looked even younger, with Chris's long hair in a ponytail and pink scrunchie, and both in designer white shorts and tank tops. I remembered the balloons that adorned the teachers' cafeteria when Monty turned thirty last year. I hadn't taken the time today to change my clothes before rushing out to meet Kira, and now my old khaki capris seemed to emphasize how long ago my own thirtieth birthday was.

"We'd have gone to the service if we'd known about it," Chris said, indicating the crowds at city hall and seeming apologetic about playing while others mourned.

Monty swept his arm down to encompass his fit body and classy outfit, his look marred only by a bandage around his calf. Or maybe that was also a fashion statement. "We weren't exactly dressed for something serious," he said. "We play almost every Sunday morning."

"Yeah," Chris said. "But I don't always beat the pants off my brother like today." She mimicked pounding his shoulder; he mimicked a severely painful reaction.

"A bad day at tennis is better than a good day working on your patio," Monty said.

"He's putting in a little brick wall and you'd think he was doing major construction," Chris told me.

"She's a tough boss," Monty told me.

"Not," Chris said, with another playful punch to Monty's shoulder.

The scene almost made me wish I had a brother.

"Hey, I called you last night, Sophie," Monty said. "I wanted to see how you were doing, after, you know, how awful it must have been to be right there when, you know, the murder and all."

"Thanks," I said. "Sorry I didn't get back to you. It was a rough night."

"I'll bet it was. Do the police know who did it? I mean, do they have any leads?" Chris asked, as if I would know. Weren't she and her brother the social media generation?

"Not that I know of."

"We thought maybe since you were right there . . ." Monty said, letting the thought drift off.

I shook my head. "I'm sure we'll be hearing something soon."

"Yeah, they've probably got everyone and his brother on this one," Monty said. "Maybe even bringing in the state?"

Since he appeared to be addressing a question to me, I answered. Sort of. "I have no idea," I said.

"I thought you had a good friend on the force," Monty said.

"Do you want to join us for coffee?" Chris asked, relieving me of the burden of explaining my relationship to Virgil. And also of informing Monty that even if I did know more than he did, I wouldn't be inclined to share it.

I declined the offer of drinks, explaining that I'd just come from the Coffee Filter, and added, "I need to get my grades done if I want to take off for a few days at the Cape next week."

"Yeah, I read about your exam grade issue on Facebook," Monty said. "You've got your work cut out for you."

"Excuse me?"

"Elysse Hutchins?" Chris said, in that way of saying something as if it were a question, but that you should already know the answer. She might as well have asked, *Are you that out of it?*

"I'm still not sure what you mean," I said, then realized I might be confirming their suspicions.

"Facebook? Elysse is pretty unhappy?" Chris said, again using her disbelieving tone.

"About what?" I asked, though I had a pretty good idea. I just needed to know if the whole Facebook community knew about Elysse's problem with me.

"It's all over Twitter, too," Monty said. "She started a Facebook page for it last night and she had, like, two hundred Likes by midnight."

Chris laughed and poked her brother. "And there's another one. You and your 'Likes.'" She turned to me. "From what I read, it does seem like you were a little harsh, Sophie," she said.

I was dazed, and not just by the bright sun. "I was harsh?" I asked, glad that the noisy crowd passing us on both sides masked my increasingly loud responses.

"You know, marking her down for a little slipup in formatting her answer," Chris said.

"It really should be about content," said Monty, who had all of two semesters of teaching under his belt. "I try to look past the small errors and go for what the kid is really trying to say. It's the substance that matters."

I made a conscious effort to relax my shoulders rather than take a swing at Monty, which would have ended badly for me.

Like many adjunct professors, Monty taught only one class, "Marketing Research," to students in our newly added International Business major. His main occupation was working for a management consulting firm in Boston, whatever that meant. I'd been over my head reading both his class description and the "about" paragraphs on his firm's website during the weeks when we on the hiring committee were reviewing his application. Terms like "estimates of market potential," "organizational sustainability," and "outsourcing management" were outside my wheelhouse. Nothing like a good, old-fashioned statistics class for clear topics: sampling, estimation, testing.

I took a second deep breath. A crowded sidewalk on Main Street in Henley, Massachusetts, was not the place to defend myself or explain my pedagogical philosophy. Especially on a day like today, with mourners in various stages of grief and relief. Besides, the Sizemore siblings each had seven or eight inches on me; it was hard to present a good argument while straining to look up at your opponents.

"Is that how Elysse put it?" I asked, as calmly as I could. "'A slipup in formatting'? There's a lot more involved than that."

"Whatever," Monty said, causing my jaw to tighten again, to the point of pain.

"She has perfect timing, too, huh? There's only about two million students getting grades this month, from somewhere or other," Chris answered.

"And maybe ninety percent of them thinking they deserved a couple more points," Monty added.

"Make that ninety-nine percent of them, if they're your students," Chris said to her brother, giving him a playful grin. One might almost think they'd rehearsed this skit.

"Well, at least they're not on Facebook with it," Monty said. Apparently the brother and sister duo forgot I was there for a moment.

Monty addressed me again. "Don't have to tell you about statistics, though, right, Sophie?" When I didn't answer, Monty continued. "Elysse has a great target audience. If she had a product to sell, I'd say now would be the time." At this point, he swung an imaginary tennis racket in the air and we all watched an invisible ball soar over our heads.

Chris seemed finally to realize that I wasn't enjoying the banter. She stopped smiling and looked at her watch. "I need some coffee," she said. "Sure you don't want to join us, Sophie?"

"I'd love to"—I looked at my own watch—"but, wouldn't you know, I'm late for a meeting."

I'd had enough of Frick and Frack. All I wanted was to get to a place where I could check out Elysse's Facebook postings. And possibly unfriend the Sizemore sibs.

As I walked, I became more and more agitated about the interaction I'd had—make that, endured—with Chris and Monty. One minute I decided to flunk Elysse outright; the next I was convinced I should give her full credit and avoid what could turn into a major hassle. My smartphone was too hard to read in the glaring sun, or I would have stepped to the side and logged on right there.

I wasn't proud of an "I'll show *you*" idea that popped into my head as I considered calling Virgil and annotating the list of names I'd given him of faculty who voted *no* on Mayor Graves for commencement speaker. "Something just occurred to me," I could tell him. "I thought you should know that Christine Sizemore stormed out of the room when we lost the vote. And, while I'm thinking of it, I heard that her brother Monty Sizemore's management consulting firm was hired by the mayor's office and then suddenly fired over a contract dispute for waste management." Take that, Sizemores.

I chided myself for vengeful thoughts and for forming an opinion about Elysse's post before I looked at the primary source.

The Sizemore team had seemed happy to aggravate me, but with a little distance I could chalk it up to their age. If one of their students had done something similar, their response would most likely have been different. They might even have joined in the thread and given the student a run for her money or simply had fun with it. How did I suddenly become old at forty-four?

Rring, rring. Rring, rring.

I took a call from Bruce. I spared him my angst over the grading issue and updated him on my itinerary.

"Watch out for the corner of Henley and Main," he said, as I approached it. "There was a demonstration of sorts in front of city hall most of the morning and I think it's still closed off."

Too late. "I'm on foot now, walking past the site," I told him, realizing how rare that was for me. And if walking meant more sidewalk meetings like the one I'd just been through, I'd stick to driving.

"Everything's peaceful here," Bruce said. "Except for a small riot in the western part of town, which the police determined had nothing to do with the mayor's death. I think some people sit around and wait for an excuse to act up. No one was hurt this time, anyway. We practically begged the city to call us in so we could get out of this trailer, but they wanted us close to the base rather than stuck out in traffic."

"And no calls from the Bat Phone?"

"A couple of people needing transportation from the hospital to rehab and back. The nurses arm-wrestled for the job."

We chatted until I reached the gate to campus, by which time I had things in perspective. It wasn't the first time a student had complained about a grade. Just the first time thousands of people knew about it before I did.

Times, they were changing.

Stepping into Franklin Hall on a Sunday was always a bit creepy, but today I had the irrational, eerie sense that someone had died here. The sickening smell of the frosting from yesterday's cake turned my stomach and caused the unpleasant reappearance of my Coffee Filter mocha.

Get in and get out, I told myself, hurrying down the hallway to my office, my footsteps echoing as loudly as a dormitory boom box.

I had my key ready and unlocked the door, surprised to see the room empty of either stale cake or a corpse. I could grab my robes and briefcase and split, or I could log on to Facebook on my computer and check out Elysse's post. I wondered if I'd recognize any of her followers. What if I did? I decided I wouldn't let Elysse bully me into panic, even in absentia; she and her post could wait until I was in the safety and comfort of my home office. So what if another two hundred people Liked Elysse before I got to see what it was they Liked.

I picked up my robes, in their plastic garment bag, and draped them over my arm, then picked up my briefcase and shut the door behind me.

Thump. Thump. Thump.

I jumped at the sound, one that should have been familiar to me. I flinched at the sudden brightness from the hallway lights being switched on. Moments later, all was well. I'd never been happier to see Woody, driving his large barrel-on-wheels.

Being on edge, on what was technically the first day of summer vacation, was not a good sign. I waited and greeted Woody as he and his supply train rumbled toward me. Did he ever go home? When his wife died last year, Woody started putting in extra hours at the college. Sometimes I thought he showed up for twice as many hours as the college paid him for. Lucky us.

"Dr. Knowles. Didn't expect to see you here."

I held out my robe-laden arm to show Woody the reason for my visit. "Thanks for helping me with Kira Gilmore this morning."

"No problem, Doctor. Sure is a shame about that young mayor. He was very nice to me."

"I didn't realize you knew him."

"Oh no, I didn't know him, met him jes' the one time, when he came by here yesterday afternoon. Did you find what he left for you?"

This may have been the shortest period of relaxation on record. Did I have another unexplained message from the mayor? Not what I needed. "I'm not sure I know what you mean, Woody."

"I unlocked your door for him. I didn't think you'd mind, Dr. Knowles. Him being the mayor and all. I hope I didn't do something wrong."

"Not at all. Did you say Mayor Graves left me a message?"

Woody leaned his elbows on his barrel, his head landing even with one of his mops, giving him a strange new hairdo from my perspective. "He came by after all the speeches were over, and the diplomas were getting handed out, and he asked me if I could let him into your office. Said he had something he wanted to leave in there for you."

I thought of the mayor's quick exit from the stage, pulling Nora with him. "Was his wife with him?"

"No, he was by himself." Woody stood up straight and looped his thumbs around the straps of the worn overall bib covering his chest. "There was another gentleman wandering around here, too, though, jes' a few minutes after the mayor came by."

"Did you recognize the second man?"

Woody shook his head, a slow *no*. "But I think he was up on that stage, too. Big man"—Woody ran his fingers over his hairless head and smiled—"bald like me, with some glasses, though. I don't need any glasses unless I'm reading something small. Not bad for someone old as I am, huh?"

I realized I had no idea how old Woody was. I hoped we

weren't breaking any labor laws by keeping him on. "That's wonderful, Woody. And it certainly sounds like a busy time for you while we were out there on that stage." My mind worked to figure out which large bald man had been hovering around my office. Woody would know anyone who was regular faculty or staff. It was a long way to come for air-conditioning or a patch of shade, if all either of the men needed was a cool spot. "Did you speak to him at all?"

"He wanted to know where the restroom is, is all, and I showed him. I didn't let him go in anywhere, if that's what you're asking, even though he had on a suit and tie and all."

"No, I'm sure you didn't, Woody."

"I wouldn't usually do that kind of thing, Dr. Knowles, letting someone into a place that's locked up. But like I said, when it was the mayor, I thought it was okay."

"Not to worry, Woody. You did the right thing." I heard Woody's long, relieved breath and felt bad that I'd put him in this stressful state with my questions, but I had a couple more. "Do you know what it was that the mayor wanted to leave for me? I didn't notice anything in my office just now."

He scratched his head, then gave me another slow *no.* "Danged if I know, Dr. Knowles. He wasn't carryin' anything I could see. Nothing big like that."

Maybe his cell phone died and he wanted to make a phone call in private. Never mind that he just happened to duck into my building. "Did he want to get into my office in particular, or do you think any office in this building would have been okay with him?"

"Your office, Dr. Knowles. He said 'Dr. Knowles's office.'"

Clear enough. "Did he come out right away?" Woody looked anxious again and I figured I'd better stop interrogating him. "It's okay if you didn't notice," I said.

"Oh, I stayed around till he come out. Even though he's the mayor, I wasn't gonna let him walk out with the furniture, you know."

Good man, Woody. He risked a tentative smile and I gave him a broad one in return.

"So how long would you say he was in there?"

I heard a whooshing-and-thudding noise at the end of the hallway, the sound our heavy doors made when closing. Woody waved his arm in greeting. I turned to see who was there, but the person had already slipped out.

"Who was that?" I asked, annoyed at my jumpy responses to every little sound today.

"Don't know, 'cause of the light coming in down there, but everybody in the building deserves a wave, don't you think?"

"You're right, Woody." I felt I was rushing the old man, and waited a beat before continuing. "Did you say how long the mayor was in my office?"

"Not long, Dr. Knowles."

"Not long," I repeated, mostly to myself.

"Didn't come out right away, either," Woody added, scratching his head, helpful as always.

I should have remembered that Woody was one of those nonquantitative types who shied away from exact numbers. I swept my free arm to indicate the roughly three-hundred-foot corridor we were standing in. "Long enough for you to mop this whole hallway?"

"No, no. Not the whole hallway. I got about to the second lecture hall, I believe, when he waved good-bye to me and left."

I'd had enough experience seeing Woody mop the floors of Franklin Hall. I estimated it took him ten minutes or so to work the patch between the end of the hall and the second lecture room. Which meant the mayor exited the building not much sooner than we all started entering it for the departments' graduation ceremony and party. Was what he left related to his earlier message on my phone? Had he called to tell me what he was going to leave in my office? Maybe that would have been the end of the *In the meantime* sentence. *In the meantime, I'm going to leave something in your office.* But what—an envelope? a book? a disk? And where—up high? down low? in the front? in the back? I was dizzy.

"You okay, Dr. Knowles?"

Not really. "Yes, thanks, Woody. I'm glad you were able to help the mayor out. Thanks for letting me know."

My head was busy with questions, none of which our poor janitor could answer. What if Woody hadn't been here? Did Mayor Graves have his lock-picking tools on him, just in case, or did he know Woody's schedule? Maybe he'd been stalking both of us. He knew I was still on the stage, so he wasn't aiming for a chat. At the time he was in my office, I was watching the Henley graduates accept their degrees. Well, more accurately, playing a word game with Fran.

What could he have left in my office that Woody wouldn't notice? It must have been small enough to carry in his pocket. How small could one make a bomb?

Woody seemed to have been ruminating at the same time that I was. He was ready to share his thoughts.

"You know, I was thinking, that might have been the last thing our mayor did, Dr. Knowles. Saying good-bye to me."

Except for whatever motivated someone to stab him in the back with a letter opener later that evening.

CHAPTER $\sqrt{9}$

As soon as Woody turned the corner in the L-shaped hallway, I was back in my office, checking for anything added. Or subtracted. Or multiplied. Just because Mayor Graves told Woody he wanted to leave something for me didn't mean his mission wasn't to take something away or manipulate an existing entity.

At first glance, my office always seemed fairly neat. I did my best to keep my physical files and books organized. I liked the look of an efficient place to work. And there wasn't time in my day to shuffle through stacks of paper looking for the one sheet I needed, such as the 3-D analysis problem I'd spent an hour working out. In the end, organization saved time.

My mother, who gave me my puzzle-maker pen name, Margaret Stone, and was quite familiar with both my home and school offices, called me a covert clutter-bug—neat on the outside, messy on the inside. Mom was probably referring to the fact that I still had copies of problem sets from

my first year teaching and all the term papers submitted by
the class of Y2K.

My computer desktop was another story. I allowed
myself a busy desktop image with a collage of Cape photos
going back to a young Margaret and a tiny Sophie frolick-
ing in the sand, all the way up to a mature Sophie and
Bruce watching the sun set on Cape Cod Bay. My screen
itself was cluttered with color-coded sticky notes—the
software kind—and the icons for at least two dozen files,
for easy access.

I ran my hands around my equipment, searching for
something different since the mayor's entry. I checked the
computer, DVD player, printers, scanner, electric pencil
sharpener, electric stapler, and—my favorite—my paper
cutter with a laser beam for alignment, a romantic gift
from Bruce one Valentine's Day. I came up dusty, but otherwise empty. I checked my bookcases. Nothing had been
disturbed as far as I could tell. No extra books had been
slipped in between *Multivariate Methods* by Tyler and
Combinatorials by Wilson. I shook out an afghan Margaret made for me in shades of Monet blues and lavenders.
Maybe Mayor Graves had tucked a slip of paper in its folds.
Nothing. I searched smaller nooks for a disk or a flash
drive. More nothing.

I opened my file drawers. My shoulders sagged as I contemplated row after row of hanging folders, holding smaller
folders, holding sheaves of papers. It would be an impossible task to sift through every single sheet of paper in one
four-drawer and three two-drawer file cabinets. It seemed
unlikely also that the mayor would have chosen that
method of leaving me a message. Unless he intended to tell
me where to look. *In the meantime* came back to bug me
again. *In the meantime, look in the folder marked "Grades
Spring 2002" in the third drawer of the large file cabinet.*
But there was no such detail available to me, which sent me
into a major funk. If the mayor had arbitrarily opened one

of my ten file drawers and stuck a piece of paper, or any other small item, in one of the folders, there was no hope of finding it, short of a miracle.

I had to switch gears.

Since Woody hadn't seen anything on the mayor's person, whatever he'd left me was smaller than a breadbox. Look who was adopting qualitative measures. In the phone message, the mayor had been specific that he wanted to talk about trouble at the Zeeman Academy charter school. I was convinced he'd left a clue to that trouble, and that trouble had gotten him killed.

I sat at my desk in front of my computer again and glanced over at my robes and briefcase on the rocking chair in the corner, where I'd dumped them after reentering my office. I'd been wearing my robes, which had no pockets anyway, when the mayor was in here, but my briefcase had been in my office from when I arrived on campus around noon yesterday until just a few minutes ago.

I rushed over, grabbed it, and emptied the contents onto a clear section of my desk. Out came notebooks, class folders, a pad of graph paper, math textbooks, puzzle books, tissues, and an embarrassing assortment of pens, pencils, binder clips, chocolate kisses, and cough drops. No secret code ring or piece of microfiche. I consoled myself that there was no bomb, either.

I went back to my desk and tried to imagine what Mayor Graves had been doing in my office for ten or fifteen minutes. Probably not trying to work the countless puzzles scattered around the various surfaces, or admiring my poster with the timeline of women in the history of mathematics. The somber look of Maria and her "witch of Agnesi," matched my mood right now. Poor Maria, born May 16, 1718, just missed a Franklin Hall party this year, since commencement weekend intervened. I doubted the mayor noted the piece of historical trivia.

Maybe he changed his mind after he entered my office

and kept the item to himself. Maybe the mayor did simply want to make a private call, or have a few quiet moments in my rocking chair, which begged the question of why he'd lie to Woody. It wasn't as if my office was the most convenient place for a break. He'd had to walk across campus, past the tennis courts and the parking lot, to get here. The college library and the back wings of the Administration Building were much closer to the stage and would satisfy any ordinary need.

And where was Nora Graves while all this was going on?

At some point, I needed to pay a visit to the grieving widow, whether Virgil liked it or not.

Before I packed up, I gave one more thought to logging on to Facebook to read Elysse's posts and see what her Friends were saying about me.

I chucked the idea. One thing at a time was enough.

I took my robes and briefcase and left my office.

I knew barely enough physics to pass the required courses for my degrees in mathematics, but I could have sworn the fountain at the center of campus had magnetic properties. I left Franklin Hall by the front door, facing the campus, drawn first to glance at the fountain, still wrapped in crime scene tape, then to walk toward it.

I stepped along the pathway in front of the tennis courts, keeping my eyes on the low concrete wall where Bruce and I had enjoyed our ice cream for a few minutes. I felt a shiver and imagined that I heard the mayor call out for me.

As the awful scene came back to me, the strangest, most unimportant details were vivid, like how I'd tossed my chocolate shake aside. I wondered where it was now. Where was Bruce's waffle cone? I knew he hadn't finished it before the mayor came stumbling toward us. Had the crime scene techs taken the ice cream for evidence? Of what? And would I ever get my white sweater back? As if I would touch it again, let alone wear it. Another shiver ran up my back.

I looked over at the faculty offices wing at the back of Admin, where humanities and assorted other disciplines were housed. I recalled that on Saturday night, a window was lit, on the ground floor. It seemed to blink at me now, like a faulty neon light. Whose office was that? If it had been Woody in there, or any of the other maintenance crew, the main lights in the whole wing would have been on until he was finished.

It hadn't hit me squarely on the night of the murder, but what if the mayor and the person who occupied that office had been in there, arguing, for example? Could it be that simple? Someone in humanities, unhappy with the mayor, reached into his pencil holder, pulled out a letter opener, and stabbed him?

I squinted, the better to count the windows from the end. I'd constructed puzzles like this. Now I pretended this was the same task. A brainteaser exercise: Match the outside window of the building to the correct interior office.

The window in question was second from the corner, which meant it belonged to the second office in from the eastern end of the building. I committed the location to memory, as if I had just left my car in a large parking structure. Ground floor, east end, second office.

I visited the faculty wing often enough. I should know the seating chart without marching up there with my briefcase and robes on a Sunday. I closed my eyes, traveling in my mind. Enter the building across from the fountain. Turn left on the cracked, worn marble floor, pass the large music room, pass the half flight of steps that led up to a corridor of classrooms, arrive at the faculty section. Oops, it would have been easier to count backward from the end of the hallway. I should have gone in the entrance on the east side of campus. It's a good thing I hadn't expended any physical energy on this puzzle.

In my mind, I saw the corner office, which belonged to
Jack Peterson, chair of the English Department. Jack's
office had only one window facing the fountain. It was the
office next to Jack's that had been lit up on Saturday night,
and it belonged to . . . I felt my whole body slump . . . Beverly Eaton, English prof, who'd taken off early, before graduation, for several weeks in Oxford with a few of her majors.
Her office would have been locked with a key that fit all the
offices in the wing. In other words, anyone on the faculty or
staff could have been in Beverly's office on Saturday night,
certain that she wouldn't show up and surprise them.

I felt like I'd run up and down the hallway getting to this
dead end. Plus, my spirit was exhausted.

My walk back to Bruce's car was happily uneventful,
except for the constant stirring of my mind, first in the
direction of Mayor Graves's visit to my office, then to his
murder, and then to the potential drama of a grievance
petition on the part of Elysse Hutchins.

At home, I resorted to eating as a solution to my anxiety
and built the tallest sandwich I could put together, with
tomato, cucumber, avocado, lettuce, and three kinds of
cheese. With Ariana away, I was out of her homemade
cookies, but I had an emergency supply of store-bought
chocolate cookies and opened a new package. It was a
good thing I had the metabolism of my skinny father and
the Knowles side of the family; the Stones had to count
calories, which I'd always thought must be a great hard-
ship, not to say boring. I had to be very careful when visiting a Stone relative not to inadvertently pick up a fat-free
something from the fridge.

I carried my sandwich, garnished with the chocolate
snaps, and a bottle of water past my den and into my office,
ready to face Elysse head-on, cyber-wise.

Rring, rring. Rring, rring.

I fished my cell out of my purse and clicked on to take Fran's call.

"Log on to Facebook," she said, with no preamble.

"I was just about to."

"You've heard, though?"

"I've heard. I'll call you after I've read it all." I longed to talk to Fran about the mayor's visit to my office, but I decided to check out the Facebook posts and call her later, when I needed advice on two issues, not one.

"Let me know if you want me to flunk Elysse," Fran said. "Because I could, you know. She's kind of on the edge in linear algebra."

"Very sweet, if unethical." I laughed, hoping no one was listening in on this conversation. It was a prosecuting attorney's dream. "I'm logging on now," I said, clicking off.

I took an unladylike bite of my sandwich and a long swig of water, followed soon by a deep breath.

I went to Elysse's profile page and saw her photo. Somehow the candid of a tall, smiling blond in cutoffs, lounging at the beach, did not win me over. I might have been more inclined to sympathize with her current plight if she'd uploaded a photograph of herself reading a math book as her profile picture.

I read her original post:

Hey, guys, here's an alert to Henley College students! If you took a class from prof. Knowles this term, check your math grade and be ready to fight. I didn't follow one little instruction and got 0 points. NADA! Zip!!! Can you say fascist???

Wrong! I wanted to shout. She did not get zero points as her term math grade; she simply got zero points for the one question that she blew on the final exam. Why didn't Facebook have a *Don't Like* button? Or a *Don't Believe This* button?

I tried to relax my jaw before taking on the Comments. I didn't even want to see the Likes. I recognized the names of one or two commenters, but for the most part they were all foreign to me. From the spelling and grammar, it seemed they might indeed have been from foreign lands. Every one of the comments had at least one typo. Not that I was looking to discredit the messages.

> *I pity all you math majrs. If this is how your get graded.*
> *That's awfull Elysse! You should send a note with your transrip telling them of this awfull injustice.*
> *Look in teh student handdbook, page 23 for how to protest this.*
> *Your kidding. 0 points!!!!!!!!!!!!!! No way.*
> *Way, my Friend.* (This from Elysse.)
> *Help Elysse, pleasse everyone.*

As if she were the victim of a violent incident or a natural disaster. Or an unnatural one, like a math professor.

There was one comment that made me LOL:

> *What do you exspect from an aged meth prof?*

I decided to forgo reading the rest of the comments for now. I had the gist of the sentiment and I wasn't happy. It didn't help my mood that my gaze kept landing on the silver letter opener on my desk, one with the Henley College seal, exactly like the one that was used to kill Mayor Graves. I couldn't remember the last time I'd used mine. I remembered thinking that we should have switched to flash drives as a parting gift for graduates. Now I thought that maybe if we had, the mayor would be alive.

I swept that ridiculous notion away, and finally also swept the letter opener into the back of my bottom drawer. I doubted I'd ever use it again. I wished both the opener and my sweater could walk on their own to the Henley dump.

I focused on the photograph of my mother and me at the Cape before she took ill. I ran my finger along the top of the frame—my favorite way to dust—and moved the photograph forward, where the letter opener had been, for better viewing.

I wasn't finished with the distasteful grading issue, however. I switched to my email and called up the correspondence Elysse and I had right after I'd made the graded final exams available.

> Elysse: I don't see why I got no points for that distribution problem!! Didn't I get the correct answers???

It seemed that Elysse and her Facebook friends spoke only in multiple punctuation marks. I'd considered responding in all caps, but had thought better of it.

> Me: The instructions were to work the problem by showing a graphical solution, and to show your work. I assume from your bare answers, with no context, that you used a calculator instead.
> Elysse: We used a calculator in class.

(No multiple periods; I was impressed.)

> Me: The instructions on the exam itself and on the separate form were to generate a graphical solution, without a calculator.
> Elysse: The proctor didn't tell me I couldn't use a calculator.
> Me: He signed the form saying he'd announced the instructions.
> Elysse: I didn't hear him.

Me: He gave you a copy of the form.
Elysse: He never gave it to me.
Me: You signed the form.
Elysse: I don't think so!!!!!!!

I'd found the form signed by both Elysse and the proctor, scanned it, and attached it to what I hoped was our last email communication.

Me: Here it is, signed by both of you. Notice the instruction NO CALCULATORS is in all caps.

A few hours later, Elysse had come back with:

OK, I see my signature. So you taught me a lesson, not to sign anything I don't read carefully, now please give me my points for the right answers!!!!

Way to win friends, Elysse, and influence your teachers.

I'd made a few more attempts to explain that the whole point of the exam question, which everyone else in the class had understood, was not to show that you could use a calculator, but to show that you'd grasped the concepts and could demonstrate them graphically.

I pointed out that even with this less-than-stellar final exam performance, she had a solid B for the term, which was a good grade. She pointed out that a B was not solid and would be one of the lowest grades on her transcript. She might want to go to grad school someday, and would need the highest GPA she could get. "And what I deserve!!" she'd added.

With all that had gone on since those emails, I'd forgotten that I never did receive closure from Elysse, not a word that indicated she'd accepted my decision.

Apparently because she hadn't. One of her Facebook posts read:

I'm taking this all the way to the greivance process. Thanks everyone FB friends for your support!!!!!

It had been years since I'd had to resort to reading the college handbook for steps in carrying out a school policy. I was aware of the good news part—that students could formally appeal only final grades, not individual exam scores. Since grades weren't due from the faculty for another two weeks, I had some time to gather my documentation, and my wits. I didn't look forward to the headache that was sure to accompany the project.

As I recalled from an early reading of the handbook, the formal process for appealing a grade was long, involving department heads and deans in a chain of decisions. The handbook needed updating, I realized, with social media now preempting much of the secrecy and substituting for notifications that used to be sent by ground mail on college letterhead.

I wasn't even sure where my copy of the handbook was these days. Probably in my office on campus.

Time to call Fran.

"Flunk her," I said. Fran laughed, fortunately hearing the laughter in my own voice. "Do you have your handbook at home?"

"I just happen to have it right here, open to page twenty-three," she said.

Sometimes just one good real-life friend is better than three thousand cyberfriends.

"Lay it on me," I said, one of Bruce's favorite expressions.

"Most of the 'Grievance Policy' section is for things like harassment and discriminatory practices, in case the school is not attending to the needs of students with disabilities, or students who feel their civil rights are being violated."

"Do students have a right to an A?" I interrupted. Then, "Sorry, I'm letting Elysse get to me."

"This is not like you," Fran said.

I left the rest of my sandwich on my office desk, grabbed my water bottle, and took it and the phone to my den. Maybe I could be more like me in a different environment. Ariana, jack-of-all-crafts, had framed and hung a new print I'd bought at a show. I looked now at the soothing watercolor, a collage of images of Boston, with a focus on the Freedom Trail that included Faneuil Hall, King's Chapel, the Old State House, and the Granary Burying Ground, where Mary "Mother" Goose was buried. Just about every schoolchild in Massachusetts had taken a field trip to the sites pictured.

In the lower corner of the print was an image of the first public school in the country, established by the Puritans and attended by Benjamin Franklin, Samuel Adams, and John Hancock, in addition to lesser lights. You couldn't get much closer to the beginnings of education in America.

I realized that what bothered me most about the situation with Elysse was my own reaction to her grievance. I prided myself on not having an us-versus-them attitude with respect to my students. I usually blamed myself instead of my students when a lesson didn't quite work. Some of my colleagues had faulted me for the mind-set, claiming that I was too friendly, with my majors especially, and that I took the students' side on most issues that came up. With needy students like Kira, I took on the role of therapist, parent, confessor.

Fortunately, most of my students were somewhere in the middle of the spectrum, between an overconfident Elysse Hutchins and a self-effacing Kira Gilmore.

I had to ask myself now—if Elysse hadn't gone all multiple exclamation points on me, and created a protest against me on Facebook, would I be more willing to give her the points and chalk it up to poor instructions on my part? It was hard to tell.

"Better you vent to me than in public, really or virtually," Fran said, still waiting for my response.

I heard pages flipping and children's voices in the background. Fran's grandchildren. "I'm keeping you from your family day," I said.

"Yes, thanks. I'm losing badly at electronic hangman." More flipping pages, then, "There's a big section on plagiarism and cheating. Is that what we have here?"

"Neither, as far as I know." I explained the details of the problem, what I'd asked for, what Elysse had submitted.

"Got it. Did anyone else misinterpret your instructions?"

"No, the other twenty-two students got it right, or at least approached it correctly."

"A big class."

"Lots of nonmajors."

"What's Elysse doing next year, anyway?" Fran asked. "I've lost track."

"She's putting off grad school. She has a biotech job in Boston."

"Not too shabby. Okay, here it is. 'Procedure for Grade Disputes and the Grade Appeal Process.' "

"That sounds ominous. What's the first thing I'll have to do if she goes through with this?"

"You know you have two weeks before she can do anything."

"It will fly by."

Fran hummed while she read partly to herself, partly out loud. Between indecipherable clucks and hums, I heard mumbled phrases involving faculty responsibility to make expectations clear, students' responsibility to know what's expected, plus a few yada yadas, until she was ready to read pertinent instructions.

"The student should consult the faculty member first."

"She did," I said. I summarized the email correspondence between Elysse and me.

"Maybe you should try talking in person," Fran suggested. "You know, face-to-face, instead of face-to-book." Fran chuckled at her Facebook send-up.

"Of course. I should have done that right away." I drew a deep breath. I really had lost perspective. "I'll try to set up a meeting with her. But I'd better hear the rest of the procedure anyway."

Fran read, "If the dispute cannot be resolved, the student must submit a written request for review to the chair of the department within which the course was offered, or to the academic dean, if the instructor against whom the grievance is being filed—"

"Is also the chair," I filled in. Lucky me.

"Right. The rest of this is what you expect. The request is formalized into a Case, capital *C*, the dean notifies the instructor, the instructor responds in writing, both instructor and student need to submit documentation, there's a review committee, a mediation committee, yada yada. There are huge paragraphs under all these headings."

"What's the bottom line?" I asked.

"I'm scanning." I heard more humming, more children's voices. I took the opportunity to imbibe a long gulp of water. "Looks like the dean then makes a recommendation, but it's the instructor's decision in the end. Hmmm. I'm surprised."

"Me, too. Remember Susan Murray's trial a few years ago?" I asked, referring to a colleague at a nearby college.

"*Trial* is a good word for it. After all the machinations, her dean had the last word and ordered Susan to make a grade change."

I blew out a breath. "Let's hope it doesn't get that far anyway."

"Amen," Fran said, and I let her return to playing hangman with her own middle school set.

CHAPTER $\sqrt{10}$

Back in my office, I gave some thought to emailing Elysse and asking for a face-to-face as Fran had suggested. I opened a Compose screen and tried several versions of *We have to talk*. I deleted all of them.

What stopped me was a new phenomenon—fear of being sued. What if my asking for a meeting was tantamount to admitting I'd been wrong in taking off points? It wasn't so much admitting defeat that bothered me, it was all the ramifications. Would Elysse be able to sue the school, or me? Could she claim emotional distress and get a big settlement that would cost Henley a large amount of money and cost me my job? Had things really gotten that bad between me and one of my students? The idea made me sad.

I couldn't take a chance. I probably should already have consulted with the college legal department. I hated the thought, but I decided that silence was my best tactic at the moment, until I could talk to the dean. Or a lawyer.

* * *

I picked up my sandwich, intending to eat it at my kitchen table, like a normal person on a normal Sunday. However, at the sight of my robes, draped over a chair, the notes of the trumpet voluntary came flooding in and I lost my appetite.

I supposed I should have thanked Elysse for providing at least one hour when I hadn't been thinking of our murdered mayor and trying to figure out why he'd pulled me into the last hours of his life.

My little cottage housed a lot of options for further distraction. Puzzles waited on every table, large and small. Some I'd made up myself; some were from other creators. My beading hobby, which Ariana oversaw, was also evident in the form of an unfinished bracelet for Bruce's niece, Melanie, and several fringed bookmarks. I knew I'd have to have something to show Ariana when I picked her up at the airport. She herself would never go a week without beading and wouldn't be able to understand if I had.

But I wasn't in a beads-and-wire mood.

I settled down instead at a website that had a long list of math games for kids. I could use some new ideas for my visit to Zeeman Academy tomorrow.

I could also use a few answers from Zeeman Academy.

I didn't remember having as many fun ways of doing math when I was a kid. I didn't recall if we even used colored chalk. We certainly didn't have a program for doing fractions with interactive pie charts. It was a wonder I went into math, with all the boring drills I'd had to recite.

I'd recently found and bookmarked a web-based game for learning to multiply. The game involved a Jeopardy-like board, where the student chose an amount to "bet" and then had to perform an arithmetic or algebraic operation, like finding greatest common factors or least common denominators. The idea was to beat a countdown clock, in which case a happy tune played and computer voices sang out congratulations. Talk about instant gratification and positive reinforcement. All that was missing was a bowl of ice cream at the end.

I got hooked on a game that required dragging and dropping a ball into several slots, each of which applied a coating or decoration to the ball, until the ball had the requisite number of extras to ring a bell. I couldn't figure what math skill was used or being taught, but it was fun to hear the different bell tones.

A more instructive app reeled me in quickly—a mystery being investigated by a pair of ten-year-old twin detectives, Kate and Kyle, who had to determine which of three bags had fake coins. I got so involved that I nearly missed the soft ring of my phone.

"Hey, Bruce," I said.

"You must be doing math," he said.

"Lucky guess?"

"Not really. You sound a lot cheerier than I've heard you since . . . well, in a while. Nice to hear."

"Sorry if I've been a pain."

"Not so much that I won't be there in a couple of hours, with dinner."

Now I was really cheery.

Knowing Bruce would be arriving soon grounded me. That he was bringing dinner gave me hope that the weekend could be salvaged. I imagined I smelled basil and interpreted it as a paranormal message from Bruce that he was bringing Italian. I guessed I missed Ariana more than I'd expected to.

It took only a moment to realize how selfish my thoughts had been. Neither the weekend nor the rest of their lives could be salvaged for Mayor Graves's family. A wife had lost her husband; a teenager would grow up without his father; and perhaps the nation had missed out on a worthy statesman.

My father had died of cancer the winter before my third birthday, and, though Margaret did her best to keep him alive for me through stories and photographs, I was always aware of the loss. As a teenager I'd been frustrated, not knowing whether I remembered his purported beautiful piano playing, or whether it was simply Margaret's mesmerizing descriptions that I recalled. Now it hardly mattered. I found myself wishing I could have told him I loved him. I was grateful Margaret had been around for me to tell her that often.

Cody Graves was old enough to be able to distinguish between reality and fiction, but I knew that living with the loss might be even harder for one who had grown to know his father.

I hoped Nora's and Cody's last words to Mayor Graves were what they would have wanted.

I had every confidence in Virgil Mitchell and his colleagues at the Henley PD, but I also had a strong urge to try to help them solve the murder case. I couldn't say why, exactly. It wasn't as though I inserted myself into every homicide case in the city. Nor into every Bat Phone call Bruce and his crew received. They had their jobs and I had mine.

If I had to put words to the feeling, I'd say it had to do with the connection that Mayor Graves had tried to establish with me at the end of his life, from his telephone message to my cell, to his nonverbal reaching out to me on the rickety commencement stage, to his seeking entry into my office, and finally, his dying attempt to tell me something as he staggered toward the fountain.

With what I judged to be uncharacteristic tunnel vision, I'd glommed on to Zeeman Academy as holding the key to

the mayor's murder. Admittedly, my feelings were partly
due to my refusal to believe that anyone associated with the
Henley campus could have been involved in the crime. I
conveniently brushed aside the nagging worry about a possible intimate relationship between Kira and the deceased.
I also dismissed the hostility between the mayor and the
Sizemore sibs. They were, after all, Henley faculty.

The controversy I'd been witnessing revolved around
the charter schools, Zeeman in particular. I ticked off the
incidents: the way the mayor had been hanging around the
Zeeman offices looking at documentation of one kind or
another, and his argument with Superintendent Collins at
the pre-graduation reception. Never mind that your average
mayor and your average superintendent might just as easily
be two guys arguing about the basketball play-offs. But
Zeeman came up again in the anger toward the mayor that
Nichole Johnson and her family had expressed at the
Franklin Hall ceremony and at the Inn at Henley dinner.

And, looming larger than life, Mayor Graves had mentioned it to me directly—I heard it again in my mind.
Something's troubling me about Zeeman.

The police had to deal with all the areas of the mayor's
life. I was sure they were hard at work unearthing motives
that members of Mayor Graves's family may have had—
perhaps there was a second cousin once removed who
owed him money. If the waste management conflict was
any clue, there must have been a host of political enemies
and business associates, and possibly every city of Henley
citizen.

I convinced myself I'd be best at tackling the one area I
had some expertise in—school issues. I planned to get to
Zeeman Academy well before my class in the morning and
see if I could get some idea of what the problems were. I
grabbed another water and went back to my office.

To get the most out of the time tomorrow, I needed to
prepare. I went online and found the .edu site for the

Commonwealth of Massachusetts. It shouldn't be hard to find a clear presentation of how charter schools were created, funded, and managed. And, I supposed, closed down.

A few basic facts would be a good start.

I clicked on glossary/definitions and immediately learned that a charter is a license. So far so good. A charter is issued by the board, I read. But which board? There were two boards referenced in the description, the Board of Elementary and Secondary Education and the Board of Trustees. One paragraph, labeled with a string of numbers, explained that the Board of Trustees was entrusted to supervise and control the charter schools, independent of the school committee. On the other hand, a memorandum of understanding governed the funding of the charter schools by the school district, and on the third hand, budgets were to be submitted to the superintendent of schools.

What? Neither "school committee" nor "school district," both of which were listed in that paragraph, had the benefit of an entry in the list of definitions. Were they synonyms? Different entities?

Apparently the superintendent, Patrick Collins in the case of Henley, had budgetary oversight of all schools, charter or not. Was he also in charge of the school committee? What about the school district? Was that simply a geographic designation, or was it another governing board? Or committee?

Highest on my list of questions was where the mayor fit into the charter school picture. Did he have veto power over all the mountains of paperwork such an organization must generate? Was he a member ex officio of any of the bodies mentioned in the circuitous narrative that passed as a page of definitions? Did he preside over *all* the bodies?

Impossible to figure out. I was sure it was my fault. Certainly the town's officers and various departments knew what they were doing. If not beyond my level of intelligence, the complexities of politics and city management were definitely outside my training and skill set. I longed for a page or two of simple text on the application of second-order differential equations to mechanical vibrations.

I thought back to Kira's claim that Mayor Graves wanted to save Zeeman Academy, to keep it a charter school but without a suspect grading system. I needed to know if he could influence that decision. Could he make or break it unilaterally, for example?

I felt a twinge of gratitude for the simplicity of the Henley College administrative org chart. Whether we liked or agreed with an official or not, at least we could always figure out who was in charge of what.

I'd done all I could. I needed Bruce to appear with dinner and rescue me from the quagmire of .edu.

Rring, rring. Rring, rring.

Not Bruce, but any interruption was welcome.

"Dr. Knowles, it's Kira. I feel like such a dope."

"Hi, Kira." Noncommittal until I learned which aspect of her life Kira had examined and found wanting.

"I've been so selfish and not even thinking of poor Cody Graves, and even Edward's wife."

There was a lot of that going around. "It's a hard thing to grasp, Kira. You seem to be feeling better, though."

"Yeah, I guess. I have a favor to ask you, Dr. Knowles. I would really, really like to offer condolences to Edward's family. I read online that they'll be receiving—that's how they put it—on Tuesday. They're setting something up at the city hall. The family will be there. Mrs. Graves is on her way back from Rome—"

"Mrs. Graves is where?" I asked, wondering who had been on the stage at Henley if the mayor's wife was in Rome.

"She took off for a charity mission in Europe right after graduation, then, of course she had to turn right around and come back after . . ."

"How do you know this?"

And why didn't I know it? Virgil must have known it when I suggested I'd be dropping in on the mayor's wife. That's what he'd meant when he said Nora wasn't home. An understatement if I ever heard one.

"It's on all the news, Dr. Knowles. Don't you get it on your browser home page?" Kira sounded disappointed in her professor. "Anyway, the whole public is invited on Tuesday morning, but I don't want to go alone."

And here I was thinking that my friendship with a cop was a better connection than the average Internet user had available.

"I'm surprised they're ready for a public memorial so soon," I said.

"The Facebook notice said something about how Ms. Eddington, the acting mayor, wants to give the city closure. I'm sure she also wants to introduce herself to the community."

I was getting a little tired of being a few steps behind on the news, both official and unofficial. And I wasn't spending enough time getting Likes on social media. That phenomenon did originate on a college campus, after all.

Once again, I came close to asking Kira point-blank what, if anything, she and the mayor had going on, catching her off topic and off guard. But she still seemed too fragile for such a confrontation. I wished Fran were on the line. She'd find a way to determine who was seeing whom.

After my talk with Kira at the Coffee Filter, I was close to concluding that the relationship was all in her mind. Either way, I didn't want to be responsible for what would happen when the facts came spilling out into reality.

In the end, I wimped out, deciding not even to ask whether there was some reason she didn't want to go to city hall alone. "Wouldn't all your friends from the campaign headquarters be attending? Or Jeanne and the others?" I asked.

"I don't exactly have a lot of friends at headquarters.

None that I can call up, anyway. And Jeanne is going to hook up with her boyfriend in Boston for the rest of the week before she starts her summer job, and Bethany is so out of here, packing for this trip out west. Nicole—I don't even want to know if she and her family plan to pay their respects. So will you come with me, Dr. Knowles?"

I needed a stall. "I'll have to see what the college administration is planning, Kira. In case it overlaps."

"Okay, I understand."

I hated that she sounded so despondent. "Is anyone around the dorms today?" I asked.

"No. I might take off myself. I have to leave by the end of the week anyway, when they close for a month. I might crash at Megan's after that. Or maybe Bethany's cousin Matt's. One of Matt's roommates might be moving in a few days. Or I might stay with a friend of Jeanne's."

That was a lot of "mights" to hang one's living arrangements on. I'd forgotten what it was like to crash anywhere there was a couch or a patch of bare floor. Between my junior and senior years in college, I'd backpacked through Germany carrying a couple of changes of clothes, a tour book, and a toothbrush. I'd made no reservations, landing here and there, connecting with other "kids" on a tour now and then, finding a hostel, or curling up on my backpack on someone's living room floor. I often didn't know from one day to the next which train I'd take to the next city, or where I might spend the night.

At some point in the last twenty years, I'd replaced that spirit of adventure with one of stability, as good a word as any to describe my current lifestyle. I was now attached to my little cottage, with its bright yellow kitchen and cozy den. I loved my home office and my lavender bedroom, even my washer and dryer. In my travels now, I traded only *up*, adding amenities like maid service and breakfast in bed. Bruce and I hiked often on vacation, during the day, but I liked the security of knowing I'd be taking my shower at night in a modern facility with towels even larger and more plush than the ones I owned.

"Dr. Knowles, will you call me and let me know if you'll go to city hall with me?"

I'd almost forgotten the start of the conversation. "I'll call you, Kira. I'd better go now and take this other call."

A call that might possibly come in. I was becoming hopeless as a role model. As I brooded over this, my cell vibrated once, spinning a bit next to my keyboard. A text from Bruce with a quick message: "ETA 15."

I left my office to put water on for coffee and set the table—the least I could do.

Buzz. Buzz.

Bruce was early. Why was he ringing the doorbell? Unless he forgot his key. I went to the door.

And opened it to the police.

Virgil Mitchell wiped his feet on my outdoor mat, out of habit, and entered the kitchen.

"I see you were expecting me," he said, glancing at the table set for two.

"Uh-huh, but I'd better add a third place, in case Bruce drops in."

Virgil laughed and plopped down on a high stool by my kitchen island, one that I had to climb up to. He was in his Sunday best—jeans and an HPD polo shirt. His old brown briefcase looked out of place at his side. I gathered it meant he wasn't off duty, simply off dress code.

"A beer?" I asked.

"Just water."

No beer, and his smile had already disappeared. Virgil was definitely on duty.

I set a large glass of ice water in front of him and took a seat on a stool opposite him. "Having a good day?" I asked, mimicking his downturned expression.

"If you mean did I keep my cool while a guy in hand-cuffs reminded me that his taxes pay my salary and if I lay a hand on him he'll get his second cousin's friend's wife who answers the phones at a law firm to figure out how to sue me and the whole department."

I pushed the package of cookies that I'd opened at lunch toward him. "Makes my day seem like a party," I said.

He snagged a handful of chocolate snaps and seemed to swallow one whole, then pulled a folder out of his briefcase. "Our tech guys spent the morning dumping the mayor's computer. These are some of the emails from the past week." He slid the folder across the counter, working around the pile of catalogs, this morning's juice glass, and a bowl of fruit that had seen better days. Bruce was due to tease me about never making good on my promise to bake banana bread with the overripe stock.

"They got to this pretty quickly," I said.

"They printed out the easy ones, still in his inbox. Now they need to go in and get the ones that were deleted. And remember, this is the mayor we're talking about. Things have a way of moving a little faster than normal."

I opened the folder and riffled through more than a dozen sheets of paper. All of them were emails from Kira to the mayor, dated within the past week. Certain sentences stood out as I flipped through, growing more agitated with each one.

> I hate to see you so miserable, Edward. Remember I'm a phone call away.
> Say the word and I can be at our spot in ten minutes.
> I wish you'd let me stay last night. You know you're my number one priority.
> I can't wait until the campaign is over and you can have a normal life. I'm here for you.

I blew out a slow breath and tucked the emails back into the folder. My theory that the relationship was in Kira's mind was now on rocky ground. "Did he respond to any of these?"

"Not that we found so far." Virgil sucked in his cheeks. A sign that he was unhappy about something. And that it most likely had to do with the person sitting in front of him. Me. "Is there something you should have told me about this student, Sophie?"

I knew he didn't want to hear that Kira was from a small town in the Central Valley of California, that she was nearly six feet tall, on the heavy side, with a short bob that resembled Fran's, but looked better on Fran. "She was one of this year's valedictorians," I offered. "With a grant for graduate work at MIT starting in about a month."

He let out an exasperated breath, which I should have expected. I wasn't trying to be difficult, merely protective of Kira while I thought about how to respond. I thought about invoking teacher-student confidentiality. If there wasn't such a thing, there should be.

"You know that's not what I'm after. I got that much and more from the interviews the officers did at the scene. I probably could have gotten it from the printed graduation program or the write-up in the newspaper. But she wasn't just another onlooker at the fountain that night, was she?" Virgil tapped the folder with his index finger. "This Kira Gilmore"—I thought better of correcting him as he pronounced her first name to rhyme with Sky-rah, instead of with Key-rah—"was one of your math majors. And I know the kind of teacher you are, Sophie. You get close. Were you aware of this relationship?"

I swallowed. "Not exactly."

He heaved a sigh of annoyance and gave me a long-practiced withering look. "Sophie?"

"There was talk." I held up my hand. "I'd hardly even call it talk. More like innuendo. Until today."

"And today?" Virgil made circling motions with both his hands, as if to hurry me along.

"Today she did mention to me that she loved him. But that's all."

"She said she loved him, and you didn't think that would be something to pass on to me?"

"It just happened this morning. And I'm not even sure there's anything behind it. If I went to you with every dormitory rumor, you'd never get any work done."

"I'm the best judge of that. Is there any other little dormitory rumor you want to tell me about?"

"No. Look, Kira may be a brilliant student, but she's very immature. I don't think she's gone on a date in the four years that I've known her, and that would include with boys her own age or with the mayor."

"You're saying this could all be in her head."

I nodded. "I think it could be, yes. My guess is that's the case."

"And you think that's enough to clear her of murder?"

I swallowed hard. Of course it was. Along with many other things, like the fact that Kira was incapable of hurting someone, other than herself. Disloyal as it seemed, I told Virgil about Kira's pitiful attempt to blame Nicole.

"She didn't even know the weapon the killer used," I told Virgil.

"That's what she made you think. She's a smart girl."

I shook my head. I couldn't seem to make Virgil understand. "Maybe when we see the mayor's replies to these emails, we'll know for sure whether there was anything real between them."

"Love how you say 'we,'" Virgil said.

I wanted to remind Detective Mitchell that he'd come to me with the folder now resting between us, not vice versa. I had the feeling that one of his prime reasons for coming was to scold me for not mentioning Kira's crush on the mayor.

The sound of a key turning in the lock, signaling the arrival of Virgil's best buddy, saved me from possible arrest for dissing an officer of the law, which I was ready to do.

Bruce, who'd lovingly arranged for a ride to pick up my car at the shop, set down groceries that smelled good even before they were simmering on the stove, then gave me a kiss. There was nothing like basil to please your olfactory glands and a kiss from your boyfriend to set things right.

"Did you follow me to the market, or do you just have perfect timing?" he asked Virgil, as they knocked knuckles.

Virgil sniffed the air, newly enriched by the presence of fennel and oregano. "Are we having Italian?"

"Love how you say 'we,'" I said.

"Touché," Virgil said.

We didn't bother explaining the repartee to Bruce, who was as busy as a housewife.

"I brought enough for an army," he said. "I think I must be psychic."

I knew I was, and I could hardly wait to tell Ariana about my remote sensing of Italian food.

CHAPTER $\sqrt{11}$

I always enjoyed dinner with Bruce and Virgil, especially when it was prepared by Bruce, an excellent cook, and served by Virgil, who'd do anything not to cook for himself.

Over a dinner of spaghetti with clam sauce, green salad, and Italian bread, I listened to the two buddies swap war stories from their work life. It was a great way to forget my own battles.

Tonight Virgil told us about a new dent on the hood of his car, made by a guy who was resisting arrest. I didn't want to think about which body part had been shoved into the hard, unforgiving metal. Bruce countered with the wrestling skills required to transport an unwilling senior citizen from one facility to another for treatment.

I was able to contribute a description of my current role as defendant in a trial carried out on Facebook.

Thanks to my long conversation and support from Fran, I managed to downplay the trauma my teaching persona had suffered. The guys had enough to worry about every day as part of their regular jobs, so I kept the Elysse Hutchins matter lighter than it felt to me.

"Kids these days," I said.

They picked up on my tone.

"Let me know if you need muscle," Bruce said, showing us his bicep.

"Remember I'm here to protect and serve," Virgil said. "If it turns nasty, call me."

I hated to think of those possibilities, but it was nice to know a couple of large men were on my side.

I walked Bruce out to his car, briefing him on Kira's plight. He was on his way home to grab a nap before starting another twelve-hour shift at nine PM. We'd spent very little dinner time talking about current events, but I wanted Bruce up-to-date on everything.

"There'll be a huge crowd at the service, or whatever it is, on Tuesday. What I can't figure out is why Kira wants me to go with her so badly."

"Other than you're good company?"

"How sweet."

"My take on it? She needs you to lend a little status to her visit. She's not just some kid showing up alone or with other kids; she's the friend of a professor. It's like having a date for the prom."

"Not so sweet."

Bruce shrugged. "You asked."

We leaned on his black Mustang, enjoying the perfect chill in the air. Rainstorms were forecast for the next few days, so we were making the most of the friendly weather.

"I just hope Virgil doesn't arrest her before then," I said. "I know Kira. She's innocent." I shook my head. "She'd never survive even an arrest, let alone anything that might follow."

"Not that you're going to do anything about that, right?"

I frowned and shook my head with vigor. "I'm just going to wait patiently to hear what they find in the mayor's emails, whether he reciprocated or acknowledged her feelings in any way. That's it."

"I'd like to believe that," Bruce said, getting into his car.

I was impressed by the stamina he had, ready to go back to work tonight. He claimed he slept through most of his shifts, but I knew he and his crew were on alert even when their eyes were closed.

"It's going to be tough going back to my little sedan," I said, patting the door of his car.

"I'll bring this muscle car around for a visit tomorrow."

"Don't forget I'll be at Zeeman Academy most of the day."

"I thought that was a one-hour gig?"

"I might stretch it out a little tomorrow."

"Because?"

Uh-oh, I hadn't meant to spill out my intentions like that. "It's the last week and I'll have some good-byes to say."

How handy that Mr. and Mrs. Sampson from two houses down happened to stroll by at that moment.

We chatted, then waved Bruce off together. I could tell that neither of them knew why I thanked them so profusely for the little visit as I turned to walk back to my house.

Early in my college teaching career I committed myself to volunteer in a school every year, in a K through 12 class. Well, maybe not K. I usually worked with high schools, leading advanced math classes for college prep students, but now and then I ventured out into the world of younger children. This was my first experience at a charter school.

"You just want to infiltrate those pliable young minds and brainwash them into being math majors later," Bruce had accused me.

Ariana had put it differently, something about young souls and old souls, but she'd meant the same thing. They were both right. You couldn't start too early to instill a love of math.

Zeeman Academy was located about fifty yards back from a busy country road on the western edge of Henley. The housing developments around the property were thought to be tough neighborhoods, but inside the fence, it always seemed safe and secure to me.

The long path to the school building was fronted by a short stubby brick wall with a bright blue and white sign announcing the entrance. A massive front lawn doubled as a playing field, which today hosted a field hockey game involving highly energetic and noisy children I recognized as fourth to sixth graders. The building itself was a modern two-story brick structure with a row of glass doors and a slanted roof.

As soon as I opened one of the front doors, more bedlam met my ears. Bad timing. But at Zeeman, a K through 8 school, it was hard to figure out the schedule. At the noncharter schools I was familiar with, classes changed at ten minutes to the hour, every hour. You could count on it. Here, students worked in groups on projects, at their own pace, and had only a few times during the week when they met in regular classroom settings, and even those comprised multigrade groups. Individual differences were paramount at Zeeman and not every child thrived with his school day divided into fifty-minute periods.

It had taken me a while to get used to the difference in overall noise level at Zeeman, not only compared to our college buildings, but also compared to other schools I'd volunteered in. One Zeeman teacher had explained to me that forcing children to be silent while moving about the hallways, for example, was a bad, stifling idea. A better approach was to replicate the home or work environment as much as possible, with an expected noise level.

"The corridors of an office building or a lab, where the students will work someday, aren't silent. They have normal noise and chatter," she'd pointed out, without specifying how many decibels she considered *normal*.

I would have preferred a level somewhere between a cloister and the kiddie park at the edge of town, where we'd take Bruce's niece, Melanie. There was no question in my mind, however, that I would adjust to any environment if it meant I could keep working with pupils. My forte was teaching math skills; I was happy to leave it to others to design the proper environment and to prepare students for the more social aspects of their future career paths.

I arrived at Zeeman at ten, an hour before Rina Flores, the Spanish teacher, would corral twenty fourth, fifth, and sixth graders into a classroom for me, probably calling them in from a fun pickup game on the back lot, or a robot-building project. I had my work cut out for me.

But first I wanted to work on that chat with the school's principal. I'd had few dealings with Mr. Douglas Richardson, and he'd been very pleasant when we met by chance in the hallway or parking lot. I'd invited him to visit my class at any time, but he had "a lot on his plate," as he explained.

I knew from newspaper articles that Richardson was my age, but he seemed older. Maybe it was the fact that his suit jacket didn't quite close around his spare tire. Also, his hair was nearly all white, whereas I was blessed with only one streak of gray, across the front of my forehead, an artifact many thought I paid regularly to have planted there. It was quite possible, too, that I had a warped view of how old I looked to others.

I'd taken a little time before nodding off last night to look over a brochure I'd received at a volunteers' orientation meeting early in the year. I didn't remember looking at it since. There was nothing like a murder to refocus one's attention.

The philosophy as laid out in the booklet seemed

forward-looking: "Zeeman Academy unites an imaginative, community-based, academic curriculum with emphasis on hands-on, experiential learning through workshops, projects, and internships."

Overall I liked the premise of the innovative curricula that charter schools offered. Though ex-military Bruce didn't approve of the lack of structure that characterized some of them, I saw the advantage of having schools that didn't follow a strict regimen, helping kids at both ends of the learning spectrum. Whether gifted or challenged, kids could profit from having the freedom to move from one subject to another without a rigid schedule.

My reason for wanting to meet with Richardson now, however, had nothing to do with the philosophy of students' obtaining work permits versus sitting still for in-class memory drills, or chatter versus silence in the hallways. I wanted to know why he and the mayor were at odds. According to Kira, the issues were grade inflation and test score fraud, but Kira had proven herself unreliable lately, and I needed to gather information at the source.

The intimate language of Kira's emails to the mayor had come to my mind often since yesterday, edging out Elysse's inflammatory Facebook posts. I wondered if I could count on Virgil to let me know what the mayor's emails revealed, especially whether Kira's affections were reciprocated. Not that I had a plan for what I would do about it, either way, except perhaps help Virgil—and Kira—evaluate the relationship.

As I approached Richardson's door I mused over how to broach the subject. Plans I'd made last night seemed too flimsy in the light of day. I couldn't seem to do any better now. "By the way," I might begin, "did you and the murdered mayor have any bad blood between you?" Or, "Did the mayor, by any chance, catch you cheating on your grade reports so you'd get continued funding?"

I heard voices behind the door now, an argument for

sure. Was it me or was there a lot of infighting going on these days? I couldn't make out the words, but I could tell there wasn't a party going on. I might have a few minutes to rework my opening after all.

Thwack!

I was stunned by a head-on, or rather head-to-chest, collision. A large mass exited Richardson's office and plowed into me, knocking my purse and briefcase into the hallway.

"Pardon me," a gruff voice said.

I stepped back, struggling to regain my footing. I looked up and saw my attacker—Superintendent Patrick Collins. His face was red, most likely from his argument with Principal Richardson. I doubted my short, small frame could have caused him to blush or made a dent in his massive front.

"Mr. Collins," I said. How awkward.

"I'm so sorry, Miss . . . ?" He looked perplexed, as if he wanted to ask how I knew him and why he didn't know me. We'd shared a cocktail party and a stage only two days ago. Clearly I hadn't made an impression. Or I simply looked different without my cap and gown.

I sprang to attention while he bent over, at considerable cost to his respiratory system, and picked up my purse and briefcase.

As he righted himself, I zeroed in on his bald head and his glasses, which nearly fell off in his struggle to retrieve my belongings.

I had a crazy thought and decided to run with it. I started with, "Did you enjoy our graduation ceremony on Saturday?"

The superintendent looked confused for a moment, perhaps surprised that I knew his whereabouts on the weekend. He recovered quickly with, "Oh, at Henley. At the college. Yes, of course, very nice. Always good to cheer on the next generation, isn't it?"

I gave him an enthusiastic nod, as if I were agreeing with a deeply philosophical and insightful statement. Perhaps we should have invited him to give the graduation speech. "I was glad you could make it. And didn't I see you in Franklin Hall afterward?" I counted on the fact that Collins wouldn't know I was still on the stage at the time, having stuck it out until the last mortarboard reached its peak in the sky, stopped, and made its way down.

"The science building?" he asked.

"Math and science," I said, with a smile. "The first floor is for the Math Department."

He managed a chuckle while still catching his breath from the deep knee bend. "Yes, I needed a fax machine and someone pointed me in that direction. You know, we're always on call these days, aren't we?" He patted his pocket, where a cell phone might be. "Wired in," he said. *Grass wasn't growing under his feet*, my mother would have said.

I gave him a sympathetic, "Yes, we certainly are," and added, "Too bad you had to trudge all the way over there. There's a copy center in the Administration Building and also one in the library, both of which would have been a much shorter walk for you."

"I guess I asked the wrong person."

Or you were looking for someone, I thought.

The superintendent stuffed my purse and briefcase into my arms without ceremony. "I'd better run to my next meeting," he said, adjusting his suit jacket and tie. He made off down the hallway as fast as his bulk could carry him, which no one would have called running.

Like principals' offices in every school I'd ever been to, including my own K through 12 schools, this one had a bench outside. I took a moment to sit down and rearrange my things, making sure nothing escaped from the outside pockets of my purse. While I straightened myself out, I mulled over Superintendent Collins's claim that he'd been looking for a fax machine. Woody, who had no reason to lie, told me he'd asked for the restroom. Maybe Collins was too embarrassed now to tell a lady, especially one he hardly recognized, that he'd needed a bathroom.

More likely, he was looking for the mayor. Since I hadn't been paying attention to him, I didn't see when Collins left the stage on Saturday. He could easily have slipped away during the exodus from the back rows right after Mayor Graves walked off, just before degrees were announced. I had an image of the bulky Superintendent Collins following the young mayor across campus, entering the building after the mayor had ducked into my office. It would have been too suspicious for him to ask Woody where the mayor was.

I regretted that I could think of no way to find out if the two met in or outside of Franklin. Or later that evening.

It occurred to me that the three times I'd seen the superintendent, he'd been irritated for one reason or another. I'd seen him arguing with the mayor at the college president's pre-graduation reception. Later, it was clear that he'd been disgruntled during the mayor's commencement address, and most recently he'd nearly knocked me over after an argument with Zeeman's Principal Richardson. An unhappy man. I wondered if he and Woody had gotten along during their brief interaction in Franklin Hall.

I stood and nearly got whacked again as Principal Richardson's door opened and he rushed out.

"'Scuse me," he said, and hurried down the hall without meeting my eyes. I doubted he knew whom he'd almost knocked over.

Two administrators, two near misses for injury.

I decided it would be safer in my classroom with the younger set.

At Zeeman, teachers were always happy to have guests drop in to their classrooms. We were welcome, as long as we walked around and interacted with the various groups of students and their projects.

I still had a half hour before my students would gather, so I stopped by Dan Sachs's class. Dan, a passionate third-year teacher, had applied for and won a grant to outfit several rooms as technology-centric classrooms, which meant a laptop for every student, large interactive screens, and enough educational software to support a space mission.

Today, Dan's students were working on a special curriculum he'd developed for teaching Shakespeare to sixth, seventh, and eighth graders. Fifteen small heads were bent over laptops, some of them lifting their eyes and moving their hands away from the keyboard long enough to say, "Hey, Dr. Knowles." One of the groups was building Facebook pages for each of the characters in *As You Like It*; another was creating a song list from the Internet that expressed the emotions of the lovelorn Silvius; a third was writing code geared to constructing a concordance of Shakespeare's comedies.

I wandered around among the groups, but participating more as a student than a teacher. I hadn't written code since the clunky days of the mid-nineties. It was a pleasure to see how far programming had come and how accessible it was to these students.

At the back of the room, Digital Dan, as we called him, was helping a group troubleshoot a faulty cable connection. Was this an English class? A vocational technology class? I'd heard Dan's pitch often enough, and knew how he would answer—that there was no need for arbitrarily defined "subjects" and that technological devices were appropriate to whatever they were studying.

"They let students learn at their own pace, teach skills needed in a modern economy, and hold the attention of a generation weaned on gadgets," he'd said, sounding like a paragraph from his grant proposal.

I saw the merit of his position, but knew also that the

results were not yet in on the long-term effect of approaches like Dan's.

There were similar questions about curricula at the college—always a back-and-forth between those who wanted to keep the offerings purely academic and those who wanted to introduce vocational programs into each department.

I felt that mathematics sat in a win-win position. We could accommodate the most abstract topics, like number theory and the construction of proofs, as well as the most practical topics, like math for machinists and computer scientists.

It seemed a bit ironic that my math classes at Zeeman were built on low or no technology, almost a throwback compared to Dan's English classes.

I teased Dan about it now as I reached the cable splicing group.

"Why don't my math classes get a shot at all this technology?" I asked.

Dan cocked his shiny, bald-by-choice head and grinned. "Math is already so interesting, you don't need bling."

How could I not agree?

CHAPTER $\sqrt{12}$

The bright part of my day was at hand, matching the brightly painted walls that characterized the school décor. I had no doubt that the students had participated in the decorating project that encompassed Zeeman's classrooms and hallways. I walked down a side hall, the walls of which were covered with children's renditions of the sun setting in the hills, houses with lawns, and a clear, starry night. Long, curvy blue lines were reminiscent of rivers, and tall rectangles with rows of smaller rectangles reminded one of a city skyline that could have been Boston.

I thought of the framed print in my den. A drawing of a large ship on one section of wall told me that Zeeman's children had been on a field trip to the USS *Constitution*, "Old Ironsides," the oldest commissioned warship afloat, from the late eighteenth century. I was always amused to recall that one of its first captains was Isaac Hull. With a name like that, what else could he have done but become a sailor? Like the handyman I hired now and then for small carpentry projects, Rick Rafter. Or like me, mathematician Sophie Saint Germain Knowles.

Just like that, a new puzzle idea came to me.

It was a good thing I liked class, or I would have skipped out and constructed a list acrostic—people who chose occupations to go with their names—then and there.

I was always comfortable in a classroom, feeling at-home surrounded by student desks, black- or whiteboards, chalk, pointers, or markers. The setup in the classroom I used at Zeeman was primitive compared to Dan's, however. Having just stepped out of his futurist model, I felt like a Luddite. I was able to use my own laptop and the whiteboard as a screen to display videos, but only three or four students could play an interactive game at the same time. We used a lottery system, and the others (I tried not to call them losers) were reduced to using actual physical manipulables and worksheets for practice in converting decimals to percents, or adding and subtracting fractions, both topics of the month.

Many of the games I'd found were disappointing. The math action seemed secondary to scoring a point in a sport. Players spent more time "building a character," that is, adding qualities to an avatar, than doing the math. In some cases, for every correct answer the player keyed in or selected, there were still several more steps to moving an icon in place to hit a home run or make a goal, having nothing to do with math skills.

At one table, I tried to encourage two fourth graders to click on a button with ten problems on adding fractions, instead of only one arithmetic operation before the football field kicked in.

"I have to give my guy some tats first," clean-cut Bobby said, choosing to place a swooping eagle on his avatar's torso.

"Yeah, and look at the bad hair they gave my guy," his partner said, though her avatar was female. "And she needs some swag."

I mentally threw up my hands.

The atmosphere in my classroom, especially compared to the up-to-date problems kids were dealing with in Dan's class, was almost enough to make me give up my hard-copy puzzle avocation and create interactive games. Maybe it was time I became part of the educational gaming world.

Either that or I'd join the opposition who questioned the need for teachers to be entertainers in the first place.

"Drill, drill, drill," they cried. Was it time to go back to that? It had worked for my mother, as she often reminded me, and in part for me, though I'd also had a taste of what was called "the new math."

So many choices and opinions. And no really foolproof way to determine what results to expect from each decision. I'd never appreciated college teaching for the piece of cake that it was. Except since Elysse and her Facebook Friends muscled their way in.

Vending machines were not my first choice for lunch food, but I decided to stay at Zeeman through the lunch hour, hoping Principal Richardson would show up. I inserted some coins, then pulled a container with a bagel and cream cheese from a revolving slot. Vending machines now came with flashing lights and high-tech money management, but the food was the same.

I took a seat at a table in the faculty lounge where Rina Flores and Dan Sachs were just settling in. I sniffed in envy as each of them in turn microwaved something that smelled delicious.

Except for my time in Dan's class, with children present, I hadn't seen either teacher since before the terrible end to Saturday's festivities on the Henley campus. Both expressed their outrage at the mayor's murder, and offered detached theories of the crime.

"Politics, you know," Dan said. "These days, there are a lot of people who think political disagreements are best settled through physical confrontation. It's all you see on TV."

Rina agreed, and added her thoughts. "A man in the public eye is very vulnerable," she said.

After a few more rounds of talk that included sympathy for the mayor's family, I went out on a limb.

"What time does Mr. Richardson usually come in for lunch?" I asked.

"You won't see him in here very often," Rina said.

I took a bite of the cold, hard, tasteless bagel with rubbery cream cheese. "I don't know why not. The food is delicious."

They both laughed and offered to share their meals, but I waved away the idea. I wanted something other than food from them.

"I wondered if Principal Richardson and the mayor were friends, and I wanted to ask him how he's holding up." It was a pretty good line, if I did say so myself, and I wished I'd thought of using it when Superintendent Collins plowed into me.

Rina, a dark beauty in her late thirties, I guessed, nearly choked on her chicken and black bean casserole; Dan threw his head back; both rolled their eyes.

"Can you say 'thorn'?" Rina asked. "That's what the mayor was to our principal. A thorn in his side. May he rest in peace, but he was always after our principal for one thing or another. Especially when his boy, Cody, was here, but it hasn't stopped."

"You got that right," Dan said. "Our principal gets special attention from high places. Attention he doesn't need."

It was clear whose side the two dedicated teachers were

on, but I suspected both were too loyal to tell me outright whether their principal was breaking the law. I had to be more direct. I braced myself.

"I've heard rumors on my campus, something about grades being reported"—what could I say that wouldn't be overly offensive?—"higher than they are."

My attempt at subtlety didn't work. Dan screwed up his mouth, his look unfriendly.

"What are you implying?"

"Just that I heard something about grades and test scores," I stammered.

"You mean how the mayor was accusing Richardson of inflating the grades for funding?" I'd never heard such an angry tone from Digital Dan, not even the last time a fourth grader spilled milk on a keyboard in his classroom. "Just so you know, as awful as it was that the man was murdered, you're not going to find many people here who will actually miss him."

Dan's flare-up caught me off guard, though I shouldn't have been surprised. Hadn't I always said how phony it was to praise the dead just because they were dead? No phoniness here.

Fortunately, I didn't have to respond right away to Dan. Rina was on me.

"I wondered why you were so chummy today, staying for lunch."

"Classes are over at the college," I said in a weak, defensive voice. Grasping at straws.

"Right," Rina said, meaning anything but. "You have no idea how hard it is to be beholden to this one and that one for everything. We don't know from one day to the next what's going to happen to the school library, or whether there will be any field trips for our kids, or any money for faculty development. Dan did great getting that grant, but it's a drop in the bucket, really."

Dan nodded, more relaxed now. "Even that grant doesn't cover maintenance or any kind of continuing ed. It's nice to have new technology, but what happens when it's all outdated next year? We'll have a graveyard of old chassis and we'll all be back to square one."

"Everything has strings attached," Rina said. "All of them—the mayor and the school committee and the parents' organization—they give us money and they think that gives them the right to tell us how and what to teach."

"And how to test," Dan added.

"Testing is a big thing," Rina agreed. "We haven't had charter schools in Massachusetts for that long. We need to be fully funded to have them work as they were meant to."

"And cut some slack to really test our methods. One person's 'imaginative academic curriculum' is another person's 'dumbed down school,'" Dan said.

"And everyone's an expert," Rina added.

I wanted to break in and tell them that I was merely asking a question, not on one side or the other. Neither Dan nor Rina was addressing me directly now. They were letting out their feelings about their school and how it was viewed by others in the education community. But it was clear that the cause of their increasing agitation had been my remark, and I wished I could take it back.

"If anyone thinks it's the worst crime in the world to try to save your school, let them come here and teach," Rina said.

"And not for just an hour now and then," Dan added, with a pointed look at me.

"You're so right," Rina threw in.

She and Dan stood together, as if they'd choreographed the move. They gave me a quick glance, tossed their unfinished meals in the trash, and walked out of the room.

I was left in the dust with the remains of a bagel so tough that not even an entire bottle of water could soften it.

* * *

I sat for a few minutes, utterly regretting what I'd done. Bruce was right. Virgil was right. I had no business trying to be an investigator. At best, I'd ruined the day for two people I cared about. At worst, I'd betrayed the trust put in me by Zeeman Academy's best teachers, stuck my nose where it didn't belong, and possibly alienated two of my friends here.

What made me think that two hours a week of volunteering gave me the right to know or to judge what went on the other thirty-plus hours?

I gathered my purse and briefcase, and left the room.

As I walked past lively classrooms, I reminded myself that while grade inflation might be what was making all this creative learning possible, and might not be a capital offense, murder was. Rina and Dan might justify the means, but not if murder was involved. I did have the best intentions—routing out Mayor Graves's killer. But that wasn't my job either.

I reached the end of the hall, about to pull on the heavy glass doors. A hulking form appeared on the other side and pushed the doors in, sending me tripping back.

"Sorry, sorry, are you okay?" asked a familiar voice. "I thought you saw me, Sophie."

Detective Virgil Mitchell. My first thought was that Rina and Dan had called the police, asking to have me arrested for meddling at the least, slander at the worst.

"I was just leaving," I told Virgil, as if he'd asked.

"I see that."

"I had my class and then stayed for lunch." I babbled, as if I'd been caught speeding and pulled over by a state trooper in his jodhpurs.

"Good," Virgil said, giving me a look that asked, *What's wrong with you?*

I slid closer to the door, first checking to make sure a third collision wasn't in the offing. "So, I'll see you later?"

"Later," Virgil said, and headed down the corridor.

I left Zeeman Academy with a few bruises to my body and spirit.

I drove home at the start of a light spring rain, predicted to turn nasty by late afternoon. I used to worry about Bruce, flying a small craft, relatively low to the ground, in stormy weather, but he'd taught me the MAstar refrain: *Four to say go, one to say no.* Each mission called for a pilot and two nurses in the helicopter, plus the preflight mechanic on the ground. Any one of them could decide that making the flight would be unsafe, and the mission would be cancelled.

I wished I had such clear instructions.

I couldn't seem to get a handle on anything the past few days. I had so many partial truths rattling around in my head, like someone had taken the pieces of five jigsaw puzzles and thrown them into one box. With no picture on the cover. I needed answers.

On top of it all, between Elysse's Facebook attack and Rina and Dan's responses in the lunchroom, I felt my whole philosophy of education was being brought into question. If I couldn't be sure of the way I taught and what I expected from myself, my students, and my administrators, what was the point?

I slammed on my brakes at a red light, which at least stopped my head from going into overdrive. The mayor's murder, and his repeated desire to connect with me, had thrown me off-kilter. Not only that, I was hungry. A couple of bites of stale bagel didn't cut it as lunch. But I could do this. I could put things in order. That was my specialty.

While I was on the lookout for food, I'd create a mental lineup of murder suspects. That should be safe territory. There was no one around to hear me and take offense.

I tapped on the steering wheel with my index finger for the first suspect. Principal Douglas Richardson. It was obvious to me that the mayor had uncovered his fraudulent scheme or schemes to get continued funding.

Maybe that's why Virgil showed up at Zeeman today, to take Richardson into custody. I wished I knew for sure; I'd have given anything to call off my own pseudo-investigation. I wondered if Virgil traveled to Zeeman Academy because he'd tracked the mayor's schedule for the last couple of days, or because I'd introduced the school into our first conversation at the crime scene. I hated to compound my accusatory stance against Zeeman by telling Virgil what I'd just learned at lunch.

In any case, it was more likely that Virgil was visiting the school today only for routine questioning, not to arrest someone. I knew from television that it took at least two cops and flashing lights to arrest a guy, and that they wouldn't want to have a perp walk at an elementary school. That's how informed I was.

I let Rina and Dan off the hook as suspects even though they had all but admitted that Principal Richardson was guilty as charged by me and that they saw nothing wrong with it. I sympathized with their plight, but, hard as I tried, I couldn't agree with them. A little exaggeration about student performance on Parents' Night was harmless, but submitting bogus official report cards up the funding chain to state and federal organizations qualified as criminal behavior in my book.

I couldn't say I'd be relieved if Virgil had evidence of fraud and could tie that crime to Mayor Graves's murder. Dan and Rina's argument and description of life at their charter school had reached me, teacher to teacher. I declined to place them on my suspect list, wanting to think their motives were pure and that they'd done nothing wrong themselves.

Superintendent Collins probably knew of the grade

inflation and that might have been the subject of his argument with the mayor on graduation day. Which side would he be on? Were Richardson and Collins in cahoots? I had no idea of the chain of command when it came to submitting grade reports. The two school administrators might have been quarreling today over why they'd had to kill the mayor. Or over the merits of chain versus independent electronics stores.

I thought of the triangle Kira had presented to me yesterday— Collins and Richardson each having something yet to be determined on the other, and both possibly having something on Graves, that something perhaps being Kira herself. A strange image came to me, from my high school chemistry text—a ring of snakes each biting the other's tail. It had something to do with how the shape of the benzene ring came to a famous (but not to me) chemist in a dream. Sometimes I had to admit that science had as many interesting stories as mathematics.

Another possibility was that the superintendent was in danger. What if Principal Richardson was killing off anyone who was aware of the fraud and didn't agree with his little scheme to keep his school open and hold on to his job? From snippets in the news and the way he cavorted with higher-ups, Richardson had always struck me as more than a little ambitious for his career. A shiver ran through me. If Rina and Dan squealed on me, I could be in danger.

I brushed away the silly thought as I checked that my car doors were locked and that all the systems displayed on my dashboard were at normal levels.

With all this dubious behavior in high places, I wondered if the city of Henley was a candidate for appropriation by the state government. I recalled a precedent. About five years ago, the citizens of the Commonwealth watched the news as the government authorized the complete takeover of a city on the North Shore, something that hadn't been done since the Great Depression. The city had been collapsing under the weight of the various mob bosses who ran the mayor and even the police. The state seized control, ousted the mayor, and installed a set of Commonwealth-approved managers to turn the city around and eventually return it to its citizens. I wouldn't put it past my home state to revive the tradition.

But I couldn't believe Henley was as bad as that. And surely Mayor Graves wasn't so corrupt. Hadn't Kira loved him? A questionable recommendation at this point.

Rring, rring. Rring, rring.

My car rang. I hated to interrupt my brilliant organizing session. I was at a stretch of busy city street where it would have been tough to pull over to check the caller ID on my phone. I'd have to either take potluck and answer through my Bluetooth, or let the call go to voice mail. It wasn't as if I were getting far with my suspect analysis. In fact, I was getting nowhere, other than a few miles closer to home. I might as well take the call.

I clicked the lever to answer my phone through my hands-free system.

"Hello," I ventured, in the suspicious-sounding tone I used for callers who blocked their ID or whose ID I couldn't see, as now. My response was meant to carry the attitude that, one, I don't like taking calls from unknowns; two, you'd better have a really good reason for calling me; and, three, if you're a solicitor, you can expect an immediate hang-up.

"Professor Knowles?"

I didn't recognize the voice, "Yes?" Wary, in case this was a call from a textbook publisher trying to influence my choices for the fall semester.

"Hi, it's Elysse. Elysse Hutchins."

As if there were more than one Elysse in my life at the moment. I felt a twinge of annoyance. If there had been a receiver in my hand like the old days, I might have hung up. Of course, now all I had to do was push the tiny off button. I didn't want to risk justifying such a move in a court of law.

"Hi, Elysse," I said, as calmly as I could.

"I think we ought to meet, don't you, Professor? I mean, sometimes it's hard to express yourself by emails."

I almost jumped in with *Yourself or myself*? But, no, I'd better think before saying anything sarcastic out loud. What if she was recording the call for future use in a deposition? Or for posting on YouTube?

"When would be good for you?" I asked. Safe enough.

"I'm going to be on campus tomorrow morning. I could meet you in your office."

I had no plans for tomorrow other than to, possibly, attend the service for Mayor Graves. I could make it easy for Elysse, or I could make it difficult.

I chose something in between. "I can meet you at eight thirty," I said. Matter-of-fact, not snarky, but fully aware of the sleeping habits of most students, recently graduated or not.

"That's kind of early."

I didn't hear a question, so I didn't respond. This was not the Professor Sophie Knowles I was proud of, letting someone stew, especially a student. Power corrupts? I hated to think it was true.

Elysse blinked first, after a heavy sigh. "Okay, I guess I can do that."

"I'll see you tomorrow," I said.

"So, are we good, Professor Knowles?"

I took a breath. "I'll see you in my office tomorrow, Elysse."

I thought of taking the leftover donuts to the meeting, but that would have been cruel and unusual.

I hoped by tomorrow morning, I'd have lost this attitude and would be ready to be "good" with Elysse.

CHAPTER $\sqrt{13}$

What should have been a twenty-minute drive from Zee-man to my home was taking twice as long as traffic wisely slowed down during heavy spurts.

I'd gotten off track with my suspect list. And I'd forgotten to look for food. At times like this, I missed Ariana. Her approach to problem solving was decidedly not logical, which was not to say illogical. How her perspective aided me in my analytical approach didn't exactly compute, but it worked every time. *What would Ariana do?* I asked myself.

She'd wisely tell me I was doing too much thinking-while-driving, especially in the rain. I took some relaxing breaths and a swig from my water bottle. I fished in my purse on the passenger seat and found a chocolate ball. Since it was wrapped in red foil, I figured it was from Valentine's Day. Only three months old. It would do.

A little stale, the candy still worked its magic and my mind was ready to shift back into gear, in harmony with

the world. Ariana would have been proud of me, making
do, without the benefit of hot tea. I acknowledged the reaction I was having to what was undoubtedly the nastiest
graduation weekend I'd ever experienced. Could it have
been only two days ago? I couldn't remember a single incident in the past when students, like Nicole Johnson and
Jeanne Flowers, had openly dissed the commencement
speaker, our own mayor, no less, at what was supposed to
be a party in their honor. Had either of them been unhappy
enough to stab him? It was hard to picture.

It wasn't hard to envision Nicole Johnson's father, Nicholas, in a heightened state of anger, however. I tapped the
wheel with three fingers, one for each suspect, but had to
withdraw the last one as I recalled again the sight of Mr.
Johnson driving off with his family. He couldn't have been
near the campus at the time of the murder, unless he traveled faster than light. I wondered if that would even do it.
I'd have to ask a physics prof.

I was left still with Richardson and Collins.

I got sidetracked, not for the first time, wondering if
Collins had gone into Franklin Hall looking not specifi-
cally for the mayor, but for what Graves left in my office.
Maybe Collins picked the lock and retrieved whatever
Graves had put in there, when Woody was out of sight. No
wonder I couldn't find it.

I sat at another light and watched the windshield wipers
do their orderly thing, back and forth. I wanted to reach out
and stop them, freeze them in one spot. My usual method
of rearranging a headful of scattered thoughts and facts
wasn't working as well as it should have. Still, I had to
continue to get all my—emphasis on *my*—suspects in one
virtual room. I needed a Starbucks; if I was lucky, one that
carried their special dark chocolate–covered grahams.
Starbucks were everywhere except when you were in desperate need of a mocha and fresh chocolate. Independents

were more difficult to spot, but I kept my eye out for a large neon outline of a coffee cup or a clever name like the Coffee Filter.

I pushed on, leaving the expressway for city streets.

The bouncy Sizemore sibs showed up in the lineup of my puzzled mind. I could see why Monty and Mayor Graves were at odds if there had been conflict of interest while they did business together.

I remembered when Monty had just been hired into the adjunct faculty and was trying like crazy to make his mark as a person of importance. He'd made a big deal of the fact that his management consulting company had landed a contract with the city's public works department. He and his colleagues had undertaken a major project: assessing and evaluating Henley's infrastructure. I'd listened as Monty took over an informal gathering at lunch, boasting about his ideas for improving road and sidewalk maintenance, outsourcing the waste management function, meeting with union reps, and, in general, being the best thing that had ever happened, not only to Henley College, but to the city of Henley as well. When the news came out that the mayor had terminated their agreement, Monty was silent. It was hard to believe that, according to Kira, it was our trash that had proven his downfall.

Was it because Monty had a reasonable motive for murder that I listed him as suspect number three, after Richardson and Collins, or was I acting simply out of vengeance, because he and his sister had sided with Elysse and her Facebook Friends instead of with me, their colleague? Maybe that was also enough to make Chris suspect number four. Why not? I needed a female on the list, and Chris had, after all, reacted out of proportion to the stakes during the vote on whether the mayor would be our speaker.

I recognized a hulking shortcoming in my method of lining up suspects. Unlike the procedure the Henley PD was tasked to follow, mine focused merely on motive. I'd been neglecting to factor in means and opportunity, which would have taken real police work.

But I doubted even the police would fare well in trying to investigate the means, a simple letter opener, unless they'd found a unique set of fingerprints on the handle. The Henley College letter opener was ubiquitous, in offices throughout the campus and somewhere in the homes of its twenty thousand or so alumnae. Or in the city of Henley landfill, into which they might have been unceremoniously tossed. There was no record or serial number on the letter openers as there would have been for a gun. No lot number or license application. No way of tracking chain of custody. The killer was either brilliant in choosing such a weapon, or incredibly lucky to be standing near it when he or she needed it.

As for opportunity, I could set myself up with a clip-board and some good walking shoes and find out who had been on campus at the time the mayor had come stumbling toward the fountain—toward me, actually—at ten fifteen on Saturday night.

At one time, even pedestrians had to log in after dark to enter a campus gate. Like overall national security in the last ten years, security on the Henley campus had gotten tighter and more sophisticated. The question was whether our system of cameras did as good a job as the old method of posting a guard at every entrance. If we'd gone with the lowest bidder on the cameras, maybe not. In any case, I was sure that, after the events of this past weekend, a high-level meeting of the college administrators and trustees was planned—or had already been held—to evaluate our entire security system. And to decide on a new present for our graduates.

I imagined the police had already looked at footage from Saturday evening. I wished I'd thought to ask Virgil about it at Sunday morning's donut feast. I doubted he'd have been any more forthcoming about being hunched over a set of monitors all night than he'd been about anything else regarding the case.

Too bad my old friend, Charlie, in the campus security office, had retired. I figured it wouldn't work to query the new guy while introducing myself to him for the first time. One more dead end among many.

I was fairly convinced that if means and opportunity had already been easily determined by either a clear set of prints on the letter opener or a sharp image of the stabbing on a security monitor, the killer would have been apprehended and we'd all know about it.

Clearly, I was on the right track by focusing on motive. It was such a heady thought that I wondered why I'd never considered entering the police academy.

Rring, rring. Rring, rring.

This time, I welcomed a distraction and clicked on without hesitation.

"Sophie? Fran here." Whew, someone on my Favorites list. "Where are you?" she asked.

"Driving back from Zeeman in the pouring rain. You sound excited."

"I'll bet you haven't heard."

"These days, you can count on that."

"They've arrested someone from the campus."

No wonder phone calls were discouraged while driving. It was all I could do to keep in my lane and not drift into a parked car. "Who?" I asked, gripping the wheel. "Who was arrested?"

"I don't know."

"Are you trying to cause an accident?"

"Sorry to get your hopes up. And I didn't realize you were driving or I'd have waited."

"No, you wouldn't have."

"Of course not. Courtney called me."

"Courtney, the dean's secretary? Courtney, the junior chem major? Or Courtney—"

"The dean's Courtney," Fran interrupted. "So, very decent cred."

Courtney Dixon was a good buddy to Fran and me, keeping us tuned to the pulse of the campus and the whims of the academic dean, briefing us ahead of time about the agenda when we were summoned to her boss's office. A young woman with the reddest curly locks I'd ever seen in person, Courtney had the level head and calm manner of an old woman with gray hair wrapped in a bun. Her cred was the best, as Fran said.

"I'm listening," I said to Fran.

"Courtney tried to reach you, by the way, but couldn't get through. I figured you had your phone off during class."

The rain was heavy and I needed to concentrate on driving or on Fran. I chose Fran and pulled over at the next strip mall. I sat facing a chain shoe store and wondered what it would be like to be a clerk there and have no homework, no students to worry about. *The grass is always greener.* I wondered why Margaret's sayings were so much on my mind lately. Maybe because she'd always seemed to have the answers.

"Tell me everything," I said.

"There's not that much to tell yet. Courtney was in the student union building going over some things with the construction crew for the remodel of the gym. You know, the girls have been complaining about the showers and the crappy lockers for the past hundred years; the boys are here one year, put in a complaint, and voilà, we fix the problem."

"What else is new?" I asked. I knew Fran would take it as I'd intended, a rhetorical question with many levels of meaning.

"Courtney happened to see a cop car out the window over by Admin. She waited a couple of minutes, then saw them come out of the building taking someone with them in the car. She was kicking herself for not being in her office, where she'd have been up close and personal to the action."

"Did she see handcuffs?"

"I don't know. Why?" Fran asked.

"They could have just been taking someone in for questioning."

"I love knowing someone with insider information on police procedure," Fran said. "I've been dying to talk to you. No one's around campus today, except a few people upstairs in Franklin. Either people are gone or they don't have a clue about the pickup."

"Lucky humanities types don't have labs to clean up and equipment to put away."

Not that Fran and I had much more than plotters and calculators to worry about. We did have assorted boxes of manipulables for our teacher training seminar, but nothing like the overwhelming number of pieces of glassware, magnets, and specimens on the floors above us in Franklin.

"Wouldn't it be great to have this ordeal over with, so we can stop worrying about our majors?"

I knew Fran meant Kira most of all. She was as concerned as I was about Kira's current state and what may or may not have been going on between her and the mayor and what it may or may not have led to. I'd told Fran about the one-way emails I'd seen, swearing her to secrecy. I knew we both had Kira's best interests at heart, and I needed all the help I could get to figure out what had been going on around me all semester.

"It will be terrific when this is all a dim memory," I agreed.

"Are you coming back here?" Fran asked.

I had no reason to go back to campus. Classes were over; I had two weeks to work on final grades. I'd planned to stop and pick up food, suddenly in the mood for real bagels and real cream cheese, and go home for a tasty, hassle-free lunch.

I tapped my steering wheel. Or I could go to campus

and spend some time gossiping with Fran; that is, analyzing the situation to death, as we mathematicians liked to
call it.

"I'm on my way," I said.

"I'm in my office, just tying up some loose ends. I'll call
around and see what else I can find out before you get
here."

"Me, too."

"It's stopped raining. We can meet at the fountain,"
Fran said, then everything seemed to come to a halt. No
normal breathing sounds from either of us. No background
clearing of throats. Just low grunts. The fountain's ledge
had been a favorite spot to sit and chat, especially when the
classroom and office walls seemed to close in on us. Once
a popular campus landmark and meeting place, the fountain had suddenly become forbidden territory.

"Is the coffee shop open today?" I asked.

"Uh-huh."

"Let's meet there."

I heard a long exhale from Fran. "Good idea. Oh, by the
way, Courtney did say she was pretty sure the person the
cops led away was female."

I gulped. "Got it. See you soon."

Since the food at the Mortarboard Café, the campus coffee
shop next to the tennis courts, was only a half step up from
what was served at the Zeeman Academy vending machines,
I knew Fran would forgive me for making a detour. With
no Starbucks in sight, I pulled up to a bagel shop a couple
of blocks from campus.

I stood in a short line thinking that I shouldn't be wasting this time. Whom could I call to seek more information
about the unidentified person who'd been taken into police
custody? Or was at least *with* the police at the moment.

It was useless to call Virgil, who was probably still at

Zeeman. Would he be in communication with whoever escorted a female from the vicinity of the Henley College Administration Building? If not, wouldn't he love to hear from me that the case had been closed? A better question: Where did I get this urge to do police work?

A sudden collision knocked me out of my mental state, into the physical present. It was my day to be battered by men, big and little.

"My bad," said a young boy with low riding shorts who looked anything but apologetic.

He'd been on a direct course to the potato chip rack, and I was a small obstacle in his way. Nothing hurt and I didn't see the wisdom of calling attention to the little mishap. The bagel clerk apparently felt otherwise.

"Hey, buddy, watch where you're going. And can you give the lady a real apology?" the clerk said, sounding like this wasn't the first time she'd addressed this problem.

The boy gave her a confused look, as if no one had challenged him in this way before. He took his bag of chips to a different clerk at the other end of the counter and flew out of the store.

"Charter school kids," the middle-aged woman said to me. "The one down the street? The Roger Williams School." She held up her hand, the better to tick off her complaints. "They don't have a regular schedule. They're in here at all hours. They're rude. They knock things over and don't pick them up." She indicated there were many more points she could make, but the exercise was exhausting her.

My first impulse was to rush to the defense of charters. Kids at any school could be rude or not rude. The same for adults. I had no time to get into it with the woman, however, and I figured my best bet was to change the topic.

I gave the woman a smile she could interpret any way she chose, and pointed to a seven-layer cookie in the display case.

"Are those new?" I asked. "They look delicious."

"Jody will help you," she said, passing me on to a younger woman with retro Goth hair, lots of silver, but no tats.

It could have been that the middle-ager's shift was over. Or she could simply have decided I hadn't appreciated her wisdom enough to be served.

"What can I get you?" asked the new clerk.

I almost said, *Mayor Graves's phone records, please*, but caught myself and ordered two bagels, a cinnamon raisin for me and an "everything" for Fran, both with cream cheese. I hoped to get to the Mortarboard before Fran settled for one of their not-quite-thawed pastries.

As I waited for the order, I scooted back into my head and thought of my suspect list, with three men and only one female. Chris Sizemore. I wished I knew whether she was the female who'd been taken to the HPD station today.

I knew I'd have no relief until I was sure that the police had zeroed in on someone else before I was forced to contemplate the placement of my star student on my suspect list. I'd been Kira's teacher for four years, and her thesis director. It shouldn't have been that hard for me to have already figured out what was going on with her. Maybe I'd have fared better if I'd had access to the mayor's emails and phone logs. I comforted myself with the fact that the police did have that access and therefore might already have enough information to close the case. As far as I was concerned, Kira was not a candidate for murder suspect. If anything, she was a victim of herself and her insecure state.

I tapped my phone on my hip. I could call Woody; he seemed to be always available these days, but I didn't necessarily want to remind him of the current situation on campus. I ran down my list of faculty friends from the Music Department, English, Modern Languages. Most of them had already skipped town for the Cape beaches or the New Hampshire mountains. I resolved to make more friends in Admin in case this happened again.

Rring, rring. Rring, rring.

Ah, Bruce. He'd be getting in from the gym, ready to take a nap before his shift.

"Hey, I miss you," he said.

"Me, too. I think you should retire and we'll run away together."

"One more year and I'll be able to buy us an island."

"Here you go," said the clerk, handing over my bag of bagels.

I reached for our lunches and headed out of the shop, still kibitzing with Bruce around our island dream. A strange theme since we were both city people and more likely to retire to the heart of Boston, or to Philadelphia, where some of Bruce's family still lived.

Things changed when Bruce said, casually, "I just talked to Virgil. I'm surprised you didn't bring it up right away."

"I wanted to talk to you first, my love," I said, champing at the bit for whatever information was circling the MAstar helipad.

He laughed. "What a surprise, huh? I'd never have guessed. She doesn't look the type at all, does she?"

"No, I heard about the pickup, but I'd never have guessed who," I said. In my heightened state of anticipation, I squeezed the warm bagels until I felt the cream cheese go to mush against the side of the bag.

A long pause. I could hardly stand it. Finally, Bruce said, "You don't know who they picked up, do you?"

I laughed in a "don't be silly" kind of way.

"Okay, bye."

"Bruce!"

"Chris Sizemore," he said.

I felt my shoulders relax. "Bye," I said.

Another laugh from Bruce, who, fortunately for our relationship, enjoyed games as much as I did.

"Go call Fran," he said.

Which is just what I did.

CHAPTER $\sqrt{14}$

It was hard to say which of my offerings Fran was more grateful for—the fresh, odoriferous bagel with light and dark seeds of everything on it, or the ID of the person of interest to the Henley PD.

It seemed to be a tie.

"I was starving, in more ways than one," Fran said, working on her second squirt of cream cheese.

"I can see that."

"After we hung up, I kept on with my telethon trying to find out who was taken away. I limited myself to faculty and staff I thought would have a good view of that part of campus. Even though the police car was outside the dorms . . ." Fran completed the sentence with a shrug and a knowing look.

I smiled, understanding her reasoning. "We don't want the students to think we're rumormongers," I said.

"No, no." Fran smiled back and wagged her finger at me. "That wouldn't be good at all. And there's nothing left to munch on in the Franklin Hall lounge"—she held up her bagel—"so thanks for this."

"I couldn't have you trudging all the way over here for last Friday's coffee and rolls," I said.

We both took a minute for bites of real food, followed by soft and contented "Mmms."

We sat across from each other in the Mortarboard Café, having bought bottled waters and packaged cookies as the price of admission to sit at a table with food from the outside. A cleaning crew hired by Buzz, the new owner, was hard at work on heavy-duty scraping and scrubbing, starting in the back corner. I hoped the sticky floor was on their list, as well as the interior brick walls, which needed a good week of sandblasting just to remove the ketchup. And if they could do something about the cooking odors from the last century, that would also be nice.

Other than Buzz, the three young women scouring tables and chairs, and two guys washing the windows facing the parking lot, Fran and I were the only ones in the place. The background music was the Mortarboard's standard pounding, backbeat fare, more suited to grunt work than to conversation.

"We should be at the beach," Fran said. "Like every sane teacher and student the world over on the Monday after graduation."

Except Chris Sizemore, I thought. I pushed my bagel aside and made a move to leave. "You're right. Let's go to the beach."

Fran laughed. "Ha. There's too much going on here."

Fran was still as excited as when she'd called me with the breaking news. "I phoned Courtney after you gave me the scoop. She called Monty right away, using a cover story that she wanted to be sure his sister was okay, but really to confirm that Chris was the one who'd been arrested. Sort of arrested. Monty didn't tell her much, as you can imagine, except that the police were simply doing routine questioning and would probably be back for another round with all of us."

"Do you think that's why they drove off with her? For routine questioning? Bruce couldn't help me with that. Maybe Monty's right and we are next. You up for a ride in a patrol car?" I asked.

Fran shook her head. Her short, silky bob showed signs of graying, but was as neatly and attractively arranged as if she'd been on her way to present a paper in Boston. "I wouldn't mind the ride, though. My grandkids would get a kick out of it. But Courtney doesn't think there was anything routine about the pickup. She said the police car pulled up right to the exterior steps of Admin on the Paul Revere dorm side, not bothering to park. She swears the car was running the whole time, though not with lights or anything, and then the two guys, one in uniform and one in plain clothes, came out with Chris, and she got in the back."

"That doesn't sound routine to me," I said.

"Anything but."

I forced myself not to be happy about Chris Sizemore's plight, but was unable to suppress relief that the female Courtney had first reported on wasn't Kira.

"Why do you think Chris would kill the mayor?" Fran asked. "Did they even know each other that well?"

"Meaning, once you get to know a person, you want to kill him?" I asked.

"That's what the homicide stats would lead us to believe," Fran said.

"When you put it that way, I have to agree."

Virgil often quoted that nearly 40 percent of murders are in a category called "homicides by intimates," adding that girlfriends were more likely to kill their men by stabbing them than by other means.

I remembered Bruce's "Good to know" when Virgil reported on this over pizza one Friday night. The two of them had shifted their chairs away from me.

The truth was that, much as I disliked her at the moment, I had a hard time picturing Chris Sizemore as a killer, of an intimate or of anyone else.

"I'm still not sure I believe Chris committed murder. Maybe they have the wrong person," I suggested.

Fran's brow turned to a seldom-seen row of wrinkles. "Think a minute. Remember how Chris ran kicking and screaming from the faculty vote? And, there's also the fact that the mayor fired her brother from the contract with the city. That can't be good for his future as a businessman in New England."

"So, you think Chris's motive could have been that the mayor ruined her brother's career?"

Fran wrapped her index and middle fingers around each other. "You know how close Chris and Monty are."

I did know. My most recent experience of their compatibility and basic agreement on issues had been during our Main Street encounter only yesterday, as they'd sympathized with my current nemesis, Elysse Hutchins. At that time, it had certainly seemed to me that Chris would have killed anyone who did her brother in, and vice versa. But, in my thoughts, "killing" was a metaphor. I hadn't envisioned a vicious stabbing.

I felt a breeze on my bare arms before I saw what caused it. Kira had opened the door and swept in behind me.

"Dr. Knowles, Dr. Emerson, wow! Hi," she said, as if she were blown away by our presence.

I didn't for a minute believe Kira's shocked look. I suspected she had a telescope trained on the campus, with nothing better to do than look out the window until she found someone to talk to.

"Imagine seeing you here, Kira," Fran said, keeping her sarcastic tone at a level too subtle for Kira to get.

"Are you guys, like, having a department meeting or something? I don't want to interrupt."

"Yes, we are talking business, but you can have a seat for a minute," Fran said, in the smooth, inoffensive way that I'd never been able to master.

"Oh, okay, if you're sure you don't mind." Kira pointed to the counter, where Buzz was busy with a spray bottle and a questionable cleaning cloth. "I'll just grab a cup of coffee."

Once Kira was at the counter, probably buying a drink she didn't want, I addressed Fran.

"Thanks for taking care of that."

"I know you worry about her," Fran said.

I nodded. I'd been worrying about Kira since she arrived in my advanced calculus class four years ago, having aced all the placement exams. She had more than the usual freshman angst, which I expected would dissolve as she progressed successfully through a demanding math major curriculum. I thought eventually she'd become more socially sophisticated and comfortable with her peers, but year after year, she continued to spend more time with her teachers than with her classmates, participating in extra-curricular activities only peripherally. She hung around with Jeanne, Nicole, Bethany, and a few other Franklin Hall science majors, but she seemed to me never quite in the inner circle.

Kira returned with a canned soda, a wise choice on a day like today, when the Mortarboard was only halfheart-edly open.

I knew it was a question of when, not if, Kira would bring up the most recent development in the murder case that affected us all so deeply.

"Getting ready for the big school across the river?" Fran asked, using our pet phrase for MIT.

That simple question was enough to get Kira started on the real reason for her alleged ad hoc drop-in. It was clear that any comment would have been a prompt for her. After all, if she'd wanted a canned soda, she could have picked one up on any floor of her dorm.

"I can't think of grad school right now," she said, seeming to hold back tears. "Have you heard what they're saying?"

"Tell us," I said. A little lame, but at least I'd finally found my voice.

"Ms. Sizemore was arrested. I must have been still in bed or in the shower or something, because I didn't see it, but the police came and took her away. They're saying the two of them, Ms. Sizemore and Edward, were, like, together"—she closed her eyes tightly at this phrase—"and he wanted to break it off and so she killed him. Or, they think it could have been the other way around, that she wanted to break it off and he wouldn't let her and they fought and she stabbed him."

Kira's words were punctuated with short breaks for lip biting and erratic breathing. I wondered which upset her more, that Chris might have been romantically involved with the mayor or that she might have killed him.

I noticed Fran flinch at Kira's referring to Mayor Graves as *Edward*, although it was Fran who'd first suggested to me that Kira and the mayor might be "seeing each other."

"Who are *they*, Kira? Who exactly is saying this?" I asked.

"Well, Bethany's roommate, Jocelyn, is an art history major, so she has Ms. Sizemore a lot for class, and she says Ms. Sizemore used to talk about Edward all the time, like just bring up things in the newspaper, and one time Jocelyn saw them in the park together or something."

It was good that Kira had never considered a career as a trial attorney.

"Did you—" Fran began.

"Then," Kira said in a loud voice, the better to interrupt Fran. "Then, Jocelyn found out the police dumped Edward's computer and supposedly found all this email correspondence with Ms. Sizemore. Jocelyn says she's one hundred percent sure of this because she has a friend in the Henley Police Department."

Hey, I have a friend in the Henley Police Department, I thought, with a bit of pique.

Kira's revelation, through Bethany, through Jocelyn, through Jocelyn's HPD friend, and who knew how many other channels, had been interesting, in spite of its shaky credentials. I'd been assuming that Chris's display of animosity toward the mayor was due to the bad blood between him and her brother. It seemed there might be a more personal basis for her display of anger.

Who said college campuses were stuffy, uninteresting places with staid professors engaged only in the research of abstruse subjects?

"Did you know about Ms. Sizemore and the mayor before this morning when the police came?" Fran asked Kira.

Kira threw up her hands, nearly knocking over her soda. "No. And I don't believe a word of it anyway. I don't care who Jocelyn's friend is."

"You don't believe Ms. Sizemore killed the mayor?" Fran asked, as if she were querying Kira about a line in the derivation of an equation. I seldom saw Fran in action with students, and I was impressed at her nonthreatening manner. I should have been taking notes.

"I don't believe the two of them were ever together. Ever. They couldn't have been. I . . . I thought he . . ." Kira drew in a long breath and then exhaled a pout. "Never mind what I thought."

I had a good idea what Kira thought. That one day she and Edward would be a twosome. I recalled the emails Virgil had showed me. I hadn't let Kira know that I'd read her declarations of love to Edward. I remembered some of them in too much detail to suit me.

I wish you'd let me stay last night. You know you're my number one priority. I'm here for you.

"Did Mayor Graves ever give you any reason to think he returned your affections, Kira?" I asked. In other words, I might have asked, *Did he ever email you back? Did he ever give you any sign at all that he received your protestations? Or is this all in your head?*

Fran cracked open a package of shortbread cookies, making a loud popping sound, spilling some crumbs, and, mostly, giving Kira time to consider how she'd answer.

"You're going to think I'm really dumb." Kira addressed this first to me, then to Fran, and then back again.

"Tell us," I said, for the second time. Talk about dumb.

"The first time I met him, I was in the campaign office and he walked in and he gave me this smile, and I knew we really connected."

I sat back, knowing I could write the rest of the script. A sheltered young woman and a man of the world—that is, the world of Henley, Massachusetts, population a mere forty-six thousand, but still larger than the California valley town Kira was born and raised in, hours from major cities like Los Angeles and San Francisco.

I listened now as Kira told her tale of working hard for the extremely important yet friendly guy who told her how talented she was, how smart, and how far she was destined to go, with her whole life ahead of her. Apparently Kira had taken that to mean that they would go far together.

I had to let Fran take the lead in drawing Kira out. I was too busy blaming myself for not monitoring Kira's social life more closely. Did I think a party a week in the Franklin Hall lounge was the beginning and end of my duty to my students? I could have made a greater effort to bring my majors together, to help Kira be more a part of the group.

I realized that in loco parentis had pretty much been voted out of schools in the sixties. Technically, I had no obligation to watch over my students the way their parents did, but that didn't mean I could brush off the sense of responsibility I felt, especially for young women like Kira, with little worldly experience.

I took a backseat and heard Kira's story through the perspective of Fran's questions. I caught the phrases I was looking for, phrases that I wanted to hear, that would ease my mind.

". . . never ever took advantage of me. He would never do that, if that's what you're thinking." (Whew.)

". . . said he wished he could show me the French Riviera. He thought I'd love it." (Who wouldn't?)

". . . treated me more like a daughter"—another whew—"which is not what I wanted, but for now, while his son was a teenager . . ."

And one that brought me up short:

". . . can't believe he'd become involved with Ms. Sizemore. Why would he want to be with an older woman?"

Fran and I stole a glance at each other at that line, thinking the same thing, I guessed—if Christine Sizemore, roughly thirty-two years old, was an older woman to Kira and her peers, where did that leave us? I couldn't wait to laugh openly about it later with Fran.

I told myself I should be satisfied that Kira hadn't given herself away completely. Maybe she'd learn a lesson from this, especially if it turned out that Chris and the mayor were indeed a couple.

I tuned in to the end of Fran's interrogation and Kira's voluntary spilling of her story when I heard my name.

"So, Dr. Knowles, are you still willing to go with me to the service tomorrow? It's at ten in the morning."

Service? It took a minute for me to remember the memorial scheduled for the mayor at city hall, and Kira's earlier request to me. I hadn't made any promises. I'd stalled. Now I had to put up an answer. I wanted to express my condolences anyway, so why not go with Kira? Besides, I had no energy to resist any reasonable request at the moment.

Finally, it would provide a natural ending to the meeting I'd scheduled with Elysse at eight thirty.

"Sure," I said. "Let's meet at the"—I caught myself before I said *fountain*—"right here."

"Okay, right here. At nine fifty tomorrow morning."

Kira took a deep breath, as if she'd checked off all the items on a long to-do list and was now ready for a good night's sleep.

So was I, although it was only four in the afternoon.

CHAPTER $\sqrt{15}$

I was glad to get outside in the fresh post-rain air. The smell from the deep fryers and the cleaning solutions in the café had bothered me more than I'd realized in real time.

In the parking lot, Fran gave me a long look, perhaps noticing my tired eyes and downturned mouth. "I have an idea," she said.

"Am I going to like it?" I asked.

"Bruce is working tonight, right?"

"Nine to nine."

"Come home with me for dinner. You need a little pampering, and a lot of distraction."

"All that is at your house?"

"Gene is cooking and our grandkids will be there."

Enough said.

Fran had been right. There was nothing like a normal multi-generational family gathering around the dinner table to put things in perspective. I'd met Fran's family before, at least briefly—Fran and Gene's daughter and son, their spouses and children. They all seemed to get along well. Even if I was seeing their "company" behavior, it was impressive.

I couldn't remember the last time I'd had a dinner like my own grandmother used to cook. A New England pot roast feast, heavy on the thyme, with potatoes and carrots, gravy, bread, and salad. All at the same meal. Was this a typical night at the Emersons'? If so, I might move in.

My question was answered when Fran explained that we were celebrating the excellent end-of-year report card of third grader Lindsay.

"Grandma told me about that," I fibbed to the little girl. One thing I loved about Fran was that she never pounded anyone with stories and pictures of her family. Photos and drawings were placed discreetly around her office, and anyone could inquire, voluntarily.

"I got all A's," Lindsay said.

"I know. And I have a present for you."

I dug into my purse and pulled out a new puzzle, an electronic maze game I'd been planning to send to Bruce's niece. I had plenty of time to find a replacement for Melanie, and it seemed to fit the moment.

"Cool," Lindsay said, smiling broadly and putting her tiny fingers to work immediately.

"I'm probably going to get all A's, too," Derek said.

"Me, too," Kendra said.

All four-year-old Ethan did was lean into me and put his head on my lap. A schemer and a charmer, that one.

I promised to send suitable prizes for all through their grandmother.

Dessert was served in the family room of the large Vermont-style house. As if we were still hungry, we all reached for an ice cream sandwich. Not the kind that came in a thin cardboard box with freezer burn, but a concoction of rich vanilla ice cream between two homemade cookies, one chocolate chip, the other oatmeal. I wished I'd packed my pj's in my briefcase.

By eight o'clock, if someone had mentioned the words "bloody fountain" or "grade inflation" or "Facebook posting," I'd have had no idea what they were talking about.

I reached my street around nine thirty, feeling that all was right with the world. It had stopped raining hours ago, but the wind had picked up and lent a pleasant, cleansed feeling to the air.

Early as it was, my plan was to download a book and curl up in bed. I wanted to stretch out the good feeling I'd gotten from family night with the Emersons.

I pulled into the garage, entered my house through the kitchen door, and punched in my alarm code. It seemed a long time since I'd been home. When I left this morning for class and, admittedly, for snooping at Zeeman Academy, I hadn't planned on getting home so late and hadn't left any lights on.

Now I flicked on the lights in the kitchen and hallway and headed toward my bedroom.

As I approached the den on the left, I felt a breeze. Had I left a ceiling fan on? I doubted it, since I seldom needed to run one in the morning.

I walked past the den, dropped my briefcase in my office, and continued to make my way back to my bedroom. The breeze got stronger with each step.

No wonder. I'd left the window open.

No, not the window. The patio door.

No, I hadn't left it open. Someone had opened it for me.

By throwing a brick through the glass.

I dropped my purse on the floor and froze in place. My ears went into some supersonic state where I seemed to be picking up sounds outside the range of normal hearing. A car door closing at the end of my street. The digital clicks and rumbles of the hard drive in my computer that often sounded like my stomach growling for food. A siren from an emergency vehicle on the expressway, a mile from my home. I even thought I heard again the sound of the train in the background of the voice mail message Mayor Graves had left me.

What I didn't hear, fortunately, was any sound of a brick thrower camped out in my home.

I stood about three feet from the foot of my bed, unable to move. The dull red brick lay at my eleven o'clock, giving off an unlikely shimmer in the light from the hallway. My lavender décor, my color of choice much of the time, took on a nasty, garish look, as if it had been violated by the smashed window and the shards of glass on the wet carpet.

A gust of wind that blew through the hole in my patio door shook me into action, and I spun around as if another brick might be coming at me from behind. I ended up flat against the wall of my bedroom, next to the door to the hallway I'd just come from. If I'd been holding a gun, one might have thought I was sneaking up on the bad guy, as I'd seen cops do in Bruce's favorite movies.

I'd neither seen nor heard anyone as I'd entered the house and walked the length of it from my kitchen to my bedroom. My alarm had been set, needing my code as I'd entered. I had no reason to think anyone was still in the house right now, but that didn't stop the shivers making their way through my body.

I finally left my wall post, holding my breath as I opened my closet door. Nothing but the new set of organizer drawers Bruce had installed for me, with my clothes stacked and hung in the neatest arrangement they'd ever seen. Next to the closet, my dresser appeared intact, its lacy scarf in place, no drawers open. A box of tissues, a few bottles and jars, and a jewelry box stood undisturbed on top, silent witnesses to what had transpired across the room.

I made my way around the room. Nothing else seemed out of place except the brick. Or what looked like a brick. It might have been foreign matter from outer space, a meteor fragment, for all the sense it made. Maybe one of those unstable satellites had disintegrated and was raining on Henley.

It took me another few minutes to adjust myself away from my fear and absurd thoughts and into a rational thinking mode. I'd been making too much of what was most likely a prank, some suburban kids on an "I dare you" mission. Most of Henley's schoolchildren were out on vacation and they had nothing better to do than cruise around creating havoc.

From the wet carpet, I figured the hole in the patio door was made before or during the showers; but the rain had been on and off most of the day and it was probably impossible to pin down when the brick had been thrown. I felt another shiver as I considered the fact that if my day had gone as planned, I might have been home when the vandalism occurred.

Though my intrusion alarm had been set, it had been useless as an alert since the brick didn't set off any of the magnetic triggers. No doors or windows had opened—Bruce would say the perimeter hadn't been breached—during the commission of this crime.

Without a lot of thought as to why I was doing it, I retrieved my phone from my purse, clicked on the camera icon, and took several pictures of the brick in situ.

I grabbed a tissue and picked up the brick, finally noticing a note attached to it with a rubber band on the underside. I picked out the piece of paper from under its shackle and unfolded a small, square yellow sticky note with a handwritten message: "SUPPORT ELYSSE."

I could hardly believe it. Had Elysse recruited a band of freedom fighters to her cause? Had she rallied union workers? Fraternity and sorority friends? Where was the Elysse of only a short while ago, the "Are we good?" Elysse wanting to meet with me in person?

I shook my head, placed the note on the floor next to the brick, and snapped a few more pictures.

Amazing that *support* was spelled correctly, I thought,

not feeling very charitable. Under the rallying cry was a URL that was a Facebook address, most likely for Elysse's page, though there was no identifying subset in the long string of characters. It was all very low-tech, from the brick to the handwritten URL. I'd have expected a flame war online, or—settling for the real-life brick and note—a simple Quick Response Code that could be scanned, instead of an unwieldy URL that was barely legible.

I imagined a crazy scenario where the brick wasn't targeted for my house at all, but was one of many bricks, thrown by a posse of Elysse's Facebook Friends, at windows and patio doors all over the city of Henley. I scrutinized the tiny note for signs of my name or any ID of me, Elysse the Victim's persecutor. Nothing. The note didn't begin with "Dear Sophie," and it bore no words that said, "This means you, Professor Knowles." At least I wasn't being immortalized that way.

What next? I could call any number of people, official and unofficial—Virgil for police intervention, Fran for moral support, Bruce for a little of both. And my insurance company for logistics.

One call I knew I had to make was to a glass replacement company. I'd do that first, before deciding how public to take this latest entry in the Sophie versus Elysse drama.

I took my laptop and a bottle of water to my den and used Google to search for the equivalent of "glass hit by bricks." I was amazed to see the number of companies that offered emergency glass services, twenty-four-seven. I seemed to have my choice of installer if I could believe the ads: One offered a tall, muscle-bound guy wearing a leather tool belt; another showed an older man who looked like every kid's favorite coach; a third, equal opportunity company showed a woman in a baseball cap, on a ladder at an upstairs window. Any of them, apparently, would come to my home or business and either board up the offending window, or install replacement glass immediately, depending on whether a custom fit was called for.

I guessed I was lucky I wasn't familiar with the multitude of such services in my own city.

Rring, rring. Rring, rring.

Bruce. I picked up too quickly, without first checking my cool level.

"Hey," I said, and then uttered a frustrated moan.

"What's wrong?" Bruce asked.

I set my laptop aside and leaned back on the couch. "Nothing serious. Just that someone threw a brick through the patio door in my bedroom." Too late to make light of the situation, but I gave it a try. "It's okay, really. I was about to call a glass replacement service. Did you know there are any number of them that will come out immediately and board me up?"

"Are you sure there's no one in the house?" I heard the man of action take over, as he had at the Henley College fountain two nights ago.

"Quite sure."

"Did you check the doors? Did you reset the alarm?"

"The alarm—" I began, intending to report on how useless it had been in the brick-through-a-window scenario.

Bruce interrupted. "I'm sure it didn't go off if the perimeter wasn't breached"—I smiled at his predictability—"but set it again anyway, okay?"

I carried the phone to the panel on the wall by the front door. "I'm doing it now," I said. I was breathing better, just having Bruce at the other end of the line.

"Have you called Virge yet?"

"No, I don't see what he can do. He's homicide, for one thing, and I know the uniforms will just want me to fill out tons of paperwork and nothing will come of it. Remember the break-in across the street this winter? The Andersons actually had things stolen and the police never found the kids or the stuff. I don't think they bother unless there's personal injury."

No response from Bruce. Had he hung up? I waited a beat. "Bruce?"

"I'm back. Virge is on his way over. Don't touch anything."

"I picked up the brick. I couldn't just leave it there."

"Okay, that's okay. Don't touch anything else, okay? And don't call the glass company yet. Wait till Virge gets there." Bruce let out a grunt. "I'd be on my way there myself, but I'm the only driver here," he said, meaning he was the only pilot on duty and couldn't leave without a major schedule disruption.

"I'm fine. I wish you hadn't bothered Virgil," I said.

"Liar." Said sweetly.

"Uh-huh," I admitted.

I told Bruce about the message on the note that was attached to the brick.

"Elysse? Is that the student who doesn't like her grade?"

"The same."

"It sounds like a ploy to annoy you. But it's odd. I don't figure college kids for that kind of vandalism," Bruce said.

"You're right. It doesn't make sense at all, especially since she called me today and wanted to meet. She sounded at least open to talking. I don't know why she would do this."

"Maybe some overzealous friends?"

"Could be."

"So how was the rest of your day?" Bruce asked, sounding as though he'd just put his feet up on what passed for a coffee table in the MAstar trailer living room–like space.

"Are we going to chat until Virgil arrives?" I asked.

"Something like that."

"Thanks."

After he read the note, I reminded Virgil of the background on Elysse and her Facebook campaign. I was proud to mention I'd handled everything with tissue, not to disturb any fingerprints, but I could tell he doubted they'd find any from the guilty party.

A crime scene tech, who'd arrived with Virgil, went about her business, packaging the brick, string, note, and a few shards of glass into evidence bags. She transferred the photos I'd taken to her own device and took several of her own. I was embarrassed to be taking up the resources of the HPD for such a minor event. I hoped no one on the other side of town was in real trouble, without a police presence, because of me.

The tech was gone in twenty minutes. Virgil settled in for coffee.

I wondered what my neighbors thought of Virgil's visits lately, more frequent than usual. Virgil wondered about the neighbors, too, but for a different reason, one I should have thought of, and would have, if freaking out hadn't been my primary reaction.

"Did you talk to any of your neighbors?" he asked when we sat with coffee at the kitchen table. I wished I could have offered Virgil one of Fran's homemade ice cream sandwiches, but all I had on hand was the same packaged cookies from yesterday.

"You mean canvass the neighborhood?" I blew out a disgusted breath. "I didn't even think of it."

"No problem. We'll take care of it. We'll find out if anyone saw or heard anything."

I pointed out the window, to the west. "Two elderly sisters live there. They're both semi-disabled and not too aware of their surroundings. They have a caregiver who comes in once a day. She may have seen something, depending on when the"—I searched for a word—"vandals did their thing."

"Caregiver's name?" Virgil had his pad and pen ready.

"Wanda. I don't know her last name. She'll be around at about ten in the morning. She stays for close to four hours most of the time."

Virgil pointed east, north, and then south, with a questioning look. I gave him the demographic of my street.

Directly east of me was the Rasmussen family with two working parents and one child in the fourth grade, so no one would have been home during the day. Virgil agreed that the brick thrower probably struck after dark, however, so it was worth checking with the Rasmussens. Across the street from me was a relatively new development with all of the houses facing into a cul-de-sac, perpendicular to my orientation. It wasn't likely that anyone happened to be looking in the direction of my house unless they were driving away, out of their street.

As I thought about it, I was uncomfortable with Virgil's plan. "I don't want to worry everyone, especially Celia and Evelyn. Obviously, the brick was meant for me. Do we really need to make a big deal of it?" This from the woman who'd been wigged-out less than an hour ago. I pointed over my shoulder to my bedroom, the crime scene. "There must have been quite a bit of noise when the brick hit my door. If a neighbor was around and heard anything, wouldn't that person have called nine-one-one, or the police station right away?"

"You'd be surprised."

"You always say that."

"Because you'd be surprised."

I decided to take a chance and move to the other reason for Virgil's frequent visits, and for my constant state of angst for the last couple of days.

"I heard on the news that Mayor Graves's wife was on a plane to Europe right after the graduation ceremony." So what if it was Kira, not I, who was tuned into the news?

"Did you?"

"I guess that's about as solid an alibi as you can have."

"Could be."

"Unless she paid someone to, uh, do the deed?" I didn't know why my mind was going in a direction I hadn't planned. My goal was to get information from Virgil, not hand him silly theories.

Virgil grinned. "I wouldn't rule that out, but using a letter opener that probably happened to be handy isn't exactly the style of your typical hit man."

"Thanks. I love hearing the insights of the HPD." I bit into a cookie. Nervous eating, since I was still full from dinner and I knew the cookies were tasteless. "I also heard that Chris Sizemore, who teaches art history at Henley, was taken in for questioning. Or maybe arrested."

"You hear a lot of things. Anything else?"

"I heard you were at Zeeman Academy this afternoon."

"Did you?" Said in mock surprise.

I laughed. "You almost knocked me over."

"Was that you?"

"Come on, Virgil. Give me something. I'm having a rough time here." For emphasis I pointed again toward my bedroom, recently visited by a nasty foreign object.

"Okay, because it affects you in a way, I'll tell you we found some email and other communications from the mayor that implied he was investigating the school as you indicated. That same grade issue you and I talked about. I wanted to catch Richardson but he'd gone for the day. You didn't happen to talk to him?"

"No, he was rushing out when I arrived."

I left out the part where I'd talked to two of his trusted employees. Why bother mentioning lunchroom chatter? It would all be considered hearsay in the end. I cringed at my amateur legal reasoning. At some point today, I must have decided that a man who commanded the loyalty and respect of Rina and Dan, two such honorable and excellent teachers, couldn't be a killer. Could he?

"Someone will be coming around in the morning to talk to you and then to the neighbors. I promise whoever comes will play the incident down to the ladies next door, not to worry them," Virgil said, moving me away from a sensitive topic.

"Thanks." *How about not worrying me?* I wanted to ask.

"The officers will have some questions for you and the usual forms to fill out. You may not think it's important, but fill them out anyway. You never know what this might connect to."

"You mean, in case there have been other bricks from the same dye lot thrown in Henley recently?"

"Something like that."

"With a reference to me on them?"

"The officers will want to know if you remember anything else about tonight. Any detail at all."

"I have to be out of here for an eight-thirty meeting tomorrow morning."

Virgil made a note. "I'll tell them to get here by seven, seven thirty. You'll be up and about?"

I nodded, resigned to the paperwork follow-up, and to failure in my attempts to help with, or intrude into, Virgil's murder investigation. He'd shared a lot more about the brick throwing than the stabbing.

In any case, our interview ended when a glass-bearing truck rolled up. Virgil opened the door to a man—closer in looks to the old baseball coach in the ads than to the beautiful people—who immediately went to work in my bedroom. Virgil chatted with him and I checked my email, taking care of some busywork, happy to find no lurking crisis.

Virgil had called a company he'd dealt with a lot and, whether because they practiced great customer service or because the request had come from a cop, my non-custom patio door was repaired in a jiffy.

"I guess you're all set," Virgil said. "I'll be on my way. Let you get some rest."

As if.

I ushered Virgil out the door. "I can't believe anyone would go to these lengths over a few points on an exam," I said.

"You'd be—"

"Surprised. I got it."

CHAPTER $\sqrt{16}$

By eleven thirty PM, you wouldn't have been able to tell that there'd been an official, police-defined "incident" at my house, except for the rather nervous homeowner inside and the unmarked cop car outside. I wondered if every brick victim got such treatment. I hoped so.

I put water on for tea and planned to relax in my newly glassed-in bedroom. I texted Bruce, in case he was catching a nap, and told him our hero, Detective Virgil Mitchell, had saved the day again. Nothing to worry about.

He called me right back, wanting to know details.

I briefed him and added, "I have a sparkling-clean patio door."

"We should get the guy to come over here. You can't even see through the trailer windows anymore."

"I believe you. Want me to throw a brick?"

"Not funny," my serious, concerned boyfriend weighed in.

"Aren't you glad I'm not still freaked out?" I asked.

"I suppose so. What's up for you tomorrow?"

I ticked off the details of my full day of meetings.

"Wait, did you say the eight thirty is with Elysse? The one who threw the brick?" Bruce's voice was rising in pitch, his tone more and more incredulous. "You're not going alone?"

I laughed. "A police escort? I don't think so. For one thing, the note says "Support Elysse," so she didn't write it. She would have said, "Dr. Knowles, Support Me," or something like that, using first person."

"You think everyone cares about grammar the way you do? I'm off at nine. Can you move the meeting up?"

"Nuh-uh. I told you, I'm booked through till after lunch. It's not a problem. I believe I weigh more than Elysse, anyway."

"Still not funny, Sophie. I'll cut out of here early. Ernie won't mind fudging his time a little."

"It's not necessary, Bruce. Elysse is not a violent person. After two years, I think I would know that. This is a prank. Committed by some kid who happens to know about our little squabble."

"Or someone who wants you to think it's a kid."

"Elysse may not even know about it. Besides, I'm not showing up to meet her with my boyfriend."

"Where are you meeting her?"

"In my office on campus."

A heavy groan from Bruce. "Think, Sophie. It's vacation time. Is it likely that there'll be anyone else in the building?"

"You're scaring me, Bruce."

"Good. Humor me and at least change the meeting to someplace public. Or even the Administration Building. They keep regular office hours right through the summer, don't they?"

"Yes, they work full-time, as our deans and staff are always reminding the faculty. Okay, I'll think of another place."

"I mean it, Soph."

"I'll change it, really. We can meet at the Coffee Filter. It's mobbed on a weekday morning with everyone stopping in before work."

I heard a relieved sigh from Bruce. I had to admit, I felt better, too, once I thought about it. Situated at the very edge of campus, Ben Franklin Hall could be creepy during the off-season. And if there was one thing I didn't need any more of this week, it was *creepy*.

I started down the hallway toward my bedroom with my cup of tea, grabbing three paperbacks from my to-be-read pile on the counter, plus my e-reader, since I wasn't sure exactly what reading mood I was in.

Once I cleared the books away, I noticed the message light blinking on my landline handset.

No way. My day was over. Wasn't it?

I turned away, stopped, and turned back again.

I knew I wouldn't be able to sleep unless I checked off all the channels in and out of my communications network. Might as well give in.

I hit the button. A computer voice told me I had two messages, then played the first for me. "Dr. Knowles. Uh, Sophie. This is Doug Richardson, principal at Zeeman, I'm sure you know. Sorry I had to rush by you at school today. I need to talk to you. Someplace other than my office. Please call me on my direct line so we can set up a meeting. The number is 508 . . ."

I pressed pound to stop the message replay. I dropped my books back on the counter and sat down on a kitchen stool. In spite of what should have been a calming sip of tea, an eerie feeling took over my body. Was Principal Richardson channeling the deceased mayor, copying his message, in spirit, and practically verbatim? Right down to using his nickname, whereas we had never even used first names before? Just as the mayor had done on the day he was murdered?

Ed and Doug, my new best friends. Except one of them was dead.

I seemed to be starring in the movie where the same thing kept happening over and over. Speaking of channeling, I was channeling poor Bill Murray. What was happening to my orderly world?

What was the protocol for returning messages to school officials? If midnight was the cutoff time, I should get on it. Or wait until tomorrow morning. I wouldn't want to wake up his entire family for some silly reason. Maybe I had left my sunglasses outside his office, or a sheet of paper from my stack slipped under his door during the spill when Superintendent Collins rammed into me.

Uh-oh. Was Superintendent Collins going to call me next and leave a message, from "Pat," that he needed to talk to me?

Something nagged at me and pushed me in the direction of returning the call now. I realized I was concerned that Principal Richardson—Doug—might die before I could talk to him, as had occurred with Mayor—Ed—Graves.

I had to call back, no matter what the hour. I couldn't stand it if something happened to Principal Richardson and I was left with another death on my hands. I played the message again, this time writing down the telephone number.

Fortified with a long swallow of tea, I dialed his number. At each new ring, I was tempted to hang up.

Finally, I heard my new friend Doug's voice. I was so grateful he was still alive, I almost cheered.

"Dr. Knowles, hello. I appreciate your calling me back." Spoken in a near whisper.

"Sorry it's so late. I—"

"No, no this is fine. Will you let me take you to lunch tomorrow? I have a few things I'd like to talk to you about," he said, still whispering. I pictured his wife and family, if he had either, in the next rooms, sleeping.

I didn't hesitate. "I'll be glad to meet you," I answered, needlessly lowering my own voice.

"Great. I'll make a reservation for noon at the Inn at Henley. Will that work for you?"

"Sure, I can do that."

"Thank you, Sophie."

A quick two-minute telephone interaction during which Doug went from Dr. Knowles to Sophie and snagged my attention with a promise of a classy lunch. No vending machines for the Doug and Sophie meeting.

I considered telling Principal Richardson on the spot that I had an inside scoop, that the police had already found evidence of grade inflation fraud and that he was a wanted man. It would save him the cost of lunch for two at the pricey Inn.

As usual, my head was foggy on the applicable law. Should I give the principal a head start? Would I then be encouraging a fugitive from justice? It was too late in the day to be having these challenges, making these decisions.

Before I could come up with an answer, Principal Richardson signed off.

I thought about my day tomorrow. I'd be awakened by police officers at seven or seven thirty, pummeled by an unhappy student at eight thirty, used by an unstable student as an escort to a memorial service at ten, and—I guessed—drawn into a charter school web at noon.

Some kind of summer vacation.

I sent a text to Elysse, telling her to meet me at the Coffee Filter instead of my Franklin Hall office, counting on the fact that she'd see the message. I could think of no one Elysse's age who would neglect to check her cell phone during waking hours. Nor anyone my age, as I'd proven repeatedly.

I settled in my bed with books and tea. Not that it did much good. Unable to read or sleep, I envisioned what must have been the catalyst for my lunch with Principal Richardson.

I envisioned a chagrined Digital Dan Sachs and a distressed Rina Flores going into the principal's office this afternoon to confess their indiscretion in essentially admitting to me that their boss was involved in grade inflation and test score fraud. Were they all worried now that I'd call the state board of education? Was there a state board of education? I couldn't remember much of my research at .edu. If the principal characters in the upset at Zeeman Academy knew how uneducated I was in the structure of their organization, they wouldn't have worried.

Besides, the issue was moot if Virgil was holding all the evidence he needed. Which didn't seem to be the case if, one, the police had picked up Chris, and, two, Virgil wasn't exactly rushing to take Richardson into custody.

It was about time I saw that there could have been two crimes—fraud by Richardson, and murder by Sizemore.

I began to drift off, then on again, wishing someone would take me into custody, and find a way to clear my head and put me to sleep.

Not yet. I heard the low buzz of my cell phone, on vibrate while it was charging. I looked up at the ceiling to see who could possibly be kidding me.

I checked the screen and saw that it was Monty Sizemore calling. It made sense that he wouldn't be able to sleep either, especially if his beloved sister was still being held at the police station. I wavered on whether to take the call, but I couldn't pass on it. Thus showing how desperate I was to get ahead of things in this case. Maybe Monty had some news that I wouldn't be the last to know.

"Hey, Monty," I said, as if it were one in the afternoon and not close to one in the morning.

"Sophie, I hate to bother you. I know it's late but I left a message earlier and didn't hear back."

I remembered now that I'd had two messages on my landline answering machine. The first message, from Doug Richardson, had consumed me and I'd forgotten to go back and listen to the second one.

"I'm sorry, Monty, it's been a stressful evening."

"I'm frantic," he said, not bothering to ask about my stresses. What happened to the "routine questioning" line he'd given Courtney, the dean's secretary? "I'm sure you heard about Chris."

"Yeah, I did. Is she okay?" I asked, feeling slightly guilty that I'd helped make Chris's pickup the buzz of the day around the campus.

Monty's strained, anxious voice was enough to soften me, and I really did hope Chris wasn't in trouble. Unless she'd murdered Mayor Graves, of course.

"I didn't know who else to call. They're keeping her overnight. I didn't think they could do that, but our lawyer says they can. They haven't charged her, but what if they do?"

Monty fell silent, as if he was expecting me to answer the question. "What can I do for you, Monty?" I asked.

"You know a lot of these small-town cops we have, right? Through your boyfriend?"

There was a time when people buttered you up if they were in desperate need of a favor. Apparently not anymore.

"What's your point, Monty?" I asked.

Monty didn't flinch, though I felt my response was on the edge of rudeness once I determined that Monty was singing the same old song. "I thought maybe you could find out why they're keeping her down there. Did they find something? They won't tell me a thing."

I almost felt bad for Monty, but no way near enough to

call Virgil or any other cop at this hour. If and when I called Virgil, we'd work through my own agenda, not the Sizemores'. Did Monty think that Virgil and the rest of the Henley PD—the "small-town cops"—were sitting around in the wee hours of the morning hoping I'd call them with a question about one of their suspects? I avoided the whole friends-with-cops issue and queried Monty back.

"Can you think of anything the police might have found? Any reason they might suspect Chris?"

Neither of us had explicitly mentioned what they might suspect her of or what the charge would be, should one be filed. The matter of the murder of Henley's mayor hung in the air.

"Chrissy wouldn't hurt anyone. Even though the idiot mayor led her on for a year and—never mind. Chrissy is simply not capable of hurting anyone."

I wished I had the gumption to quiz Monty on the relationship between the mayor and *Chrissy*. It was the season of nicknames. I wished I had one, other than *Soph*, which only Bruce and close friends were allowed to use.

It would have been nice to know that Mayor Graves and Ms. Sizemore had a full-blown affair, which would mean the deceased mayor wouldn't have had time for Kira.

I groaned at my own petty focus, as if the only important repercussions of such an affair were those that affected me and mine. I needed some sleep. Which meant getting Monty off the line. I felt like a hostage negotiator.

"If Chrissy is innocent as you say, then I'm sure she'll be on her way home soon," I told Monty, with an air of finality, as if I was convinced of the infallibility of our justice system.

"You don't understand."

"What don't I understand?" I asked. "Chris is not in jail; she's simply being questioned. If she tells the truth, that will be the end of it."

"You know, Sophie, this was a mistake. I don't know

what I was thinking. You've had your own stressful evening, as you said, and I shouldn't have called. Have a good night."

With that, Monty hung up.

Strange. In a period of much strangeness. I wondered if Monty was making the rounds of faculty, or calling just those of us who were known to hang around cops. I doubted I'd heard the last of him, though his "Have a good night" had sounded close to "Have a good life."

I switched my phone to *nothing*. Off. No ringing, no beeping, no vibrating.

I lay down and looked across the room at my new patio door. Not that I could see it, since my lavender drapes were drawn. But I knew the doorframe now held glass that was shatterproof, like the newest house on the block. It was cleaner than any glass since Margaret bought the house decades ago. I also knew a cop was on alert on the other side of the drapes.

Those facts alone seemed to be enough to put me to sleep.

CHAPTER $\sqrt{17}$

Unlike Virgil, the two patrol officers who rang my buzzer at seven thirty on Tuesday morning did not bring donuts. I was sorry I'd tossed out the old ones. I knew for a fact that microwaving did wonders for stale junk food.

On the other hand, these officers looked like they ate only healthy salads and yogurt and started every day with a rigorous workout with a personal trainer. The new breed of patrolman?

"Morning, ma'am," said officer number one and officer number two in quick succession, making me feel very old. I wondered if their combined ages added up to mine.

Too bad I'd had to abandon my usual very chic look today and dress for a memorial service. A black skirt, closed black flats, and a dark paisley top didn't have much to recommend them other than a mourning look. The brightest part of my outfit was a string of brown and gold beads created for me by Ariana.

I could hardly wait till my friend and beading tutor

returned. If Ariana had been home, I'd have shared every last detail of the downer events of the weekend and beyond. I also would have had fresh home-baked treats to offer my uniformed guests, which seemed to be the only kind of guests I'd entertained lately.

Fortunately for the young officers, I remembered that I had one of Ariana's delicious blueberry loaves in the freezer and could serve it now.

The officers accepted my suggestion of a coffee break and my apology for not having more choices of snack. I emphasized that the bread had only the freshest organic ingredients, which was true, with 90 percent certainty.

"That's okay, we just had donuts, ma'am," officer one said.

Officer two punched him in the well-muscled arm and laughed. I followed suit, with the laughing, skipping the punching.

"I'm Officer Nolan and this is Officer Coyne," I heard, as the guys remembered the protocol.

Officer Nolan, who filled out his short-sleeved uniform shirt nicely, handed me two flyers from two different glass companies. "These were in your driveway, ma'am," he said.

I took the damp papers from him and scanned the full-color ads, one with a screaming red background, the other a dull blue. I'd never seen the flyers or heard of the companies or needed glass before. I wasn't a big believer in coincidence.

"I don't understand how these flyers got here," I said.

Officer Coyne shook his head. "Vultures," he said. "They know you had a problem with a window or door and they're knocking one another over to get your business."

"I already have new glass. And, anyway, how would they know?"

Officers Nolan and Coyne took turns explaining what was clearly one of their pet peeves.

"They want your business the next time, or they want you to recommend them to someone else who needs glass."

"And they go 'round looking for this kind of thing. They may have seen the workman's truck outside here last night."

"If you'd called us directly, you'd have had more flyers than you could fit in your trash."

"Plus people showing up on your doorstep with special deals. They all have scanners these days."

It was another world out there in Vultureland. I thought it sad that young officers like Nolan and Coyne were so smart about the worst aspects of people's behavior, and that they had to be, to do their jobs. I found myself wanting to teach them math and give them both A's, to show that some people were fun and kind, like mathematicians, for example.

"We need to go over the incident here last night," said Officer Coyne, who seemed to be slightly senior. I nodded in acknowledgment that we had business to do. "We know Detective Mitchell took care of getting the evidence in, and talked to you. Is there anything else you can remember about it? You came home and . . ." He drew circles slowly with his wrist to prompt me.

I thought a minute, taking no pleasure in reliving the experience. It had taken all this time to relax and forget it; now it was back in the form of official police business. I knew I should be grateful that my little problem was being handled, but the sooner it would disappear, the better.

I tried to conjure up some detail that would help the officers. I'd been out all day, so there was no way I would have seen either a stranger or an unfamiliar car lurking in my neighborhood.

Finally, I shook my head. "Nothing comes to mind. I just came home and there was the brick." I pointed over my shoulder and down the hall to where the brick had entered my home.

Officer Nolan pulled a sheaf of papers from a large

envelope. "I understand, ma'am. In that case, would you please read over this description by Detective Mitchell, including your own statement of last night and, if you agree, and have nothing to add, please sign at the bottom?"

I loved the smell of boilerplate in the morning.

I took the papers to my kitchen island while the officers continued with what might have been their first or their third breakfast, depending on when their shift started and how many acts of vandalism they'd been assigned to follow up on.

I read Virgil's summary, but just barely. The form itself was intimidating, with categories like "Involved Persons" and "Affected Property. In the "Narrative" section, words like *penetrated* and *shattered* stood out and made me nervous.

I trusted Virgil. I didn't need to edit his prose. I noticed he'd already had the photos printed and had attached them to the file. Unlike me, apparently, the man made good use of his sleepless hours. "This looks fine," I said, signing the pages and returning the package to Officer Nolan. "Are you going to talk to my neighbors?" I hoped Coyne and Nolan had been briefed on suburban sensibilities.

"Yes, ma'am. Detective Mitchell advised us to be especially careful with the ladies next door." I was impressed to see that Officer Nolan pointed in the correct direction for Celia and Evelyn. "We're going to come back at ten when their caregiver, Wanda, last name unknown, will be present."

Officer Coyne took over, pointing to our newest housing development across the street. "We should tell you, we already talked to a neighbor in that cul-de-sac"—he checked his notebook—"a Mr. Lawrence, who left late for work yesterday morning, around nine thirty, and says he saw a silver SUV pull away from in front of your house. He says they were in a hurry. He could not say how many were in the vehicle, nor could he describe them."

"That make any sense to you?" Officer Nolan asked, his Adam's apple on the move.

"I don't know anyone who owns a silver SUV, if that's what you mean."

"What time did you leave here?"

I thought back to what seemed like ancient history, when I left my house yesterday for Zeeman. I'd wanted to be there by ten, so I left . . . I drew in my breath. "I left about nine thirty," I said. "I just missed them?"

A new brand of shiver went through me as I contemplated the arrival of criminals in broad daylight. How would I have dealt with meeting them in person? Would they have aimed the brick directly at my head?

Officer Coyne seemed to sense what was going through my mind. "They probably waited around the corner for you to leave," he said, in his low, comforting voice. "That's what they do."

"I would have thought they'd wait till it was dark."

"Well, ma'am, this is good news in a way. It shows they didn't want to take a chance that you'd be home. They weren't out to hurt you," Officer Coyne said. His partner nodded reassuring agreement.

"Thanks," I said, returning to my normal breathing. "Both of you."

As the officers took their leave a short while later, I made a note to tell Virgil what a good job they were doing at the police academy these days.

I couldn't afford useless dallying, running different brick scenarios through my head. I had a meeting to get to. I checked my phone and found a text from Elysse.

"C U at CF."

Message received. Did Elysse figure out why I'd switched the meeting to CF? Was she happy that her brick-

throwing plan worked, and frightened me—or, rather, my
boyfriend—into choosing a public place? Did I care?

I checked Elysse's Facebook page before I left and was
relieved to see that action had slowed on her wall. *Whew.* I
was already old news. Her friends had moved on. To
vandalism?

I'd taken Elysse's initial phone call as a sign of concili-
ation. Now I questioned her motives. I could hardly wait
to find out what else she had in mind. If the brick was
some kind of opening salvo, she had a lot to learn about
negotiating.

I parked on campus and walked past the Student Union
building and out through the gate behind the Clara Barton
dorm, where Kira was still in residence. I wondered if she
was up yet, and how she'd react at the Graves memorial in
less than two hours. I was glad yesterday's rain was short-
lived. Services for lost loved ones were sad enough without
a downpour from the sky. At least Kira would wake to
bright, pleasant weather.

Let's take care of one student at a time, I reminded
myself. Elysse Hutchins was next. But as I crossed Main
Street, I allowed myself thirty seconds to clear my head of
all student issues and focus on the magnificent median
strip. A riot of orange and yellow daylilies with profuse
green foliage lined the street for several blocks in either
direction. It was enough to make me want to take very
early retirement and do gardening full-time.

The Coffee Filter was busy enough that Bruce wouldn't
worry for my safety—he'd already checked in to make sure
I kept my promise about meeting my antagonist in a public
place—but not so crowded that I couldn't get a good table

that allowed for me sit with my back to the wall, eyes front, to spot Elysse when she came in.

At almost all surrounding tables were people working on laptops or other electronic devices. I noted only one table with two women talking to each other without technological assistance. Like all the coffeehouses of today, the Coffee Filter served a whole different purpose from even a few years ago. Instead of asking, "Cream and sugar?" which were now off on a counter for self-service, customers were offered the Wi-Fi password with their drinks.

I made it a policy never to arrive unprepared to wait for a meeting to start, whether a whole academic department or only one other person was involved. I kept a thin leather travel portfolio stocked with printouts of puzzles, some to solve, some on the way to completion for my puzzle magazine editor. Often, I'd become so engrossed in a conundrum or a math game or a twisty puzzle, I'd forgotten that a meeting had been set up.

Today was no exception. I arrived at the Coffee Filter at 8:17, ordered a latte and a cheese Danish, and settled in for a puzzling session. It was a much more reasonable way to spend the time than fretting over what Elysse might want or what my strategy should be, especially regarding the brick incident.

I pulled out a set of riddles sent by a grad school friend who had moved back to his hometown in Iowa. We'd been mailing occasional challenges to each other for many years. I wondered why this set seemed particularly easy, until I read the accompanying note. John was offering riddles that I might use for my younger Zeeman Academy students. I whipped through the first few.

What word is heavy when written forward and not when written backward?
Answer: Ton.

On to the next one.

The letters in the phrase redo now can be rear-
ranged to form one word. What is it?

The answer was too easy, even for fourth graders: *redo*
now is an anagram for *one word*.

I appreciated the value of fun-filled wordplay to help
sharpen the critical-thinking skills of young minds, but I
needed something more difficult if I was going to steer
clear of worrisome thoughts.

I abandoned the grade school riddles and started working on a seven-by-seven grid wordplay puzzle. I kept coming back to the day's meetings, however, projecting ahead
to Elysse's arrival, to the memorial service, to lunch with
Principal Richardson. To many questions. Was Elysse
going to be packing another brick and try to ambush me in
the Coffee Filter's ladies' room? Would the service for
Mayor Graves be formal or informal? I'd dressed for in
between and hoped I'd blend in. Was Principal Richardson
going to fire me? I'd grown to like the younger kids and
hoped to do another volunteer year at Zeeman Academy.

I'd already run through several possible openings for
the moment when Elysse plunked herself down across
from me. My practice dialogue ran the gamut from sarcastic to pleading to threatening.

Thanks for the new window.

I'm so sorry, forgive me, please don't ruin my reputa-
tion as a good, fair teacher.

Back off, or we'll rescind your degree.

Here's your A, now go away.

On second thought, I've given you zero points on every
problem, retroactive to your full two years.

I was contemplating *Can you help me get more Friends*
to Like my cause? when Elysse showed up, dressed scantily
for a chilly morning—two or three pastel tank tops over a

pair of denim shorts. I considered it a lucky break for me since I wouldn't have to be concerned that she was wearing a wire. And her pixie haircut was too short to hide any ear device. So far, so good.

"Hey, Dr. Knowles."

"Hey, Elysse."

An awkward silence followed the "hey" volley, but I felt it was her turn. I couldn't remember ever being so intimidated by a student. I'd had my share of complaints before, especially about grades, but I'd always been able to work it out. More often than not, the student was successful in convincing me that I'd misjudged or been unclear about an aspect of an assignment or exam. For years, I'd done this amicably, without the help of social networking or messages dispatched in unconventional ways.

Elysse had picked up an iced coffee on the way to the table and set it down now, nearly tipping it over in the process. Maybe she was nervous, too. Or it could have been simply that her loose backpack gave her an unstable center of mass.

"I got your message," she said. She cocked her head from side to side. "Duh. Of course I did. That's why I'm here"—she pointed in the direction of Franklin Hall—"and not there." Her expression turned serious. "And I got your other message, too."

"What other message?"

I wished I'd looked over our email communication again so I'd be ready for whichever email or text she was talking about.

But apparently she was referring to something altogether different.

She reached into her pocket for a piece of paper, folded into one quarter its size. "This one," she said.

My first shock was that Elysse's tight shorts could have held such a thickness. My second shock came when she unfolded the sheet and showed me a note, neatly typed on the paper.

You'll be sorry if you continue this fight.

S. K.

I stared at the paper. "What does this mean?" It took a beat for me to realize why she was showing me the note. And much longer than it should have to realize that *S. K.* were my own initials. "You think I sent this?"

"It was slipped under my door. It was there when I woke up yesterday." She pointed to the letters at the bottom of the note and frowned. "S. K. That's you, right?"

I shook my head, slowly, trying to make sense of the message and the presence of my initials. "I don't even know where you live right now, Elysse."

"I'm crashing with my cousin until my apartment in Boston is ready." She sat back. "That's right. How would you know that?"

"I wouldn't."

"Kira didn't tell you?" She frowned. "Wait. I don't think Kira knows yet. Then who sent it?"

"I don't know. It must be some other S. K," I offered.

"But I'm not fighting with anyone else."

"Are we fighting, Elysse?" I took out my phone and opened my photo gallery to the pictures I'd taken of the incident that became the subject of a Henley PD police report. "Now that I think of it, I guess we are."

I placed the phone to face her, showing her first the photo of the shattered glass of my patio door, then scrolling to the brick and the note, then back. I doubted she could have faked the horrified look on her face.

Elysse pulled the phone closer to her and scrolled back and forth herself, stopping at the glaring "Support Elysse."

"Is this your house, Dr. Knowles?" The question was pitched high, with the word *house* at the highest pitch of all, from a very upset young woman.

"Elysse—"

"I know I started this with Facebook and all, but I never, never would do that." Elysse pointed to the phone and the offending photos, then pushed the phone away and crossed her arms over her chest. "I never meant for things to get this far. I'm on Facebook, you know, like all students, and we vent. It's just to vent. Do you think my friends are doing this? I mean my"—she made quotation marks in the air—"'Friends' on Facebook?"

"I don't know what to think, except that we should settle this issue once and for all before we leave here. I'm sorry—"

"I'm sorry—" Elysse said at the same time, and broke into tears. "Never mind the grade, Dr. Knowles. Really, all this over a stupid grade? I can't believe I was so . . . so . . ."

Young, I wanted to say, but decided to keep things going in the direction of progress.

Elysse had a lot more to say about Facebook and how she hated flame wars and couldn't believe she'd started one. While she talked on and on, because she had to, I had the strangest flashback to the watercolor print in my den. One of the images was of a circle of cobblestones in front of the Old State House in Boston. The tiny monument commemorated the Boston Massacre of 1770, in which a minor dispute between a young American man and a British sentry turned into a riot. The crowd, some of whom had no idea what started the fray, grew angry. British soldiers fired into the crowd, killing five colonists. At least, that's the way our American history teachers told the story.

Historical accuracy aside, I thought there was a lesson in the narrative. If not settled early, a small dispute grows bigger and hurts a lot of people.

I took Elysse's hand and held it a moment. "I was thinking we'd meet each other halfway. What if I give you half the points for that problem? I believe you honestly misunderstood the instructions and had no intention of getting away with anything by using the calculator. Giving you half credit makes sense, and I can live with that in terms of fairness to the other students who worked the problem as I intended. This way, you'll still have your A for the class."

At which point, Elysse's sobs became loud enough to attract the attention of some, but not all, of the people around us, clicking away on their computers, notebooks, pads, touches, and phones.

As for the Friends, whoever they were, who had planted the note under Elysse's door and thrown a brick at mine, I knew if I found them, I'd show no mercy.

CHAPTER $\sqrt{18}$

I had some time before meeting Kira at the Mortarboard, the campus's poor cousin to the Coffee Filter. I wished I'd thought to change my meeting with Kira also, if only for the sake of good coffee, but it was probably too late. I decided to walk back to my office and spend the interim on end-of-year odds and ends. The first order of business would be to make the adjustment to Elysse's grade.

Though I was happy to be closing that chapter of the school year, I couldn't help wishing there was a way to address the faceless alleged friends who'd escalated things.

I called Bruce from my office, reported on my morning visit from the HPD, and gave him happy news for once.

"Elysse and I are good again," I told him, and relayed the details of our meeting.

"Then who threw the brick and who put the note under her door?"

"I have no idea. Maybe one of my Facebook friends has a silver SUV."

We both laughed at that idea. My presence on social networking sites was only through the Henley College page and those of various professional groups I belonged to. I kept putting off establishing my own page since I didn't see the point. I wasn't looking for a job; I had all the flesh-and-blood friends I needed; I had nothing to sell. For now, I was fine without pokes from capital-F friends.

"I'm going to look into it," Bruce said, his chuckling over.

"What can you do, other than write a message to every one of Elysse's friends individually and ask for their alibis?"

"I can start by talking to Virge."

"Bruce, Friends are all over the world. They're in Omaha and Singapore and Brazil. Not even the Henley PD can track them all down."

"One of them came to Henley, Massachusetts. He didn't toss a brick from Shanghai."

"Good point. But I still don't see how you can find him. Or her. My neighbors didn't get a license plate or see who was driving the vehicle. There's not enough to go on."

"That's Virge's job. He'll help me figure something out. Meanwhile, just be cool."

I promised I'd try.

I was ready to drop the brick episode and let Bruce and Virgil do their thing, except that every now and then I looked out my campus office window at passing traffic, checking for a silver SUV. The Lawrences were new to my neighborhood. I wondered how they'd feel if I showed up on their doorstep and queried them further about the vehicle they'd seen speeding away from my house.

I sat at my desk, from which I sorted and tossed paper after paper—homework sets from classes gone by, articles that were years out of date, memos with college policy changes that had been superseded ten times over by now. I made a note to alert Woody to the extra poundage for the trash this week. The promised paperless office never quite made it to Henley, at least not to the first floor of Benjamin Franklin Hall.

All the while I was sorting, I'd checked each piece for one that might have been left by the deceased Mayor Graves. Nothing. How many more times was I going to try? How many more *nothing*s would it take before I'd drop the fantasy that the mayor had left a clue to his murder in my own little office?

I thought about the undefined evidence Virgil had mentioned. Sight unseen, I tried to convince myself that the police had already found whatever important, or incriminating, communication there was between Richardson and the mayor. I would love to have concluded that whatever the mayor was trying to tell me—in person, on the phone, in my office—had now been cleared up. I figured it would be at least an hour before I questioned it again.

On the way to the Mortarboard to meet Kira, I walked past the tennis courts, where Monty Sizemore was hitting neon green balls against the backboard. Maybe it was because I was aware of his current mental state, but he seemed to be slamming the ball with more force than necessary. I felt sorry for him, knowing he was missing his partner. Then not sorry when I recalled his repeated calls and nagging.

He stopped when he saw me and indicated that I should meet him at the gate to the courts. He trotted over to the entrance to the courts, a white towel around his neck and a bottle of water in his hand.

"Hey, Sophie. I hoped you'd come by today. I figured you'd be going to the service and you'd maybe stop at your office. I was watching for you, but I didn't see you go into the building."

The idea of Monty's stakeout gave me an irrational, uneasy feeling. "I went in through the side door," I explained, curious that he didn't simply call me back after last night's hang-up. I looked at my watch. "I need to meet someone in about five minutes in the Mortarboard."

"Let's walk and talk," he said, and put his hand under my elbow, as if I couldn't guide myself along the path. I slipped my arm away as soon as I could without letting on that I didn't like the feel of his hand on me. Over the years, very few people had made it to my "do not like" list. Monty and Chris were headed for it, nearly doubling its length. At some point, I'd have to stop and figure out why. I hoped I didn't simply envy their youth and closeness.

"Sophie, I'm so sorry I was all wound up last night. I certainly didn't mean to be so . . . whatever. I hope I didn't offend you."

What thirty-year-old these days used that term? Offend? Maybe business schools kept to old-time terminology. "No offense," I said.

"It's just, I'm so frustrated."

"I'm sure you are. I take it Chris is still at the station?" *In custody* seemed too harsh for the guy, though I remembered how harsh he and his sister had been with me when I'd become Facebook's witch du jour. I was bigger than that, I told myself. Especially after the amicable settlement with Elysse, I really didn't want to spoil my day with vengeful thoughts or deeds.

"She's still down there. My lawyer says she could be out by noon. That is, if they don't charge her." Monty took a long swallow of water. "I know you're tight with that cop in the HPD. There must be something you can do?"

Monty was the ultimate broken record. I'd have to match him. "I'm really very sorry, Monty. But we keep our professional and social lives separate."

Liar, liar. I chided myself. But in the matter of Chris versus the city of Henley, I really didn't have any official information. It had been Kira, not Virgil, who mentioned emails between Chris and the mayor as the reason for her current status, and even that was second- or third-hand campus gossip only.

Once he'd released my elbow, Monty had begun a strange kind of routine, which included running ahead of me a few steps, then turning around to face me. He'd walk a few steps backward, then repeat the sequence, talking all the while. I found it disconcerting, but with only a few yards and a few minutes to go, I wasn't about to complain to him.

About ten feet from the door to the Mortarboard, Monty stopped, blocking the entrance. I let out a sigh, this time not bothering to conceal a touch of annoyance.

Monty held his hands up, as if he was surrendering. "Okay, I didn't want to say this, because it could sound bad," he said. "But I'm sure if I share this with you, you'll want to think about it and find a way to help, no question."

"Monty—"

"Just listen," he said, clenching his water bottle until it popped. I was surprised it didn't crack open. "I know what the police have on her. Or what they think they have on her."

"Oh?" Now I was listening.

"Chris was in there with Ed. In the humanities office that night. The night he was killed. They were in Bev Eaton's office. It's where they've been meeting the last few weeks. Chris has a roommate, and Ed has a . . . well, had a wife, you know, so they'd meet there."

An English professor's office as a trysting place? It made for a bizarre scenario, unless, like Ed and Kira, they were just talking. I remembered tracing back the one light that was on in the Administration Building on Saturday night to Bev's office. I had my own feelings of regret now. If I'd told Virgil about the light right away, he might have

been able to rush in there and . . . and what? . . catch a
killer who had nonchalantly waited around to be caught?

"The mayor dumped my sister for good that night,"
Monty continued. "It had been coming on for weeks. He'd
been hinting that he considered her just a good friend, but
when he finally came out with it, how he had a wife and son
he'd never leave, and all that drivel, she was devastated.
Never mind that Chris had given him her heart. Plus a major
chunk of money to his campaign. Our aunt Tess died and left
us each"—Monty waved away the story as if it was a gnat
aiming for his face—"never mind that. Chris was destroyed.
But she didn't kill him. She saw him walk away. I swear."

If nothing else, Monty would make an excellent, persua-
sive character witness for his sister.

"Did Chris tell all this to the police?"

"I don't know. I don't think so. Unless she told them
yesterday when they picked her up. I haven't talked to her
since then. It's driving me crazy."

Watching Monty hop in place in front of the Mortarboard, I didn't doubt him for a minute. "What about your
lawyer? Shouldn't she or he be able to have Chris released
if she hasn't been charged?"

Monty mopped his brow, having generated his own heat
on what was a cool spring morning. He threw up his hands.
"He's supposed to be working on it. Whatever that means.
I know Chris freaked out when she heard Ed had been
murdered; that's when she told me she was probably the
last person to see him alive."

I thought of the list I'd given Virgil of those who'd voted
no on the mayor as speaker. Chris had been on it, though I
hadn't highlighted her, or any of the faculty, as Virgil had
wanted. "Did the police interview her?"

"Yes, and I advised her not to tell them about that night.
Even though she had nothing to hide. You know how cops
can be." I nodded as if one were not a close friend. "Now
I'm kicking myself. I feel like I'm to blame for this mess

she's in. Maybe if she'd come right out and admitted she was with him just before he was killed, they'd have believed her and it would be all over and she'd be here now."

"Chris made her own choice, Monty. You just have to let her work it out."

Monty gave me an angry, questioning stare, as if to ask if I'd been listening at all. "Are you saying you won't help? You won't at least make sure the police know that she withheld information only on my advice, that she did nothing wrong? Maybe I could just take an obstruction of justice charge myself and that would be it."

I was spared from having to decline once again to intercede on Chris's behalf by the presence of a figure in black who came up to us on the pathway. Twenty-one-year-old Kira Gilmore had outfitted herself head to toe with the color of mourning, looking like the old Italian woman who lived on my street when I was a kid. With the specks of beige and gold in my paisley top, my outfit seemed gaudy in comparison.

"Hi, Mr. Sizemore and Dr. Knowles," she said, then, "Are you coming with us, Mr. Sizemore?"

Though I hadn't verbalized it, Monty realized I still hadn't made a commitment to help him out. I wasn't sure why not myself, except that I had no reason to believe in Chris's innocence, but every confidence in Virgil and the HPD's ability to figure it all out.

Monty barely acknowledged Kira. He glared at me again. "I hope you're not sorry about this, Sophie," he said.

It sounded too much like a threat this time. Was he going to start another Facebook attack? I was beyond being intimidated, no matter how great the difference in our heights and weights.

"Have a nice day," I said.

"You never say that," Kira said, once Monty had taken off. She was clearly confused by what she'd happened upon. "I thought you hated that expression."

"Extraordinary times," I told her, and we headed toward city hall.

I couldn't remember the last time I was in Henley City Hall. Possibly three years ago when I was maid of honor, complete with a tacky fuchsia dress and matching heels and bouquet, for a friend who wanted a civil ceremony. The inside of the building was no match for the impressive exterior. It was as if the city had run out of money after applying the expensive coat of gold leaf to the magnificent dome, in imitation of the lavish golden dome of the State House that was one of Boston's great attractions.

Inside, the city hall was like any other government building, with modest wooden floors and moldings and a collection of statues in the great entryway. Paul Revere, John Quincy Adams, Edward Everett Hale, and a host of other patriots watched over us all.

The building may have been ordinary, but I shouldn't have been surprised that the gathering in Mayor Graves's honor was unlike any other memorial service I'd attended. It seemed every cop and firefighter in Bristol County was present. I hoped everyone who depended on them was safe. This would be the perfect time to throw a brick through someone's patio door.

Nora and Cody Graves sat on a stage at the front of the large assembly room that had been outfitted for the service with jardinieres and banks of flowers. I wondered if Mrs. Graves was thinking back only three days to a time when she shared a simpler stage setting with her husband on the Henley campus.

Surrounding the mayor's widow and son were about a dozen people I recognized as city council members, not from lunch dates with them, but from the political literature strewn around at election time. Bruce was more in tune with the VIPs than I was. He'd once served—he would have said hobnobbed with—state and national celebrities and politicians when he worked as a pilot for a private helicopter company. I seemed to remember that Superintendent Collins had been among them at one time. If prompted, Bruce could go on and on, without naming names, about CEOs who played golf during working hours and rock-star women who slipped away for a weekend, allegedly with the girls.

I sat on a folding chair, but not on the stage this time, with a subdued Kira next to me. I wondered how either of us would ever get close enough to Nora to offer a personal greeting. Or, in my case, ferret out a clue that might help find her husband's killer.

With Kira not interested in conversation, I scanned the assembly for people I knew, spotting a few Henley faculty members, but no Principal Richardson or Superintendent Collins. I figured they'd had their secretaries send flowers and counted that the end of their obligation.

I tuned into the buzz around me, picking up bits of the low-level chatter that precedes any formal gathering. I realized I had a de facto list of words that reached my ears with particular clarity and bias. I heard them now, in succession.

A man behind us to my left complained to his companion, "I should be at a board meeting right now. Services like this are a waste of time."

Waste. I thought of the city's contentious waste management contracts.

The mother of a middle schooler, both of whom were sitting in front of us, took the opportunity to bond with her daughter. "Dad and I are so proud of your report card, sweetie. Your grades are so much better than last year."

Grades. I wondered if the girl was a Zeeman Academy student whose grade was inflated.

Two young women next to me chatted in vivid detail about the faults of their current boyfriends. "Sometimes I want to kill him," the first said.

Kill. When her friend nodded and exclaimed, "Totally," I wondered if they'd end the day with a plot to murder each other's problem guy. I figured this particular association was due in part to the many times I'd watched Hitchcock's *Strangers on a Train* with Bruce and Virgil.

But on the whole, it was the murder of Mayor Edward P. Graves, and not movie references, that had seemed to consume my mental energy since Saturday night. I was in the middle of a self-inflicted rebuke about this when two voices behind me seemed to rise above the others in my vicinity.

"Thomas is dead," said the man who wished he was at a board meeting.

"Long live the Stewart Brothers," said the other.

"Money talks," said the first.

"Unless you're dead."

I hoped no one else had heard the exchange, utterly inappropriate at a memorial service, even if it was late getting started.

Their words bounced back to me, striking a chord in my head. I'd heard the combination of names, Thomas and Stewart, before. Kira's soft sigh reminded me of when— during her tutorial on the waste management dispute between the mayor and Monty Sizemore. Mayor Graves had wanted to give the contract to the Thomas Company and Monty had preferred the Stewart Company. Or vice versa. I closed my eyes and tried to remember. It came to me. The W. Thomas Company and the Stewart Brothers, that was it. Apparently the mayor's death ensured the Stewart Brothers victory in the battle.

Could they have killed Mayor Graves? But why, if the contract had already been awarded?

I leaned into Kira, whispering, "Did you tell me that Edward gave the waste contract to Thomas?"

The question, out of context to say the least, shook Kira awake. She gave me a confused look. "They hadn't closed the deal yet. Edward just gave them a verbal last week."

Was this an *aha* moment? A suspect I hadn't thought of? "Thanks," I said to Kira.

"Why—"

"We'll talk later," I said, cutting her off and giving her hand a squeeze.

I hoped Kira would forget the issue by the time the service was over. If it would only begin. Now I was eager to leave to pursue my new line of inquiry. Monty had popped up on my suspect list because he wanted to have the contract, probably getting a kickback. But why not Stewart himself? Or themselves, if there were really brothers involved. I felt handicapped that I had no clue who the owners of the offending company were, but I liked the idea that the murderer might be someone completely disconnected from Henley College.

I wondered if Virgil was up to speed on the contract dispute. Surely, the HPD would go through all of the mayor's outstanding negotiations, but what if the waste management issue was at the bottom of their stack?

The question was whether I should tell Virgil also of what Monty had spilled out about Chris's confrontation with the mayor on Saturday night, minutes before he was stabbed. Perhaps Chris had already confessed. If not, would I be getting her into more trouble than her emails did?

Rushing out to call Virgil with both bits of news was an option I considered seriously, but howling feedback from the mic told me the service was about to start and my exit would be awkward. I couldn't claim this was an emergency. In fact, the way things had been going lately, Virgil might already have released Chris Sizemore and brought in the Stewart Brothers.

I wished I could have said that the speeches in honor of the mayor were better than his own at the Henley graduation. In both cases, however, the words hardly seemed to matter, except to those most affected. For the most part, the prayers and hail-fellow commentary seemed part of just another day in the life of the attendees.

Acutely aware of Kira at my side, I was ready to intervene if she acted out in any way. But she seemed to evolve before my eyes, sitting up straighter and straighter through the eulogies, frowning in concentration as if trying to put everything in perspective (this might simply have been my projected wish for her), and respectfully bowing her head at the appropriate times.

As I predicted, the reception line in the assembly hall was about as long as the famous rope around the earth in the problem I gave my middle school classes every year. To my relief, Kira questioned the wisdom of standing for an hour simply to shake the hands of Nora and Cody and be summarily rushed away.

"If you don't mind, Dr. Knowles, I think I'm ready to leave," she said. "I contributed to the flowers the kids at campaign headquarters sent and I signed the card. That's probably enough."

I heartily approved of her choices and was proud of my student. I took Kira's behavior as a sign that she'd come to terms with the fact of Nora Graves as Edward's legitimate wife and herself as a useful sounding board for him. I hoped today ushered in a return to reality for Kira.

And for me, too, as I had a moment of truth that I should be following her example. Here Bruce would have sung a line from a musical, something like, "If you're a teacher, by your students you'll be taught." My own condolences were represented by the hefty wreath sent by the college, and that was the only appropriate response for me. I was embarrassed that I'd ever considered trying to insert myself personally into Nora Graves's life for the purpose of interrogating her or her son, and relieved that I hadn't had a chance to follow through.

It wasn't lost on me that this was far from the end of it for Nora and Cody. There would be a funeral, of course, and an undetermined amount of time before the mayor's case was resolved. As far as their returning to a normal life, I guessed it was too far off to contemplate.

"It was a nice service," I said, testing my theory that Kira had crossed a threshold.

She nodded. "I'm glad we did this. Thanks for coming with me, Dr. Knowles."

"No problem. Too bad we couldn't get through the line."

"I'm not disappointed. I'm glad I was part of the mayor's life. I learned a lot, but that's over now. In fact, I have a lot to do. I'm going to start packing up today." Kira gave me a big smile. "It's time I got off campus, don't you think?" A sheepish look took shape on her face. "I didn't want to tell you, but my place at MIT has been ready for a couple of weeks."

I held back on the yelps of joy, but gave my star student a big hug.

We parted ways when Kira went left toward the Clara Barton dorm and beyond and I went right toward the side gate to Ben Franklin Hall.

Things were looking up. I was good with Elysse Hutchins and thrilled that Kira Gilmore was on her way to adulthood.

CHAPTER $\sqrt{19}$

Thanks to Kira's epiphany and our abbreviated time at city hall, I had nearly an hour before my lunch date with Principal Richardson. I figured I should practice calling him *Doug*, just in case he reverted to the form he'd used on the phone, like the deceased *Ed* before him.

On the way to my office I was aware of every vehicle rolling up and down Main Street, on a meaningless search for a silver SUV, possibly with a pile of red bricks on the passenger seat. I was frustrated that I couldn't focus on the beautiful, sunny weather, or the new spring blossoms on the colorful median strip. I couldn't seem to shake off the feeling that I was being stalked.

It was too early to call Ariana in San Diego—besides, I hadn't heard from her in a couple of days and took that as a sign that her social life had picked up. I knew I'd have a full report soon enough. I hesitated to call Bruce, who'd gotten off work at nine this morning. Chances were good that he'd still be napping. A text message would be unintrusive, however. I gave it a try.

"U up?" I texted as I walked. In the swing of things, since the street was crowded with others from the memorial service, nearly all of them with buds or phones at their ears or thumbs working rhythmically.

A minute later, my cell rang, Bruce calling me back. As great as it was to hear his voice, he was no help in distracting me from the brick-throwing incident.

"There are more silver SUVs than you'd think in Henley," Bruce said, sounding despondent.

"Shouldn't you be sleeping?"

"I got a few winks in. It's especially hard to trace a car not knowing the make and model. But Virgil has guys working on it."

"How?" I asked, giving in to Bruce's choice of topic. I imagined young Officers Nolan and Coyne traipsing around the city knocking on the doors of all silver SUV owners. I hoped they didn't mention Professor Sophie Knowles as the cause of the inconvenience.

"They'll generate a list and then see if any of them has been linked to a crime, or maybe try to match it with campus people. I don't know exactly, but I'm sure they've done this before."

"The people in that car might not even have been the ones to throw the brick, Bruce. The SUV might not even have been silver. As I understand it, Bill Lawrence saw the vehicle briefly as he was flying out the door himself. The car could have been pale blue or gray or who knows what color."

"I think they allow for that in their search. I told Virge about the note Elysse got under her door, too, and they're trying to put it all together. It can't hurt, Sophie. I'm surprised Virge hasn't called you about it, but I guess he's busy bringing in the big education gun."

"What gun?"

"Oh, I figured you knew."

I wanted to scream, *I don't know anything until it's practically all over.* "What gun, Bruce?"

"Collins. The superintendent? They picked him up early this morning on a tip from someone. Anonymous, of course."

I stopped short, nearly getting rear-ended by the family of four walking behind me. "Superintendent Patrick Collins has been arrested?" The littlest child in the group, apparently the one with the sharpest ears, gave me a funny look. I attempted a comforting smile, in case she was worried.

"Yeah. You didn't know?" Bruce's rub-it-in routine, which ordinarily I'd enjoy. But not today.

"What happened to Chris Sizemore? Has she been released?"

It didn't sit right that I'd received most of my information on the principals in the case from Kira and Bruce, and now I was begging more information from Bruce when, after all, I was the one the mayor had reached out to. Good thing I wasn't the pouty kind.

"I think Chris is still in custody," Bruce said.

"They're both being held? Chris and Collins?"

"Looks that way. Anyway, with all that, I'm glad Virge is willing to give some time to your brick. It's not a trivial incident, and it wasn't random, Sophie, especially with that note attached."

"You're right. And I should be glad the HPD is trying to find out who got in the middle of Elysse and me. I just want them to find the mayor's killer and not be distracted by vandalism or petty—"

I stopped, a new thought bursting into my head. What if my brick incident was related to the murder? Not that I had a clue how that could be. But I couldn't let go of the idea.

Suppose the person who stabbed Mayor Graves thought I was onto him. Never mind why she or he would, since I certainly had done nothing but think up a list of suspects and motives. And talked a lot to Virgil. Maybe that was it.

The killer assumed I was working with the police and might be instrumental in his capture. I tried to picture the same person who viciously stabbed a man now resorting to tossing a brick through my patio door, then figuring out where Elysse lived and slipping a note under her door.

It didn't make a lot of sense, especially if the very large, rather clumsy Superintendent Collins was the culprit, even if he was on my short list of suspects. But not much else made sense either.

"Soph?" Bruce asked, as in, *Are you still there?*

"I'm here," I said. "Approaching campus."

It was too soon to mention this latest brainstorm to Bruce. I needed more information on why Superintendent Collins was taken into custody, or invited for an interview, or whatever category he fit in.

I reminded Bruce about my lunch with the Zeeman Academy principal. "We'll be in broad daylight at the Inn," I told him. "No need for a bodyguard."

"That's what I like to hear. You busy for dinner?"

"I'm expecting my handsome boyfriend. I'll even cook his favorite pasta primavera for him."

"He'll be there at six."

I entered Franklin Hall through the side entrance in time to wave to two other faculty members who were boarding the elevator to take them to the biology floor. I'd noticed them at the memorial service and figured they were getting in a bit of work before lunch as I was.

I was dismayed to realize how relieved I was not to be alone in the building. I should have been comforted by the fact that the police had detained not one, but two suspects in the mayor's murder. It was safer than ever on the mean streets outside the police station. Still, I hurried down the hall to my office, entered, and quickly shut the door behind me.

More than ever, I wanted to call Virgil. The list of things to tell him was growing by the minute. There was Chris's meeting with the mayor in Admin the night he was murdered, the Stewart Brothers waste company benefitting from his death through a lucrative contract, and the newly forming connection in my mind between my brick incident and the murder.

It should have been easy for me to arrange a sit-down with Virgil and run all these things by him in a give-and-take. I'd order pizza and share my theories; he'd lay out for me the current status of the case. I longed for Virgil to explain to me why he told me he had evidence against Principal Richardson, but had picked up Chris Sizemore and Superintendent Collins. Had this been a conspiracy of three committing murder? The idea was unappealing.

Clearly, I was missing a key piece of the puzzle. Together, Virgil and I could solve the mystery of who stabbed Mayor Graves on the Henley College campus. If only I were a cop.

I doubted that my dream scenario would work, since I didn't have a badge, but I decided to call Virgil anyway. Maybe I could wrangle a few tidbits from him.

I punched in his number and was disappointed that my call went to his voice mail. I stumbled through a message about having some new information on the mayor's murder case, and mentioned that I'd be free this afternoon and could stop by his office. I thought of inviting Virgil to dinner, but it had been a while since Bruce and I had some quality alone time together, not since our ill-fated ice cream stroll on Saturday night.

There was still about a half hour before I'd have to leave for the Inn at Henley and my tête-à-tête with Principal Richardson—my friend *Doug*. A little research was in order, but not as prep for that meeting. If I was going to talk about waste management with Virgil, I should know a little more about it than what day of the week to have my blue container at the curb for pickup. I booted up my computer and searched online for the W. Thomas Company.

Kira had it right—there was a lot of money in trash. The W. Thomas website listed more ways than I could have guessed for a waste management company to make money from your trash. You could rent a Dumpster, fill it, then pay to have it hauled away. You could order special pickups for things like spent fluorescent lightbulbs and batteries. You could order (that is, buy) a kit into which your special waste could be inserted before you paid to have it hauled away.

You could do all this for your private residence, for your office building, or for your multinational corporation. W. Thomas was ready to handle your medical syringes and your pesticides, your outdated heavy industrial equipment and your construction debris. All at reasonable rates, of course.

I noticed the value added by W. Thomas, which Kira had mentioned, offering an extra pickup the day after a major holiday, at little additional cost. Was that feature enough of a reason for the mayor not only to choose them, but to fire Monty when he disagreed with the choice?

I skipped over to the Stewart Brothers site and skimmed through the text and images. Now that I was fluent in waste vocabulary, I saw a slightly more obvious approach to green solutions for waste disposal, but nothing so significant that Monty Sizemore would be willing to lose his job over it. Both companies hauled away, bought, and sold anything the citizens of Henley no longer wanted.

I sat back. What had I expected to find in this search? A clue to the conflict between the mayor and Monty? I figured it had to be about money. I glanced once more at the Stewart Brothers page, open on my screen, as if I might spot a FAQ section listing the opportunities for kickbacks from the company who landed the contract for handling of the city's refuse. I envisioned a table, with the names of the waste companies at the top and the short list of two advocates, Mayor Graves and Monty, along the side. The boxes would be filled with dollar amounts indicating how much payoff money was involved in each choice.

When had I starting using mathematics to support a pessimistic worldview?

As usual when I was in front of my computer, I thought of one more thing to look up. I searched on Google for the superintendent of schools to see what I could find out about Patrick Collins. I wondered if his website had been updated to include his current custodial state.

After learning that I was the 1253911th visitor to the site, I clicked on the home page of the school district. The most prominent text was a long letter from Collins, inviting the six thousand students now ending their school year to have a safe, happy summer. I read through data on the improvement in literacy rate over last year's classes, the decrease in dropout rate, and the superintendent's renewed commitment to the children of the community.

A thumbnail of Collins showed him at a desk with the American flag behind him; he was sitting straight, smiling formally. I tried to imagine him in an orange jumpsuit.

Collins's bio read like a prose version of the standard resume of an educator's career. He'd held many leadership positions in urban education, special education, and professional development organizations. The only personal note was that Collins spends his time between Henley and Chatham—a more affluent town on the Cape than I'd have thought a government employee could afford.

I was tempted to click around and read about the district's student health services, the school calendar, the yearbook office, and the policy on bullying, but I couldn't see any advantage as far as gaining insight into what might have gotten the superintendent picked up by the HPD.

I made one side trip to my favorite Internet news site and saw nothing yet about a possible arrest in the Graves murder case. It was always hard for me to leave the

Internet, but it was time to go. At least I hadn't bought a
useless home storage product or an unneeded pair of
sandals.

The quarter-hour chimes rang out from the clock tower.
If I didn't hurry I'd be late for my lunch date. I shut down
my computer and dashed down the empty hallway and out
to the parking lot, noticing every wastebasket and trash
container inside and outside of Franklin Hall.

The Inn at Henley was no less elegant at lunchtime. I
thought of the lunchroom at Zeeman Academy, with its
Formica tables and old-model microwave, and wondered if
two of its teachers, Rina Flores and Digital Dan Sachs,
were responsible for my date today. I'd soon find out if the
loyal employees, formerly also my friends, had rushed to
warn their principal that they'd essentially incriminated
him and themselves, admitting to the crime of fraud.

Doug Richardson was waiting for me at a table against
the wall and perilously close to the large tropical fish tank.
I questioned the Inn decorator's choice to display the tiny
striped and patterned fish at a venue that served up their
larger, plainer cousins on steaming platters.

The principal stood as I approached. He gave me a hesi-
tant, uneasy smile and ran his hand over his full head of
white hair, smoothing it. He checked his tie and dropped
his napkin, as nervous as if we were on a blind date and he
was worried I wouldn't like him.

"Sophie," he said, extending his hand.

I greeted him, noticing that today's suit, a navy pinstripe,
fit much better across his middle. Had I rated a new outfit?
It felt strange to be in a situation where the principal of a
school seemed to be trying to make a good impression on
me. I, on the other hand, made no attempt to apologize for
my lackluster mourning outfit. I had to admit I was enjoying
the dynamic. I had too many memories of being on the

opposite end of the principal-student scenario as I'd made my way from K through 12. I had to keep reminding myself that I was now the same age as a school principal, probably within a year or two of the one sitting opposite me.

We went through the small-talk ritual of traffic (heavy with the lunchtime crowd), weather (*Beautiful, isn't it?*), and ordering (crab salad for both of us, iced coffee for me, merlot for him).

One sip of wine later, Doug was ready to jump in.

"I'd like to explain a little about why I called you." I flashed an agreeable, expectant smile. "I realized in retrospect that you might have wanted something from me yesterday, and I rudely rushed by you."

Another first. A school principal was apologizing for not paying attention to me. I was sure Doug wasn't springing for a four-star meal so I'd forgive him for not hanging around to tend to my needs yesterday. I smiled again, sipped my refreshing iced coffee, and waited him out.

"This is a little awkward," he said.

The better part of me won out and I decided to help him through the ordeal. "You mentioned that you needed to talk to me about something," I said. Then the worst part of me took over. I wasn't perfect. "Was it about the argument between you and Superintendent Collins that I overheard?"

Doug blanched, apparently buying into my suggestion that I knew what the fight was about. I realized I had no idea if Doug knew the superintendent was in custody. I wished I could call Kira or Bruce, the most informed friends I had, to find out if Collins had been charged or released or neither.

"Pat and I, we have our differences. He was never on the front lines. He's been a bureaucrat all his life, with no idea what it's like to wrestle with the day-to-day operation of a school." Doug leaned toward me. "Sophie, may I tell you a little about charter schools?"

"Certainly," I said, in spite of feeling I knew enough

about them already. It was only fair to let Richardson have his day in my court. I could definitely say that charter schools were more important to me than waste handling, although I might not stick to that position if disposal services were suspended for any length of time.

Understandably, Doug began with all the positives about the charter school model—more hands-on learning, students on all levels working together on ungraded projects, internships for older children in the business track.

"Did you know that our students manage small businesses right at Zeeman Academy? They run the snack bar at the back of the cafeteria, buying and selling the cookies and drinks and handling the money. Another group runs a car wash in the parking lot on Saturdays. Our drama group puts on plays for the community and donates proceeds to emergency relief all over the world. How many regular schools"— here Doug made quote marks in the air—"even know what's going on in the world outside their little soccer teams?"

"But that's not what you and Superintendent Collins were arguing about, is it?" I tried not to sound too smug, lest Doug call my bluff.

"We're always arguing. It's not a new battle. Do you know how Zeeman is funded?"

"I got a taste of it from a couple of teachers," I said. "I know it comes from everywhere and nowhere."

Doug shot me with his index finger. I took it as confirmation of my assessment. "Most of our teachers buy supplies with money out of their own pockets. They'll do anything to help improve the performance of our students. Theoretically, federal grant money is available to charters to implement turnaround plans for underperforming schools. But good luck getting the funds unless your school qualifies with good test scores."

I nodded at a familiar catch-22. "You have to be performing well to get money to improve your performance."

Doug slapped the table, lightly, in deference to those

around us, I surmised. The Inn was much less crowded than it had been on graduation night, the music more mellow and suited to the office crowd I picked out. "You got it. Makes a lot of sense, doesn't it? The state can close the school if we don't reach certain grade levels. They could do something to help, but they don't; they just keep making recommendations. And threats. Lots of threats."

"So you have to make the numbers look good," I coached.

Doug nodded, seeming pleased that I was following his winding argument toward exoneration. "Take the student-teacher ratio. You're going to read that Zeeman has a ratio of twelve to one. That's what I submitted. But that's because we include every teaching assistant, every college intern, and every parent who spends time with our students."

"And me?" I asked.

Doug blushed. "And you."

"What's the real number?"

"More like twenty-three to one, and with cuts next year, it will be up to twenty-six to one."

I wouldn't have guessed that more than grade inflation was involved in the fraud. There was the teacher-student ratio, and probably a host of other line items on the school's report card.

By now, I could write my own blog on the perils of charter schools. Time to dig deeper. I waited until the servers departed, leaving behind overflowing salad bowls, a new basket of warm bread and butter, and a refill of drinks. It was hard to concentrate amid such luxury.

"Neither Superintendent Collins nor Mayor Graves saw your predicament, did they?" I asked, counting on the fact that Kira was right about her *Edward*.

Doug inhaled deeply and let out a long breath. "I won't belabor the issue of whether tweaking the grades is the answer to the problem. I never saw it as a long-term solution, but at the moment I see no other way to save the

school and I don't regret my decision. I know you talked to
Dan and Rina, and . . . uh . . . well, that's that, and I don't
know what your plans are for spreading the word, but . . ."
He threw up his hands, a gesture I took as both a question
and a plea not to turn him in.

I gave Doug points for creativity in describing his crime
as *tweaking the grades*. I did what I always do when I'm
unsure of how to respond. I stalled.

"I didn't mean to upset Rina and Dan, or pry into school
matters," I said. "I'm simply eager to see Mayor Graves's
murderer behind bars."

Doug dropped his fork and sat back, seeming genuinely
surprised. "And you think we have something to do with
Ed's murder? Me? My teachers?"

I gave him a look, neither *yes* nor *no*. "What did the
mayor think of your tweaking?"

"He was no more sympathetic than Pat." Doug leaned in
toward me. "What do you know about the mayor, Sophie?"

The truth? Not much while he was alive.

Had he been worthy of Kira's admiration and affection?
That had to be put in perspective, given Kira's personality
and nearly cloistered upbringing. I knew what Monty told
me—that the mayor, who was a husband and a father, was
seeing Monty's sister and had just dumped her, taking a
large sum of her money with him. But, again, that was
someone else's—Monty's—perspective. The only other
thing I knew was that he'd wanted the W. Thomas Company to take out his trash for the next ten years.

"Why don't you tell me about him?" I asked Doug.

"Ed Graves is dead, and in a very violent, ugly way. So,
it's tough to talk about him objectively. You know how we
canonize people once they're gone." I nodded agreement.
"He wanted truth and honesty when it came to some things,
but he had his hand out when it came to his own pockets."

"His hand out, as in, he could be bought off? Can you
be more specific?"

Doug used another bite of bread and butter as cover for preparing his answer. I was familiar with the trick.

"You've read about the waste management contract dispute?"

I nodded, feeling confident since my Internet search.

"There's a reason Graves wanted the work to go to Thomas, and it wasn't because their containers are prettier."

"Your only beef with Mayor Graves was that he might have been taking a payoff for a contract award?" I asked.

Doug looked sheepish. "Okay, he also threatened to report me to the district. It would have meant my job. Now here you are taking his place."

"You think I'm going to report you?"

"I don't know." He shrugged and bit his lip. "I thought I might be able to give you my side of the story. I have a wife, a family."

I never understood why that would matter. Were married parents to be excused just on that basis while single, childless people could be put in jail willy-nilly? I let Doug go on without querying him on that matter.

"I know you're on friendly terms with the HPD," Doug added.

Why was I not surprised? If I were a less self-confident person, I'd be bemoaning the fact that my chief value as a friend or colleague was that I was on a first-name basis with an HPD homicide detective.

I thought of recommending that Doug speak to Kira or Bruce, who were much better sources of insider information at the moment, seeming to be on the front lines of communication with the HPD. Instead I ignored the remark and asked my own question.

"What about Superintendent Collins? Is he about to report you?" From his jail cell, I might have added.

"I've taken care of that. He no longer has credibility."

I frowned, concentrating. Bruce had mentioned that the HPD had acted on information from an anonymous source.

Was I sharing a basket of bread with the tipster? A murderer?

Before I could relax enough to work out the chain of events, picturing Collins and Richardson pointing fingers at each other, a hubbub at the front of the restaurant caught my attention, and that of all the diners.

Two uniformed police officers became the main attraction in the dining room through their large and bulky presence. But it was the plainclothes detective in front of them who set my head buzzing. Virgil Mitchell had entered the building.

They were headed for our table. For me? Of course not. I hadn't done anything wrong.

Doug, who'd had his back to door, was now turned one-eighty. He stood and dropped his napkin on the table. The two uniforms hung back, there for backup, in case the person of interest put up a fuss, I figured. One of them hung his head, not looking at the person of interest. Maybe he was a former student and couldn't bear to arrest his principal?

I had to admire Doug's response, one befitting an educator and administrator. He must have assumed, though incorrectly, that I'd summoned Virgil, but he still spared me any embarrassment by walking toward the police contingent.

I couldn't hear the words exchanged as the four men left the restaurant. Had the cops read Doug his rights? Or simply asked him to accompany them downtown?

Doug Richardson had surrendered himself—I wished I knew to what—causing a minimum of disruption to the upscale diners.

All eyes then turned to me. An accomplice? The moll? I wouldn't have minded so much what anyone thought if I hadn't also been left with the check.

CHAPTER $\sqrt{20}$

I wanted badly to drive straight home. I needed a shower. From the weather, which now bordered on hot, and from the heated activities of the day, beginning with a tricky negotiation with Elysse, and on to the ambush by Monty, and then a lunch date with an unhappy ending, all cushioned only by a memorial service stuck in between.

But I also needed groceries for the dinner I'd offered Bruce. With so much mental confusion to sort out, the idea of dealing with anything as mundane as pasta and vegetables was frustrating, but a promise was a promise.

As I drove toward the small market near my home, my mind was busy making connections and putting things in order. Why would the police be involved in what should have been a school board matter—unless they saw a motive for murder in Doug's fraudulent reports to his funding sources?

I revisited my suspect list, drawing lines and arrows on the imaginary whiteboard that seemed to live in my head. I labeled my work the "CGR Theory," for Collins, Graves,

and Richardson, with a corollary of "MCS," for Monty and
Chris Sizemore. Having specific unknowns always made
an equation or algorithm seem simpler.

I thought of the ring of crimes I'd constructed from
Kira's information what seemed like weeks ago, but was
really only over the past couple of days. I played out my
theory, adding the meager details I'd gleaned today. It was
a simple matter of combinations and permutations.

C and G point to R: Superintendent Collins and Mayor
Graves learn about Richardson's fraud and threaten to
expose him. At the same time, R and C point to G: Richardson and Collins are aware that Graves has shady dealings to conceal vis-à-vis waste management. And finally, G
and R point to C: Graves and Richardson know something
about Collins that gets him taken into custody.

Maybe not a simple matter, after all.

Either Collins or Richardson takes care of Graves by
killing him; Richardson takes care of Collins by calling in
a tip about—what?—something that gets Collins arrested
so the police won't believe him if he tattles on Doug.

Too many loose ends.

First, it seemed the police did believe Collins, since
they came for Doug. Second, why would Doug kill the
mayor but take such a risk with Collins? Why not kill him,
too? Third, if Collins and Graves both wanted to squeal on
Doug, what were they arguing about at the reception before
commencement and why did Collins follow Graves into
Franklin Hall?

I despaired of fitting Monty and Chris Sizemore into
this circle; they each had their own motives, ranging from
unrequited love to Henley's trash pickup.

If I'd been at a real whiteboard I'd have taken up a red
dry-erase marker and x-ed out the theory. Maybe someone
entirely outside the circle was taking care of the great men
of Henley.

I was certainly behind the curve in helping catch any

wrongdoer associated with the mayor's case. Maybe it wasn't my job to solve the puzzle in the first place. What a concept. Bruce and Virgil would be proud of me for thinking of it.

I arrived at the market parking lot, wondering how I'd gotten there. *Very bad.* I had to stop losing focus on what was in front of me, like the road.

It would help my focus if I knew whether all three—Collins, Doug, and Chris—were being held at the police station. I had the crazy thought that if I could talk to them, I could figure out which one was a murderer.

I pulled out my phone and called Bruce, who should be awake at one in the afternoon.

"Hey," he said, sleepy voiced. It was a sign of my current frenetic state that I felt little sympathy. "Are you cooking?"

"Something like that. I'm in the lot at Al's Market. Anything special I should pick up for tonight?"

"I assumed pasta primavera, salad, good bread? Ice cream. I can get that. Mmm, I can almost taste it."

"That's still the menu but I thought there might be a special veggie or—"

"Sophie?"

"Yeah?"

"You want to know what's up at HPD?"

Busted. "Well, it's either you or Kira."

Bruce laughed. "Zucchini."

"What?"

"I'd like some zucchini in the primavera."

"Bruce." My tone was as serious as I could ever make it when Bruce was in a joking mood. I was also a little envious at how he could go from sleepy to funny in a matter of seconds.

"Okay, give me a minute."

I waited a very long minute for Bruce to return.

"Soph?"

"I'm here."

"Here's the latest. Doug Richardson—your lunch

date—just arrived at the station a few minutes ago. Don't
know why. Probably the grade fraud you've been talking
about."

That much I knew. "Did you tell Virgil where to find
him? That I was having lunch with him at the Inn?"

"My lawyer advises *no comment*."

"I'll take that as a *yes*. Go on. Is Collins still at HPD?"
I asked.

"Oh yeah. Pat Collins, you wouldn't believe. They're
getting ready to indict him for embezzling city funds to the
tune of a quarter million dollars. That anonymous tip I told
you about sent the cops to a storage locker in Hopedale,
rented under another name. Looks like Collins has been
buying personal items with Henley money and also buying
and selling stuff on eBay for a couple of years."

I opened my window for air, warm and humid though it
was. It would take a while to process the picture of Superintendent Collins sneaking around the city's books, siphon-
ing off funds for himself. I wondered if the image I was
constructing should include a snapshot of him tossing a
brick through my patio door, though I couldn't imagine why.

I found it hard to imagine a person leading a double life.
I hardly had time for a single one. Besides, it always
amazed me when high-profile people took the risks they
did, especially when punishable offenses loomed on the
horizon. Did big shots think they were above it all, that
their infractions would go unnoticed? Didn't they realize
they had a better chance of getting caught than low-profile
people, like college professors?

Which reminded me. "Are they still holding Chris
Sizemore?"

"As far as I know. Looks like Richardson for fraud, Collins for theft, and Sizemore for murder. Not Henley's finest
hour."

I flinched. I knew Bruce hadn't meant to be careless

about a homicide, but the whole crime wave was setting us all on edge and clouding my perspective.

Every time I tried to put the case behind me, Mayor Graves's voice rang in my head. I heard his plaintive cry at the fountain, and his simple request to talk to me on my voice mail. I was glad the HPD was cleaning things up, ridding the town of thieves and frauds (all without my help, miraculously), but I couldn't quit before someone, if not I, put his killer behind bars.

"I'm sorry, Sophie, that sounded pretty insensitive. I know this is personal for you."

Of course, Bruce would understand. He dealt with similar situations day after day. He didn't know the man who died in the car crash on Saturday morning, but he felt as bad about the loss as if he'd been his soccer coach, and as much a failure as the EMT or surgeon who couldn't save him.

"I'm okay."

"Hey, don't you want to know about the brick?" Bruce asked.

I'd almost forgotten. Probably because I hadn't reentered my house since this morning. "Did they find fingerprints? Or trace it to the one store in Henley that sells them?"

"It's not *Law and Order*, unfortunately. Your brick is garden variety, so to speak, like the ones you'd use in small garden projects, not big buildings. But they're still working on it."

I couldn't think of anyone I knew who had a garden project going on, other than the guys who lined Henley Boulevard with magnificent blooms. One more dead end among many.

A signal that it was time to zero in on pasta and veggies.

But not until I was finished with Bruce, my confidential informant. I had one more question. "By the way, Bruce, my love, how are you coming by all this up-to-the-minute information? Are you and Virgil joined at the hip these days?"

And if so, why can't I be, too? "I remember a time when you guys would talk about anything other than your jobs."

"It's not just me now. It's the demographics of MAstar personnel. Every guy in the trailer has a buddy on the force. Three of the guys were EMTs, another couple of them came over from the fire department, another was in boot camp with a few cops, and on and on. It's like HPD annex here."

"So, you all sit around and talk about police cases?"

"What else is there to talk about? Our new special medical interiors, our high-skid gear, the intensity searchlights we just installed, the more than twenty thousand radio frequencies that enable us to communicate with any agency?"

I faked a yawn. "I see what you mean."

"There are only so many chores to keep us busy between emergencies. After we dust all the furniture, iron our flight suits, polish the silverware—"

"I get it, thanks."

I might finally believe Bruce when he said his job was boring between dispatches, that medevac pilots and their flight nurses worked at EMS—*earn money sleeping.*

Anticlimactic though it was, ten minutes later I stood in the checkout line at Al's with the handles of a red plastic basket cutting into my arm. My goal at any market was the same as what Bruce described as the rules of a skirmish: Get in and get out. But I'd inadvertently chosen a lane with a chatty checker and a customer who was needy. I tapped my feet and perused the environment. I scanned the tabloid headlines, but saw no name I recognized, no "famous" bride or groom who'd sold their wedding photos, no unexpected split-up I cared about.

My eyes were drawn to a large barrel in the corner of the store, one that I'd seen before, where customers could drop in donations to a food bank. I was sorry I hadn't remembered to pick up a couple of canned items to add to the container. Next time for sure. The plain brown barrel, made of super heavy cardboard, had a crude sign taped to it—a letter-size piece of paper with the words "NOT TRASH" in thick black marker. I hadn't noticed it before, but I saw the wisdom of such a warning, given the trash-can-like appearance of the container.

I smiled as I thought of Woody's "TRASH" and "NOT TRASH" signs in Franklin Hall and the amusing origin of the practice, going back to Fran's messy pile of research papers.

I missed my girlfriends. I hadn't talked to Fran today or to Ariana since the weekend. I realized they didn't know about the brick or even the outcome of the Elysse Hutchins situation. I'd debated whether to call them several times, but fortunately thoughtfulness and reason won out as I let them have some time with family (Fran) and new friends (Ariana). Eventually, they'd both hear all my sorry tales.

The needy customer in front of me described to the clerk what she was going to do with the mushrooms, bread-crumbs, and onions in her basket. Bored as I was, I thought of taking a phone photo of Al's Market's version of "NOT TRASH" and sending it to Fran. I pulled out my phone and clicked on the camera icon. I framed the picture, centering the sign.

A flash went off, but not from my camera. From my brain, which finally put itself in gear, and I knew what our deceased mayor had been doing in my office on graduation day. More accurately, where exactly he was doing it. He'd hidden something—evidence I assumed, though of what I wasn't sure—in the "NOT TRASH" pile. The one place I hadn't looked.

In retrospect, it was the smartest place he could have chosen, essentially directing me to it. *Look here*, he was saying. *It's not trash.* He knew that no self-respecting jani-tor would toss something labeled "NOT TRASH."

The only thing left for me was to dig it—whatever it was—out of the pile, and I'd have all my answers.

I was so excited about going back to my office, I almost missed my turn when the needy lady left.

My trunk loaded with four plastic bags from Al's Market, I drove toward the college. Still early. I could make a quick trip to my campus office before heading home. Thanks to Bruce's taking charge of the ice cream, nothing I'd bought was perishable, unless you counted the freshly shaved Parmesan.

I wondered if the old-fashioned radio in my car was up to the task of reporting news in a timely way. If nothing else, the radio would give me a less complicated focus on the current crime wave than the theories I kept dreaming up.

I caught the end of a story involving the ribbon-cutting ceremony for an important building in Taunton, about twenty-five miles away, and an upbeat feature on how Stoughton, another neighboring town, had been chosen as the site of a statewide swim meet at the end of the summer. I turned up the volume when I heard the start of local Henley news.

Police searched a storage locker belonging to Superintendent Patrick Collins this morning. They found evidence of over one hundred items billed to the school district, including software, furniture, valuable coins, diving gear, and decorative birdhouses.

"Birdhouses?" I asked the empty car. There was no accounting for what robbers found attractive. Maybe they were eBay's hot item of the month.

I tuned back to the female voice.

Through his lawyer, Collins insists that he's innocent, claiming that the allegations are payback for his refusal to hire as his assistant the nephew of Principal

Douglas Richardson of the Zeeman Academy charter school.

The temperature tomorrow is expected . . .

Enough. I punched the button for an all-Chopin station, in honor of my piano-playing, mathematician father. I hoped Cody Graves would eventually be able to enjoy good memories of his father also.

Rring, rring. Rring, rring.

My Bluetooth rudely interrupted a lovely concerto.

"Hey, Sophie." Worse, it was Monty's voice. Hadn't he hung up on me the last time we talked on the phone? "Sorry to keep bugging you. I really need your advice. Do you think I should go to the police and tell them that Chris was there? You remember, right? What I explained to you about the fight in Admin that night and how Graves left her, very much alive?"

"You know this because she told you, right?"

"Yes, as soon as it came out that he'd been killed. She called me and I rushed to campus."

Surely Monty realized that a devoted brother wasn't the most credible of witnesses. I didn't know what advice to give. I didn't see how his statement would help Chris. It wasn't as if he could alibi her. But I didn't want to be the one to dissuade him from going to the cops either.

All I could do was repeat an old refrain. "I'm really sorry I can't advise you, Monty. Maybe you should just trust your sister, that she's told the police the truth, and if she's innocent—"

"She is innocent."

"Then she'll be fine."

I tried to put a tone of conviction, but not in the legal sense, behind my words, as if it were as simple as the quote etched above the entrance to the Henley courthouse: "The truth will set you free." Hearing the catch in his voice, I was moved to give Monty something a little more concrete.

"Actually, if you can just be patient, I'm on the trail of something that might clear Chris." For all I knew, what I found in my office might implicate his sister further, but I wasn't about to tell Monty that. This was me, bolstering up a distraught colleague.

"Wow. Wow," Monty said. "I knew you'd come through. What is it, Sophie? Can I help? Wow."

Loud and excited as it was, Monty's voice was nearly overridden by sudden noise in the background, what sounded like carnival music. "Are you at Disney World?" I asked, lightening the mood now that we seemed to be less antagonistic toward each other.

Monty laughed. I really had made his day, and hoped I could deliver. "My window's open. My office building overlooks the kiddie park on the east side. It's kind of fun hearing the kids have such a good time."

Melanie loved to go to the park when she visited. She went for the rides; we went for the fresh, hot kettle corn. Henley had something for everyone. But the juxtaposition of the kids running wild with cotton candy and the cool-but-sophisticated professional didn't quite jibe with my image of Monty Sizemore. It could be that I'd been too quick to judge him.

"Let me close the window," Monty said. I heard a thud, after which the sound of screaming kids, newly freed from school, went away. "There, is that better?"

"Yes, but I have to go, anyway. I'll talk to you later, Monty."

"You'll call if you find something that would help Chris? I'll do anything, make it worth your while. Name your price."

What was that about? Did Monty think I'd work harder if there were a carrot dangling in front of me? I guessed he never did leave his bottom-line businessman persona far behind. I figured I'd better hang up before Monty talked himself back to the usual low place he had on my list of respected academics.

CHAPTER $\sqrt{21}$

I parked in my usual place near the tennis courts and walked to Franklin Hall. As I inserted my key in the front door, I wondered when the spring semester would really be over and I wouldn't be coming into work every day.

I walked toward my office, my excitement over the "NOT TRASH" pile abating. I started to doubt my initial reaction to the sign at the market. What a silly idea, thinking a town dignitary had stashed an important message to me in an innocuous pile of papers in my office.

I entered the room and looked immediately toward the mound of filing, some of which by now was actually "TRASH." My office felt colder than usual at this time of year, and I wondered if Woody had forgotten to turn off the air-conditioning. The chill might also have come from the looming paperwork in the corner. I changed into a pair of jeans that I kept in my tiny closet, made myself a cup of tea from the supplies in the bottom drawer of my desk, and took a seat on my rocker, diagonally opposite the heap of

paper. I longed to stay on the chair, Margaret's blue afghan
around me, close my eyes, and have a quick nap. But that
would have been a stall, putting off disappointment. If the
"NOT TRASH" pile was a bust, I had nowhere else to go.

I took a few deep breaths and headed for the pile when
my phone rang. A legitimate stall. Someone was helping
me procrastinate.

Kira Gilmore. I hoped she wasn't back to looking out
her dorm window, waiting for company.

"I don't want to bother you, Dr. Knowles. I saw your car
and I just want to say good-bye. I'm going to spend a couple of weeks at home with my family, and then move into
the apartment in Cambridge. I'm really excited about it."

"That's great news. I'm excited for you, Kira."

"I have a little thing I want to give you. I'm right outside
Franklin. Can I stop in for a minute?"

I could hardly refuse a present. I eyed the small moun-
tain of "NOT TRASH," which seemed to be taller each
time I looked, and left my office.

I let Kira in through the front door. We took seats in the
large lecture hall nearest the entrance instead of walking
all the way back to my office. In jeans and a flowered top
that was new to me, Kira seemed to stand taller today.
Most likely because she'd lost the hangdog look and attitude I'd become used to.

"I'm going to miss this place," she said. "But, you know,
I'm kind of through with it." She put her hand to her mouth.
"I didn't mean it that way, Dr. Knowles."

I gave her a broad smile. "Not to worry, Kira. I'm glad
to hear it." In fact, it was music to my ears.

Kira spent a few minutes telling me about her new
apartment, which was only a short walk from the MIT
Museum, with its fabulous (her word) holograms and an
exhibit of Harold Edgerton's high-speed photography,
groundbreaking in its day. She loved her new roommate, a
grad student in physics, and couldn't wait to walk around

her new Cambridge neighborhood. I couldn't have been more thrilled.

"Well, I'm sure you wouldn't be here if you didn't have work to do, so . . ." She reached into her tote and pulled out two items. She handed me the first one, the sliding block puzzle I'd given her at one of her worst hours.

I saw that the puzzle had been completed, displaying M. C. Escher's *House of Stairs*, in its black-and-white glory, with unidentifiable creatures crawling around a complicated set of steps and walls.

"Done," Kira said, and I know she meant it on many levels.

Next she handed me a small box, wrapped in tissue. "When I saw this, I had to get it for you, Dr. Knowles."

I opened the package and let out a gasp of pleasure, much to Kira's delight. On the white cotton batting lay a piece of costume jewelry, in the steampunk style, with a montage of flowers, leaves, brass curlicues and findings, and a tiny silver heart on a ring. Best of all, in the center was a small replica of a crossword puzzle. A disembodied feminine hand adorned with a lacy glove held a thin yellow pencil. The piece was about two inches across, larger than any in my collection, with a sturdy pin on the back.

"It's perfect," I said.

We tried pinning it to my paisley shirt, but the fabric was too thin and slippery to hold the extra-thick pin. "I'll have to wear something tonight that will show this off in a way that it deserves," I said, putting it back into the box.

"Maybe I should have chosen—"

I held my hand up, staving off an apology from the old Kira. "This is perfect," I repeated.

Kira and I shared a hug and swapped thank-yous. A special moment.

As I let her out of the building, I realized Kira and I had just had a conversation where the deceased Mayor Edward P. Graves didn't come up.

Between my reconciliation with Elysse Hutchins and my pride in witnessing Kira's growth, I felt like the school year was coming to a satisfying close.

Now if I could only say the same for the murder case.

Back in my office, I was almost surprised to see the mass of paper still in the corner. One might have thought I was endowing it with magical powers. In any case, I was ready to tackle it.

I figured I was looking for something very small, or it would already have stood out to me during my previous searches of my desk, bookcases, and filing cabinets. It was going to be a tedious job, and I needed to approach it in a positive manner, as if I were solving an extra-large word search puzzle. It wouldn't daunt me; neither should this task.

A wire basket resting on the floor in the corner held the embarrassingly high, approximately eighteen-inch stack. One more sip of now-cold tea and I approached the pile. I knelt on the floor and went to work, sorting as I picked up each piece. Some were headed straight for the real trash—long-ago movie reviews, old memos, out-of-date coupons. Some were to be filed eventually—conference programs, receipts, folders, journals, catalogs. About half the height of the stack came from an assortment of features on everything from differential equations to the best place to get cannoli in Boston, from puzzles to correspondence to hotel reviews.

I found photos I'd forgotten about, waiting to be framed, plus a paperback I'd accused Fran of not returning.

I did my best to be patient, taking each piece out, one at a time. If it was a journal, I held it by its edge and shook the pages; if it was an envelope, I checked inside; if it was a sheet of paper, I turned it over, in case the mayor had written out his message.

Finally, my due diligence was rewarded. More than halfway down was a crisp, new white envelope, one that hadn't come through the mail. The imprinted return address was of Henley City Hall on Main Street.

I sat back on my heels and opened it, holding my breath. Inside was a small, flat blue plastic item, barely one inch on a side.

An SD—Secure Digital—memory card. I let out my breath, excited and happy to have something, uncertain what it contained. I turned it over and over in my fingers, as if I could read it through my skin. Wouldn't it be wonderful if rubbing it forced it to give up its secrets?

In the real world it was going to take an electronic device like a camera or a computer. But the only camera I had was an app on my phone. And my campus computer was about two years out of date and had no adapter to read an SD card. My home laptop had a USB port and an accessory that would work, but I was miles from it. I felt that after all this time, I deserved instant gratification, but it seemed it wasn't to be.

To my surprise, I couldn't decide between rushing home to my laptop or taking the SD card directly to Virgil. So unlike me.

I wanted more than anything to see what was on the card, to be the first to see it. And I'd thought Kira had acted childishly! But I had a plausible excuse—what if there was nothing on the card but pictures of Cody Graves's seventeenth birthday party? Or another boring speech by the mayor himself? Shouldn't I screen the card before taking up the valuable time of a detective in the HPD?

On the other hand—maybe it would work to my advantage if I showed the kind of diffidence and responsibility Virgil would like by taking it to him immediately. I might get his attention and agreement to share with me. A bargaining chip, in the literal sense.

I wanted to review my suspects—that is, his

suspects—with him. Without more information, I might as well put "Collins," "Richardson," and "Sizemore" labels on a dartboard and see what stuck. It seemed to come down to money for the two men, love for the woman. I wondered what the statistics were on those combinations.

The answer had to be on the card I held.

Still undecided, I put the envelope, unmarked except for the Henley address, into a plastic sleeve meant for a three-ring binder. I'd get in my car and see where it took me. It wouldn't be the first time I'd used such a sophisticated method of decision making.

I flashed back to Saturday, picturing Mayor Graves in my office on graduation day, having sweet-talked Woody into letting him in, probably hearing the applause across the campus as young people symbolically started a new life. Did he think back to his own graduation, to his hopes for the future? Did he ruminate on how much simpler things were then, when he didn't have to skulk around hiding things in piles of "NOT TRASH"? One thing I was pretty sure of: He didn't know he'd die on this campus that same day.

I wondered again why he would have chosen such an inglorious method of presenting me with evidence, if that's what I was holding in my hand. Why not hand me the envelope at Zeeman, or at the president's reception? Or send me an email and meet me for lunch. Not that the most recent lunch I'd had with an official turned out very well.

Why does anyone do what they do in a perceived or real crisis? Nothing that has to make sense. My mother did some strange things at the end of her life. In the days before she died, I might find her ironing tablecloths or restocking the soap in the laundry area, as if they were the most important tasks left for her to do. She set out large bags, stuffed out of my sight, for the trash pickup. Instead of sharing stories of her life, she made me promise not to look through the bags.

"What's in them?" I'd asked her. Since I'd been the one dragging them to the curb, I'd felt I had a right to know.

"Never mind."

"Hmm. Love letters to someone other than Dad?" I'd teased.

"If that's what you want to think," she'd said, inscrutable. In her last weeks she'd become harder and harder to read.

It wasn't very satisfying, but eventually my curiosity faded away as I tried to hold on to only the unambiguously good memories.

I ran my finger along the SD card through the plastic sleeve. Was I holding the key to the mayor's murder?

As I exited the building, the SD card tucked in my briefcase, my cell phone rang. I looked at the screen. Monty. *Not now, Monty. I have an important errand to run.*

My better self won out and I answered, thinking I might get rid of him quickly by telling him that yes, I did find something and that I'd get back to him within the hour.

I walked toward my car and slid my phone open.

"Hey, Monty."

"Sophie, I'm just calling to, you know, check on things."

I was about to announce to him that I'd finally made some progress and that he'd better not hold me up if he wanted the results anytime soon. But something stopped me. The background noise on the phone. There was none. Why the lack of noise reminded me of the presence of noise, I couldn't say, but I remembered the sounds as clearly as if they were playing in stereo.

First, the sound of the train in the background of the call to me from Mayor Graves on the morning of graduation. Second, the sound of the kids playing in the park below Monty Sizemore's business office. One of main attractions at the kiddie park was a small train that ran around the perimeter of the area. Kids could sit in the colorful little cars and ride around the track. Melanie loved it. The pint-size wooden train made a sound like the grown-ups' train.

It all fell into place. The mayor had made the call after noon from Monty's office. I imagined he got in somehow when Monty wasn't there and took the SD card, perhaps from a camera he knew was in place, or from any number of repositories. I already knew he was good at getting into empty offices.

Monty's story about his sister was true. Chris had let the mayor walk out of the room in Admin after he called an end to their relationship. But Monty had been waiting nearby and didn't let him off so easily.

My head ran the video, as if I were directing a screen-play to a movie set on my own campus. I could picture exactly where Monty must have been standing, exactly where a faculty member's desk held a mug of pens and pencils. And a letter opener.

"Sophie?"

I couldn't let Monty know what I suspected. I stammered into my phone. "I'm in kind of hurry, Monty."

"I can see that," he said, sending a chill through me.

I looked up from the screen. A man in white was approaching from the direction of the Mortarboard Café. I squinted against the strong sunlight. Monty, with large shades.

I knew it would be a close race to my car as I quickened my pace and made dramatic gestures toward my watch: *I'm in a hurry!* And Monty did the same, breaking into a run. He held up his hand and showed me his fingers. *I only need five minutes.* Whom did he think he was kidding?

If the respective distances we had to travel had been different, I might have made it to my car, pretending not to understand his five-minute gesture, pretending not to have figured out who killed the mayor. But Monty was closer to my car and had longer legs, so the math worked out in his favor.

"Hey, Sophie," he said from a few yards away. "I thought that was you. Did you find anything?"

Could Monty possibly not know what I had in my briefcase? Could this be just another innocent if pesty encounter? It was worth a shot.

"No, I . . ." I stammered. "I was just doing some work on—"

"You're a lousy liar, Sophie. You'd never make it in the business world. I knew it was just a matter of time before you either figured it out or found that video."

"What video?"

But there was no fooling Monty. I could tell by his anxious expression, and by his determined pace as he closed the gap between us, towering over me.

And, finally, by the gun he held in his right hand.

CHAPTER $\sqrt{22}$

In seconds, the air on campus went from hot and sunny to icy and overcast, a heavy dark cloud passing over the tennis courts and over our heads. Monty's visage took on an ominous look. He might as well have been wearing a dark cloak instead of his tennis whites.

"Hand it over, Sophie," he said, his face pinched. "I knew you wouldn't give up until you found it."

I couldn't have been more surprised at the turn of events in the last two minutes. I felt winded and weak at the same time. I thought I'd fall over on my face. I moved toward the grass in case I did take a tumble. As if the gun pointed at me wasn't a much bigger threat to my well-being.

"Monty, what's going on? What are you doing?"

He held up his hand and yelled, "Enough! I know you found it and I'm protecting myself is what I'm doing." He held out his gun-free hand and wiggled his fingers. "Give me the card, Sophie."

"Monty—"

He grabbed the briefcase from my hand and tried to undo the flap. He ended up dropping the briefcase and making every effort to right it, while still training the gun on me. If he hadn't been holding a gun, I'd have said he was as nervous as I was, but the balance of power gave the lie to that.

"Please let me—"

I wanted to explain that I hadn't seen what was on the card, that I never had to see it, that I'd swallow it whole if it would make him put the gun away and let me get in my car and be on my way. But each time I began a sentence, his look became more frantic, his eyes more threatening.

I perked up at the sound of a vehicle. I snuck a look to my left, in the direction of the library entrance. Monty heard the sound, too, and we both watched as the car, a nondescript sedan, drove toward us. I tried to play it out quickly. I could scream but would the driver hear me? Would Monty dare shoot me in broad daylight? He looked wild and unstable enough to follow through, taking his chances on escaping. All the driver would see would be a tall guy in a white suit and a petite woman in jeans crashing to the ground.

My heart fell as the car made a right, heading for the parking lot near the dorms. I was surprised to find I was still holding my phone, technically still on a call with Monty. If my life weren't on the line, it would have been a funny moment.

Monty was unnerved by the arrival of the car and what could have been his undoing. For me, the event had been a roller coaster of hope and despair as the car went on its way to the other side of campus.

"Get in your car," he said, his voice nothing like the confident, often cajoling businessman-instructor that I knew. He used the gun to nudge me along the few yards to my car. This Monty was ready for a serious institution of the mental kind.

Where was everyone? It was the middle of the afternoon. I knew very well where everyone was. On vacation. At home, catching up with all the things that got neglected during the busy end-of-year days. My colleagues were doing laundry and paying bills while I was held captive outside my own building.

What could I do to get away? I fingered my cell phone, now in my jeans pocket, wondering if I could manage a nine-one-one call without looking at the keypad. First I'd have to mute the sound or Monty would hear the dispatcher's voice. I felt around my phone to determine its orientation. I found the long edge that had no portals, which was on the right side of the protective case. That would put the mute switch on the upper left. I used my fingernail to tuck the lever to the left.

There were still many more steps to go. I'd have to click the button on the bottom, slide the lock to the right, find the phone app, then the keypad, then . . . tears welled up in my eyes. It was hopeless.

As much as I hated to, I followed Monty's deadly instructions and climbed into my car.

"Drive," he said.

I tried to adopt a pleasing, cooperative demeanor. "Of course. Where are we going?" You might think we were headed for a getaway at the beach.

Monty had difficulty entering my car, what with the pesky briefcase and the gun to manage. He placed the briefcase on the floor between his legs. I couldn't imagine why he was having trouble finding the SD card since the plastic sleeve that held it was simply stuck between two folders of the same size.

I put my car in gear and coasted toward the library gate. Surely someone would be coming in at this time. I could drive into him. A fender bender, which Massachusetts was famous for, would help my cause. Or get the other guy killed also, I feared.

Maybe I could alert the guard at the gate, if there was one. During off-season, sometimes we swiped our ID cards to enter and exit. I looked ahead to the checkpoint. And, wouldn't you know, we were in the unmanned season.

"Use my card," Monty said, retrieving his from his pocket. I shouldn't have been surprised that he was prepared. After all, he'd brought a gun. He probably learned his lesson on the night of the murder when he'd had to improvise with a letter opener. Looking at him on the seat beside me, I had no doubt that he had the strength to plunge the blade into a man's back.

I turned right, toward the police station, though we weren't even close. "Make a U-turn," Monty said, waking up to his responsibility to give me directions.

With my vast experience with crime dramas on television I knew the key to survival was to get your captor talking. But I couldn't get started. It was not a good time to be tongue-tied. Monty helped me out.

"He deserved it, you know."

The mayor, I assumed. "Why do you say that?"

"Not just what he did to my sister. That was the last straw. He stiffed me on the waste contracts, then fired me. As if his contracts were all aboveboard. He was in bed with the CEO of Thomas. That guy was one of his biggest campaign contributors, so, big surprise, Graves wants to throw the city's waste business his way."

"But you'd already made a deal with the Stewart Brothers." That was me, making an educated guess.

"So?"

"I just wondered, that's all," I said, my voice faltering, but still sympathetic.

Was Monty really asking why kickbacks on city contracts were wrong? Was he also telling me that all the rumors of the mayor's dirty hands were true? I hated to think things were this bad in Henley, that business as usual meant money changing hands in all the wrong ways.

Monty let out a mean chuckle. "You really don't know what's on that card, do you?"

I shook my head. Monty might be willing to deal now that he knew I hadn't read the card. "I could—"

Monty dug the gun into my ribs. "It doesn't matter whether you read the card or not. I can't very well let you go now. I had a good thing going. Not just with Stewart. The mayor was in on a deal or two. If it weren't for the conflict on the waste contract, we'd still be doing business together."

Shaky as I felt, a puzzle was a puzzle and I had to know. "The mayor's dealings are also on the card?"

"Sure they are. I told you, he took money from Thomas for the dump contract." Monty seemed angry that I hadn't learned the lesson he was trying to teach me.

"I remember now. That's terrible."

"No kidding. Then out of the blue he gets an attack of conscience. I think the attention from all those cute and adoring campaign workers went to his head and he started to believe he was some kind of hero. He gets my secretary to let him into my office, plants a camera, and catches me in a ton of meetings. Financial meetings that should have been secret. Tells me he's ready to pay for his one or two indiscretions as long as it stops me cold. He was willing to take a little heat for his own actions, just to see me crash."

My mind was a jumble of thoughts and questions; my body shook with fear. Even in my panic, I tried to put the jagged pieces together. I finished the story in my head. The phone message started with Zeeman but it was really all about city contracts. I imagined the end. I'd mistakenly focused on *Something's troubling me about Zeeman*, but the important part had been cut off and he was probably in too much of a hurry to start over. *In the meantime* should have ended with *I left an SD card nailing Monty Sizemore in your office in the "NOT TRASH" pile*.

How different this moment would have been if he'd

been able to finish his message. I made a resolution: If I
lived, I'd immediately change my message length to
infinity.

Monty was reliving another moment. "He never knew
what hit him. I stood there in the office next door, listening
to His Honor dissing my sister. I knew they were meeting
and I figured this was the Big Dump, you know, and I
wanted to be there for her."

"I know you love Chrissy, Monty. You just wanted to
protect her."

Sympathize, sympathize, I reminded myself, but Monty
continued as if he were alone. Except that the gun was
meant for me.

"The letter opener was on the bookcase by the door with
a bunch of mail. The thing was shining, from the lamp
outside the window." Monty rubbed his eyes and for a
moment the gun pointed straight toward the roof of my car.
If he'd only keep it that way. "It's like the thing was blind-
ing me."

He shook his head so hard it must have hurt. He wasn't
quite finished with his story. "I let him go, you know? I
could have finished it then and there, but I'm not a bad
person." I tried not to react to Monty's self-assessment. "I
watched him stumble out the door and I almost hoped he'd
make it, that he'd find help and survive. I just wanted to
make him suffer."

I felt like Monty was telling his story not to me, but to
himself.

I'd made the turn to drive east on Henley Boulevard,
trying to guess where we were headed.

The airfield that was Bruce's base was northwest; the
police station was due west; my home and Zeeman Academy were southwest. The only thing east was . . . I shud-
dered . . . the city dump.

I couldn't let this happen. I couldn't drive myself and
my killer to the most ugly, remote part of town. I couldn't

bear the thought of someone I loved being called to iden-
tify my body, clothed in garbage.

We were still on a relatively busy street, three lanes
wide, but soon we'd be isolated. If I were going to make a
move it would have to be now.

I saw a signal light in the distance, probably the last one
before we left the main part of town. I checked the traffic
around me. It was light, but it would do. Timing now was
everything. It was a good thing I remembered the rate-
time-distance equation; math and science could save my
life. I couldn't stop a small smile from forming. Or my
stomach from churning.

Monty must have noticed my thinking, planning,
puzzle-solving look because he said, "Don't do it, Sophie.
Whatever you're thinking. I have nothing to lose. I want
this to be over, for my sister's sake. I never intended for her
to suffer for what I've done. If I'm going out, I'd just as
soon take you with me. One less busybody on campus
would be a service to all."

His remark unnerved me, but the setup was falling into
place. Unstoppable.

First I had to adjust some things in my pockets. I pretended to be reaching for a tissue, an action that provoked
only mild irritation from Monty.

"No funny business," he said.

Of course not.

Next I had to distract him. He'd been fishing around my
briefcase on and off through the trip and still hadn't found
the plastic sleeve with the SD card. I needed to help him.

"Let me tell you where the card is," I said.

"No funny business," he repeated. I felt more than saw
his strange, suspicious look. "Why would you be helping me?"

I let out a heavy breath. "Okay, Monty, I admit I'm hoping you'll change your mind if I make it easy for you to get
what you want." He seemed to be considering this. I spoke

quickly before he could figure out my plan. "Turn the briefcase so the flap is toward you."

He obeyed. A good start. "Yeah, okay," he muttered,
ready for the next step.

"See that lineup of folders? There are two yellow ones
in front."

"Yeah."

"Now just separate the two yellow folders."

While Monty was busy, ever so slightly relaxing his aim
with the gun, I reached into my pocket and pulled out the
pin Kira had given me. It had taken some amount of dex-
terity to remove it from the box and unlock the clasp, but
the tissue ploy had given me access. I gave a silent nod of
thanks to Ariana for forcing me to do the finger exercises
necessary for beadwork.

"Way down, between the two yellow folders . . ." I
began, grateful that Monty obliged with a slight bending of
his head.

I oriented the pin with the fingers of my right hand and
jabbed the sharp point into Monty's neck. Even though I
closed my eyes at the last fraction of a second before stabbing Monty, my aim was good and I heard the scream I was
hoping for.

I jammed on the brakes inches behind a blue Camry. I'd
arrived at the light, third in line in my lane. It had turned
red, but I would have slammed to a stop no matter what the
signal was. The gun fell to the floor as Monty clutched his
neck, from which blood was shooting out. I clicked off my
seat belt, opened the door, and . . .

I think I screamed. Or fainted. Or both.

CHAPTER $\sqrt{23}$

I'd always wondered what it would take for the president of Henley College to send me flowers. Not really, but the arrival of a large bouquet in a lovely vase was quite a surprise. Though the note read only "Wishing you a speedy recovery," I suspected she meant, *Thanks for getting* Heinous Murder on Campus Still Unsolved *off the front page*.

With the mayor's killer behind bars, the crimes of fraud and embezzlement, by Principal Richardson and Superintendent Collins, respectively, had moved to the top spots on the news. The college, now free of investigative activity and bloodstains, slipped off the chart.

It felt pretty good, being pampered over a simple sprained ankle—apparently I'd fallen out of my car, miraculously avoiding being run down by the vehicle in the next lane. I wished I could thank the unknown person who saw the wounded Monty try to run, and flagged down a cop.

Ariana, just back from San Diego, hadn't even unpacked before heading over to bring her special teas and mantras.

It had disturbed me that I'd had to sacrifice the structural integrity of my beautiful puzzle pin, but Ariana assured me she'd have no trouble repairing it. Or teaching me how to.

Many students and faculty sent congratulations or get well emails. Elysse's included a special message:

> I hope you noticed my complete apology on Facebook, Dr. Knowles. I wish I could take it all back. You're the best.

Kira, who'd heard the news from her former dorm mates, called from California. I knew that of all the Henley College community, Kira would be most thrilled to have this closure. Someday I'd tell her how I overcame a tall, fit tennis player using her gift to me.

Visiting hours at my home were flexible, and on Wednesday evening there was a modest gathering. Bruce and Ariana hovered; Fran brought a complete dinner to match the one she'd served in her home, down to the homemade ice cream sandwiches I'd been bragging about; and Virgil was exceptionally forthcoming in tying up loose ends.

I couldn't have been happier. Driving my own car to a possible unfortunate end while being held at gunpoint by a crazed killer seemed a small price to pay.

We sat around my expanded kitchen table. Virgil looked even happier than I did as he asked for more gravy on his pot roast. I seized the moment. I had two questions, which I labeled "The mysteries of Chris and the Brick."

"Did Chris know what her brother had done?" I asked Virgil.

With his meat and potatoes newly drizzled with excellent gravy, thanks to me (by proxy), how could he refuse to answer a simple question?

"Looks like she didn't have a clue. She said that after the fight with the mayor that night, she'd gone straight to the ladies' room down the hall to fix herself up, and by the time she was ready to leave the building, there was a commotion down by the fountain."

"She must be pretty broken up," Fran said.

"Oh yeah," Virgil said. Wordy for him.

"I guess we can safely assume that Monty was responsible for the brick that crashed through my door and the note under Elysse's door?" I asked Virgil.

He nodded. "Monty was hoping to distract you. Give you something else to think about. He wanted it to look like a kid's prank. Then, later, what he wanted from you was that little card."

I was grateful for Virgil's pouring out of information, relatively speaking, when he didn't have to. "Thanks, Virgil," I said. "More gravy?"

"I can't believe I missed all this," Ariana said.

"Wait till you hear the long version," Bruce said.

Later, Bruce and I snuggled on the couch in my den.

In a typical philosophical mood, we moved beyond the events of the past few days. As if anyone would ask us, we mused over what Henley historians might write about the main players in the case.

"That two guys supposedly working for our schoolkids were out for themselves and a better retirement," Bruce said.

"That Chris Sizemore blames herself for the outcome," I said.

"She probably thinks the mayor would be alive today if she'd simply dealt more maturely with his rejection."

"And the third in the line of the Graves mayors, Edward P.?" I asked. "What will history say about him?"

"That he was not a simple man," Bruce said.

"He was on the right side, the students' side, of the law on education issues," I said.

"But on the wrong side of graft."

"Then there was his ego."

"You mean what drove him to befriend and perhaps mislead young women?" Bruce asked. "I get that."

A punch in the ribs and a long kiss ended that thread.

"One thing we know," Bruce said. "He picked you out of the crowd to trust. That tips the scales in his favor."

I couldn't have asked for a better solution to a puzzle.

ᶠᵁᴺ(EXERCISES)

Sophie Knowles doesn't expect that everyone will be able to unwind with arithmetic, but she feels that doing puzzles, brainteasers, and mental arithmetic keeps you sharp, and improves your memory and your powers of observation. Here are some samples of puzzles and games that exercise your wits.

Browse in your bookstore, library, and online for more brainteasers, and have some fun!

BRAINTEASER #1

Here's the first exercise, a brainteaser, a classic with many variations: "The Fox, the Chicken, and the Sack of Grain."

You have a fox, a chicken, and a sack of grain. You must cross a river with only one of them at a time. If you leave the fox alone with the chicken, he will eat it; if you leave the chicken alone with the grain, it will eat the grain.

How can you get all three across safely?

BRAINTEASER #2

In this puzzle, three numbers, 16, 14, and 38, need to be assigned to one of the rows of numbers below. To which row should each number be assigned? (Hint: This is not a mathematical problem. The numerical values are irrelevant.)

A	0	6	8	9	3
B	15	27	21	10	19
C	7	1	47	11	17

RIDDLES

1. Here's a riddle for the junior high set:
Why should you never mention the number 288 in front of anyone?

2. And another for kids:
Who's the fattest knight at King Arthur's Round Table?

3. And a more challenging one for adults:
Two friends, Peter and Jenny, are chatting:

"Peter, how old are your children?"

"Well, Jenny, there are three of them and the product of their ages is 36."

"That's not enough information, Peter."

"The sum of their ages is exactly the number of sodas we've drunk today," Peter added.

"That's still not enough."

"Okay, the last thing I'll tell you is that my oldest child wears a red hat."

How old were each of Peter's children?

MATH PUZZLES

Here are two math puzzles that ask you to figure out the next in the sequence:

A. What's the next number in this series?

11

21

1211

111221

312211

13112221

B. What's the next number in this series?

11   1,331   161,051   19,487,171

ANSWERS

ANSWER TO BRAINTEASER #1

Take the chicken across (the fox can be left with the grain) and come back alone.

Take the grain across and come back with the chicken.

Leave the chicken and take the fox across (the fox is with the grain again—hope he's not starving!) and come back alone.

Take the chicken across.

Done!

ANSWER TO BRAINTEASER #2

The numbers are organized by shape. In Row A, all the numbers have rounded shapes. In Row C, all the numbers have linear shapes. Row B is a mix of curves and lines. Therefore, 16 goes to Row B, 14 goes to Row C, and 38 goes to Row A.

ANSWERS TO RIDDLES

1. It's too (two) gross!

2. The fattest knight is Sir Cumference. He got that way from eating too much pi. (Sophie can hear your groans!)

3. Let's start with the known product, 36. Write on a sheet of paper the possible combinations of three numbers giving a product of 36: 6, 6, 1; 6, 3, 2; 9, 2, 2. Knowing that the sum is not enough must mean that there's more than one possible combination with the same sum. That brings us to either 9, 2, 2 or 6, 6, 1. Since we learned further that the "oldest" son wears a hat, it is clear that the correct combination of ages is 9, 2, 2, where there is exactly one of them who can be oldest, the other two being twins.

ANSWERS TO PUZZLES

A.

ANSWER: 1113213211

SOLUTION: Each line describes the line above. The last line is: one one (11), one three (13), two ones (21), three twos (32), and one one (11), or 1113213211.

B.

ANSWER: 2,357,947,691

The numbers are 11 to the first power, 11 to the third power, 11 to the fifth power, and 11 to the seventh power. The next number would be 11 to the ninth power, or 2,357,947,691.

What is the only word in the English
language that ends in *-mt*?

BOOKS CAN BE DECEIVING

-A Library Lover's Mystery-

JENN MCKINLAY

Answering tricky reference questions like this one
is more than enough excitement for recently single
librarian Lindsey Norris. That is, until someone in
her cozy new hometown of Briar Creek, Connecti-
cut, commits murder, and the most pressing question is whodunit . . .

"A sparkling setting, lovely characters, books, knitting,
and chowder . . . What more could any reader ask?"
—Lorna Barrett, *New York Times* bestselling author

facebook.com/TheCrimeSceneBooks
penguin.com
jennmckinlay.com

M981T0911

FROM *NEW YORK TIMES* BESTSELLING AUTHOR
JENN MCKINLAY

-The Library Lover's Mysteries-

BOOKS CAN BE DECEIVING
DUE OR DIE
BOOK, LINE, AND SINKER

Praise for the Library Lover's Mysteries

"[An] appealing new mystery series."

—Kate Carlisle, *New York Times* bestselling author

"A sparkling setting, lovely characters,
books, knitting, and chowder! What more
could any reader ask?"

—Lorna Barrett, *New York Times* bestselling author

"Sure to charm cozy readers everywhere."

—Ellery Adams, author of the Books by the Bay Mysteries

facebook.com/TheCrimeSceneBooks
penguin.com

Bethesda Regional ~~Li~~
~~74~~ ~~ton R~~
Bethesda, MD 20814

M1145AS0712